DIAGNOSIS MURDER

THE
PAST TENSE

Lee Goldberg

BASED ON THE TELEVISION SERIES CREATED BY

Joyce Burditt

A SIGNET BOOK

SIGNET
Published by New American Library, a division of
Penguin Group (USA) Inc., 375 Hudson Street,
New York, New York 10014, USA
Penguin Group (Canada), 90 Eglinton Avenue East, Suite 700, Toronto,
Ontario M4P 2Y3, Canada (a division of Pearson Penguin Canada Inc.)
Penguin Books Ltd., 80 Strand, London WC2R 0RL, England
Penguin Ireland, 25 St. Stephen's Green, Dublin 2,
Ireland (a division of Penguin Books Ltd.)
Penguin Group (Australia), 250 Camberwell Road, Camberwell, Victoria 3124,
Australia (a division of Pearson Australia Group Pty. Ltd.)
Penguin Books India Pvt. Ltd., 11 Community Centre, Panchsheel Park,
New Delhi - 110 017, India
Penguin Group (NZ), Cnr Airborne and Rosedale Roads, Albany,
Auckland 1310, New Zealand (a division of Pearson New Zealand Ltd.)
Penguin Books (South Africa) (Pty.) Ltd., 24 Sturdee Avenue,
Rosebank, Johannesburg 2196, South Africa

Penguin Books Ltd., Registered Offices:
80 Strand, London WC2R 0RL, England

First published by Signet, an imprint of New American Library,
a division of Penguin Group (USA) Inc.

First Printing, August 2005
10   9   8   7   6   5   4   3   2   1

Copyright © 2005 Viacom Productions Inc.
All rights reserved

The Edgar® name is a registered service mark of the Mystery Writers of America, Inc.

 REGISTERED TRADEMARK—MARCA REGISTRADA

Printed in the United States of America

Without limiting the rights under copyright reserved above, no part of this publication
may be reproduced, stored in or introduced into a retrieval system, or transmitted, in
any form, or by any means (electronic, mechanical, photocopying, recording, or otherwise), without the prior written permission of both the copyright owner and the
above publisher of this book.

PUBLISHER'S NOTE
This is a work of fiction. Names, characters, places, and incidents either are the product
of the author's imagination or are used fictitiously, and any resemblance to actual persons,
living or dead, business establishments, events, or locales is entirely coincidental.
    The publisher does not have any control over and does not assume any responsibil-
ity for author or third-party Web sites or their content.

If you purchased this book without a cover you should be aware that this book is stolen
property. It was reported as "unsold and destroyed" to the publisher and neither the
author nor the publisher has received any payment for this "stripped book."

The scanning, uploading, and distribution of this book via the Internet or via any other
means without the permission of the publisher is illegal and punishable by law. Please
purchase only authorized electronic editions, and do not participate in or encourage electronic piracy of copyrighted materials. Your support of the author's rights is appreciated.

Praise for the *Diagnosis Murder* novels

"Even if you never watched the TV show, read these mysteries! Sly humor, endearing characters, tricky plots—Lee Goldberg's smart writing is what makes these terrific *Diagnosis Murder* books something to tell all your friends about."

—Jerrilyn Farmer, author of the bestselling
Madeline Bean mysteries

"The *Diagnosis Murder* novels are great reads. Intricate plots and engaging characters combined with Lee Goldberg's trademark humor make for page-turning entertainment."

—Barbara Seranella, author of the
bestselling Munch Mancini novels

The Past Tense

"What a great book! I enjoyed it tremendously. It's a clever, twisting tale that leaves you guessing right up to the heart-stopping ending."

—Lisa Gardner, bestselling author of *Alone*

The Waking Nightmare

"Can books be better than television? You bet they can—when Lee Goldberg's writing them. Get aboard right now for a thrill ride."

—*New York Times* bestselling author Lee Child

The Shooting Script

"This is the *Diagnosis Murder* we all know and love. Even if you've never seen a moment of the TV series, you are bound to be caught up in the twists, the thrills, and the fun on every page. From start to finish, *The Shooting Script* is a damned entertaining read."

—Eric Garcia, author of *Anonymous Rex* and *Matchstick Men*

"Fans of Dr. Mark Sloan will not be disappointed. If anything, *The Shooting Script* is an even more compelling showcase for the good doctor than the television series."

—Rick Riordan, Edgar® Award–winning
author of *Southtown*

"Rx for fun! Lee Goldberg's *Diagnosis Murder* series is the perfect prescription for readers looking for thrills, chills, and laughs. I know I'll be standing in line for my refill!"

—Meg Cabot, author of *The Princess Diaries*

continued . . .

The Death Merchant

"Dr. Mark Sloan returns in a crime story that seamlessly inter-weaves two radically different story lines while taking the reader on a roller-coaster ride through the delights—and dangers—of Hawaii. If you liked the broadcast episodes, you'll love *The Death Merchant*."

—Jeremiah Healy, author of the John Cuddy Mysteries

"This novel begins with tension and ends with surprise. Throughout, it is filled with gentle humor and a sure hand. *Diagnosis Murder*, the television series, could always be counted on for originality and a strong sense of humor, particularly when Lee Goldberg's name was on the scripts. This is not just a novel for fans of the television series."

—Stuart M. Kaminsky, Edgar® Award–winning author of *A Cold Sunrise*

The Silent Partner

"A whodunit thrill ride that captures all the charm, mystery, and fun of the TV series . . . and then some. . . . Goldberg wrote the very best *Diagnosis Murder* episodes, so it's no surprise that this book delivers everything you'd expect from the show. . . . A clever, high-octane mystery that moves like a bullet train. Dr. Mark Sloan, the deceptively eccentric deductive genius, is destined to join the pantheon of great literary sleuths. . . . You'll finish this book breathless. Don't blink or you'll miss a clue. A brilliant debut for a brilliant detective. Long live Dr. Mark Sloan!"

—*New York Times* bestselling author Janet Evanovich

"An exciting and completely satisfying read for all *Diagnosis Murder* fans. We were hooked. . . . Goldberg's skill in bringing our favorite characters to the printed page left us begging for more."

—Aimee and David Thurlo, authors of the Ella Clah, Sister Agatha, and Lee Nez Mysteries

"For those who have, as I do, an addiction to Mark Sloan, Lee Goldberg provides a terrific fix. . . . Will cure any *Diagnosis Murder* withdrawal symptoms you might have had."

—S. J. Rozan, Edgar® Award–winning author of *Absent Friends*

To Dr. D. P. Lyle, for creating the illusion
that I know what I am talking about

AUTHOR'S NOTE AND ACKNOWLEDGMENTS

For the purposes of these books, Mark Sloan and his son, Steve, are younger than Dick Van Dyke and Barry Van Dyke, the actors who played the characters in the TV series. Mark is in his sixties and Steve is in his early forties . . . and through the magic of fiction, they never age. It's a shame we can't all be fictional characters, isn't it?

A major portion of this story takes place in February 1962. While the events and characters are fictional, one thing is true: Southern California was pounded by a devastating and deadly series of storms that caused enormous damage and killed two dozen people. The historical and meteorological events described in this story actually occurred, though some artistic license has been taken with the chronology and some of the geography.

I am indebted to Zoë Sharp, Rhys Bowen, Stephen Booth, John Baker, Lee Child, Jan Curran, Ralph Spurrier, Twist Phelan, Gen Aris, Stan Barer, Paul Bishop, Ann Tomlin, Robbie Schwartz, and everybody on the DorothyL mailing list for their technical, cultural, and historical advice. Special thanks to William Rabkin and Tod Goldberg, my unofficial editors, and to Dan Slater, my official one, and to Gina Maccoby, my agent with a license to kill.

But despite all those contributions, this book would not have been possible without my wife, Valerie, and my daughter, Madison, with their love, support, and home-made cookies.

I would like to hear from you. To contact me, visit www.diagnosis-murder.com.

PROLOGUE

It was a good day for killing.

Dark clouds covered the sun like dirt on a coffin. The streets were muddy rivers. The sewers were clogged with trash, leaves, and unread newspapers. There was no one on the boulevard except the young woman. The rain had driven everyone else indoors. Even a slight drizzle threw Los Angelenos into confusion. A genuine rainstorm generated panic.

She wasn't dressed for rain. Nobody in LA ever was. They couldn't imagine a day without sunshine and felt naked without sunglasses. But those same people could blithely accept living in a place where they breathed poison, where the ground could suddenly heave under their feet and lay waste to everything.

She was one of those people. Los Angeles was where she was born and raised and where she would die. He knew her entire life story, beginning and end.

He was the end.

She walked into the wind, clutching her jacket closed over her blouse and short skirt, as if she were afraid the buttons might not hold.

She was oblivious to everything but her own discomfort, cursing out loud at her miserable fate. If she'd actually known her fate, she wouldn't have been cursing. She would have been screaming. But she didn't see the man in the car, parked at the curb of a side street, across from her.

She stopped at the bench on the corner and looked up and down the street, clearly hoping to see her bus on its way. She gave him a fine opportunity for a full appraisal. She was in her late teens, with fiery red hair. Her legs were long and pale, her body thin but with some unexpectedly generous curves that her wet clothes only accentuated.

He put the car into drive and slowly eased out into the street, timing it so he would reach the intersection in front of her just as the traffic light turned red.

It was a long light and he was right at the curb. His windows were slightly fogged, just enough to obscure his face. Even so, he knew she was looking at him, dry and warm and comfortable. He knew she was imagining how nice it would be inside his big car, surrounded by all that rich leather and wood, away from the cold and the rain.

He glanced casually in her direction and caught her staring at him. She turned her head, pretending to check again for the bus she knew wouldn't be there. And when she looked back, soaked to the bone and shivering, the passenger-side window of the car was already down, and there he was beyond it, smiling at her. Without even being aware of it, she took a step towards the car, beckoned by the open window and drawn by the warm air escaping from inside like the heat from a fireplace.

He knew he had her then, even before he offered her a ride, even before she saw his face and made her choice. Her body foreshadowed her intent, betraying her one last time.

She got into the car, slammed the door shut, and buckled up, thanking him for his thoughtfulness.

The light turned green and he moved slowly into the intersection, rain beating down on the car. The rhythmic swish of the windshield wiper blades, repeatedly swaying across the glass, was strangely soothing, almost like soft music.

After a moment, she sunk into the plush seat and let out a contented sigh, relaxed and grateful, feeling absolutely no fear at all.

That would come later.

He wasn't in any hurry. He was calm, completely at peace. Perhaps she sensed that. Perhaps that was what fooled her. Perhaps that was what fooled them all.

It felt good to be killing again.

CHAPTER ONE

Dr. Mark Sloan awoke that February morning to an empty house, feeling as if he hadn't slept at all.

He hadn't slept well the last few nights. It could have been the rain, which had pummeled the house all night long. Maybe he wasn't accustomed to the sound anymore, the rainstorm coming after one of Southern California's prolonged droughts, which had left the hillsides brittle, dry, and prone to wildfires.

Only a few days ago, the newspapers had been full of dire warnings about the parched soil, about catastrophic crop failures and uncontrollable fires, about the desperate need to conserve water before Los Angeles withered away from thirst.

Now, after three days of rain, those concerns were gone. Instead, everyone was worried about the water-saturated soil, about deadly flash floods and gigantic landslides, sweeping power outages and gridlocked freeways. Sandbags were being handed out at firehouses across the county. TV stations were interrupting regular programming with live "Storm Watch" reports, as if the city were facing an imminent hurricane instead of a common rainstorm.

Sometimes Mark wondered if what really worried people was having nothing to worry about.

It wasn't raining that morning, though the dark clouds

remained, exhausted from the long night of thundering and pouring, gathering their strength before unleashing their mayhem again.

As Mark made himself coffee and looked out at the beach, covered with seaweed, driftwood, shells, and trash churned up by the stormy seas, he realized he'd been sleeping poorly for a while now.

It had started when he'd witnessed a woman leaping out the window of her office building. She'd survived, but the memory of that horrible moment tormented Mark's sleep until he discovered what had driven her to attempt suicide and then solved the problem for her.

But even after that, sleep didn't come easy. He'd broken his arm in a car accident, and the cast made it difficult for him to get comfortable in bed. Once the cast was removed, his arm was sore for weeks, making it hard to get a good night's rest.

Perhaps it was age, he thought. As much as he hated to admit it, he wasn't a young man anymore. He was in his sixties. His days of eight hours of deep, uninterrupted sleep might be gone for good.

He took his coffee to the kitchen table and sat, watching a flock of seagulls circling over the sand and picking at the enormous clumps of seaweed. He listened to the crash of the waves, the squawk of the gulls, the settling of the house, and the windlike *whoosh* of cars passing by on the Pacific Coast Highway.

He was acutely aware of the emptiness of his Malibu beach house, which seemed to double in size whenever his son, Steve, was away.

Steve lived on the first floor, but lately he had been spending more and more nights at his girlfriend's apartment.

Although his son's job as an LAPD homicide detective kept him busy and out of the house a lot, Steve's presence had been there even if he wasn't. If Mark didn't run into Steve at night, or on his way out in the morning, there would always be signs that he had passed through. Dishes in the sink. Sandy tennis shoes on the deck. Case files on the coffee table. Recently, however, the house looked the same in the morning as it had the night before.

Maybe it wasn't the rain, or his arm, or his age, that was causing him to rest so uneasily, Mark thought. Maybe it was being alone.

He immediately rejected the idea. Loneliness couldn't be the problem. His life was full of people and activity. Between his work at the hospital and consulting on homicide investigations for LAPD, he had very little time alone. The more he thought about it, the more he realized he should be savoring the time to himself.

Or was that what he was afraid of?

Was all the work simply a way to avoid being alone? *Ridiculous.*

Mark set his empty coffee cup aside. As a doctor, he knew the best prescription for what ailed him: a brisk walk on the beach, followed by a scalding shower and a big, healthy breakfast rich in fruit and fiber. Two hours from now, he would feel rested and energized and ready to work. All this moping would be forgotten.

Until tomorrow morning anyway.

He changed into an old pair of jeans, a faded sweat-shirt, and his most comfortable pair of ragged tennis shoes and hurried down the steps from his second-floor deck to the beach below.

Mark paused on the bottom step and took a deep breath, luxuriating in the crisp, clean air, rich with the ocean mist. That was one of the great things about a storm—it washed the gunk out of the air. Of course, that meant the muck was dumped onto the streets, where it was swept into the gutters and out to sea, where—

He abruptly dropped that line of thought, deciding it was better to just enjoy the fresh air than to think about how it got that way.

The sand was pleasantly thick under his feet, soaked and pockmarked by raindrops. He was dismayed by the amount of trash that had been washed ashore amidst the seaweed, driftwood, and palm fronds. Styrofoam cups, fast-food cartons, newspapers, candy wrappers, cigarette stubs, beer bottles . . .

It could be worse, he thought. A few years back, the morning surf had littered the shoreline from Manhattan Beach to as far north as Ventura with thousands of used syringes that'd been illegally dumped into the sea.

As he worked his way around and over the obstacles in his path, his walk became more of a slog. Ahead of him, the seagulls picked and fluttered and fought over a pile of kelp resting above the berm. From the smell drifting his way on the ocean breeze, Mark guessed that the carcass of a seal had washed ashore, tangled in the rubbery vines and tiny bladders.

As he got closer, he saw the hint of a fin and the silver glint of scales. It wasn't a seal after all, but rather some kind of large dead fish.

Mark turned, and was about to continue on his walk, but curiosity got the better of him. No fish he'd ever seen had a tail fin quite so perfect or scales that shone so bright. He had to know what it was.

So he grimaced against the stench and crouched beside the mound of seaweed, scattering a thousand flies and infuriating the gulls, which continued to hover low over him, squawking their fury at his intrusion.

Using a stick of driftwood, he brushed away dozens of hungry sand crabs and carefully parted the strands of seaweed to get a better look. First he saw the long, graceful fin, tapering to a fantail at its point. Then, as he cleared more kelp, he saw a mane of fiery red hair.

For a moment, he simply stared in disbelief.

It was a mermaid.

Her face was ghostly pale, almost translucent. Her eyes were wide and green, her lips slightly parted, her slender throat slit from ear to ear.

*　　*　　*

It started to rain again just as the crime scene techs finished erecting the tent over the clump of seaweed where the woman's body had been found.

While she was being kept dry, scores of officers and forensic investigators were getting drenched as they moved slowly up and down the beach, looking for clues in a race with the rain and tide, both of which threatened to wash away any remaining evidence.

Dr. Amanda Bentley, the medical examiner, squatted beside the body, waving away the swarm of flies and sand crabs that stubbornly refused to give up their claim to the corpse.

"She isn't a mermaid. She's wearing a costume," Amanda said. "And those big openings on either side of her throat aren't gills."

"I figured that much out for myself," Mark said, studying the body.

The only reason that he was still allowed to be at the crime scene was that Dr. Amanda Bentley worked for him, too. She was staff pathologist at Community General Hospital, where her lab doubled as the adjunct county morgue. Amanda not only juggled two jobs but also was a single parent, raising a six-year-old son. And she did it all with seemingly boundless energy and enthusiasm. Mark couldn't figure out how she pulled it off.

"It's not going to be easy determining time of death," Amanda said, "but judging by the lividity, the shriveling of the skin, and the lack of bloating, I'd say she's been in the water no more than eight to ten hours. I'll know more after I get her on the table."

"This may come as a shock to you," a familiar voice said, "but I'm actually the homicide detective in charge of the investigation."

They turned to see Steve Sloan entering the tent, water dripping from his umbrella, his hair surprisingly dry. His badge was clipped to his belt.

"I know it's just a small technicality," Steve said, "but shouldn't you be saving your report for me?"

Amanda shrugged, tipping her head towards Mark. "He was here first."

"That's only because the body washed up in his front yard," Steve said.

"Isn't it your front yard, too?" she asked. "Come to think of it, weren't you wearing those same clothes yesterday when I saw you at the beheading?"

"*Beheading*?" Mark asked.

"Never mind," Steve said.

"This couple, married for thirty years, is sitting down to dinner," Amanda said. "The husband turns to his wife and says that the casserole she made for dinner is too salty. So his wife does the natural thing. She smacks her husband with a cast-iron frying pan, cuts off his head with an electric carving knife, and tosses it out the window."

"What happened to the casserole?" Mark asked.

"She's not one to waste food. She kept it and offered to serve it to us while we worked the crime scene." Amanda glanced at Steve. "I didn't think it was salty, did you?"

Steve shook his head.

Mark stared at his son in disbelief. "You *ate* the casserole?"

"It wasn't the casserole that killed the guy," Steve said.

"In a way it was," Amanda said.

"Could we please move on?" Steve said.

"You're right," Mark said. "Let's stick to the point. Steve spent the night with his girlfriend."

Steve groaned.

"What girlfriend?" Amanda said. "He's never mentioned a girlfriend. Who is she?"

"Her name is Lissy," Mark said. "She used to work nights as a technical support operator until her job got outsourced to India. Now she's studying for her real estate license. He made her a coffee table. Not from scratch, of course. One of those snap-together things from Ikea."

"They don't just snap together," Steve said. "There's fifty parts you've got to assemble with hundreds of special screws and interlocking bolt thingies using only this tiny little tool they give you that's impossible to get a good grip on . . ."

Mark and Amanda stared at him, making him feel self-conscious. He cleared his throat.

"Do you think we could discuss something else now?" Steve motioned to the body. "Like, for instance, this dead mermaid."

"She's not a mermaid," Mark said. "It's a costume."

"Thank you, Dad," Steve replied. "It's nice to know I won't have to go to Atlantis to interview suspects. What can you tell me, Amanda?"

"I'm not a forensics expert, but I'm certain this wasn't where she was killed."

"Because there are no signs that she bled out here?" Steve asked. "The blood could have been washed away by the surf."

"It's not the lack of blood," Amanda said. "It's the body. She's covered with postmortem scrapes and some deep, ragged gashes. She didn't get them from being splashed by the tide on a soft, sandy beach. This body was slammed against a rocky shoreline a few times before washing up here. I'd bet she was in the ocean most of the night."

Mark sighed. "Which means that for the moment the victim herself is the only evidence we have to work with to solve her murder."

"We?" Steve asked.

"She did wash up in my front yard," Mark said.

"That doesn't mean you've got the right to start investigating her murder."

"Of course it does," Mark said.

"I have the strangest feeling I've experienced this conversation before," Amanda said.

"Send that mermaid costume down to the crime lab as soon as you can, okay?" Steve said.

"Sure," Amanda replied. "If you like, I can also finish your end of the argument for you. I think I know all the lines by heart. I can even tell you who wins."

"I know who wins," Steve said, leading his father out of the tent, putting his arm over his shoulder and sheltering him from the rain under his umbrella. They headed for the beach house.

"You've got some kind of luck, Dad."

"What do you mean?"

"A couple months ago you walked in on a murder at the house next door. Now a corpse washes up on the beach, practically on your porch."

"*Our* porch," Mark corrected.

"If I was one of your neighbors," Steve said, "I'd move."

CHAPTER TWO

Russell "Cork" Corcoran liked to tell the rookie life-guards under his command that he was the inspiration for David Hasselhoff's character on *Baywatch*. He told Steve Sloan the same thing as they drove in his lifeguard patrol truck to the southern edge of Point Dume state beach. Steve would have had an easier time believing Cork's story if David Hasselhoff was thirty pounds overweight and tried to hide a bald spot under six wispy strands of hair combed over from the other side of his head.

The rain had stopped, but it was just an intermission while the scenery changed in the meteorological show. Dark, heavy clouds were lumbering up to their marks onstage.

"Normally the currents run north to south," Cork explained as they bounced along the deserted beach in the bright yellow pickup, surfboards and rescue floats strapped to the bed. "But if there's a southern swell, like with the storm we've had the last couple of days, the current runs the opposite way."

After leaving his father's house, Steve had contacted the county lifeguards, hoping someone over there could use tide tables and currents to help him pinpoint where the dead woman might have been dumped into the sea by her killer. Cork had volunteered for the job.

"So you're guessing the body was dumped south of where it was found on Broad Beach," Steve said.

"There's no guesswork involved. I've been doing this job twenty years," Cork said. "I can feel how the currents are moving just by looking at the water."

"So if we know the direction the currents were moving, then it's just a matter of calculating the speed and working backward from her approximate time of death."

"The lateral current runs about a quarter knot per hour," Cork said. "That's about the equivalent of one mile per hour. But then you got to figure in the wind speed, which is going to have a much bigger impact on how far, how fast, and in what direction the body floated."

"How fast was the wind blowing?"

"Fifteen, twenty miles per hour," Cork said. "But you've also got to factor in the tide and lots of other variables. For instance, when there's a southern swell, the current moves a little faster. Plus the wind speed isn't constant; it tends to change based on the time of day. The wind also changes direction depending on what corner of Santa Monica Bay you're talking about."

"This is starting to sound like one of those tricky math questions we used to get in grade school," Steve said. "I flunked math."

"Me too," Cork said.

"Great," Steve said. "You happen to have a calculator in this truck?"

"I don't rely on numbers anyway," Cork said. "I prefer instinct."

Cork stopped the truck at the southernmost edge of sand, where the beach gave way to large, jagged boulders that spilled out into the sea, creating a natural breakwater. They got out of the vehicle and trudged a few feet to the shoreline, close enough to feel the ocean spray as the waves crashed against the rocks.

"Where we're standing, the wind runs west to east,"

Cork said. "My instincts tell me the girl had to be dumped here."

"If the wind blows east," Steve said, "wouldn't that drive the body right back to the beach?"

"You'd think so," Cork said. "But the bay curves in the same direction, so the wind actually runs parallel to the coastline, which, given the factors at play twelve hours ago, would have carried the body north."

Steve wasn't sure he understood Cork's thinking, but his instincts told him this was the right place.

It was a great spot to dispose of a body. There was a public parking lot that ran most of the length of the beach, which would have been pitch-black and empty last night, particularly in the midst of a storm. The location provided easy access and good cover, with the added benefit that the wind, the rain, and the tide would probably wash away any evidence the killer inadvertently left behind.

Steve glanced at the waves, churning and frothing against the boulders. It wasn't just his instincts, or tide tables, or lateral currents that made this spot feel right to him. The location fit with Amanda's theory that the victim's postmortem abrasions came from being dumped along a rocky shoreline.

Still, it was only his gut feeling. He didn't have any proof that this was actually the place where the woman's body had been tossed into the sea.

He looked back at the parking lot. It was about a hundred yards from the lot to the rocks. Either she had walked out to the rocks and then was killed or she was dragged or carried across the sand. If she was dragged, there was a slim chance that some evidence might have been left behind that hadn't been washed away, particularly higher up the beach away from the surf.

That was when Steve noticed the man moving methodically along the beach, waving a metal detector over the sand in front of him, stopping every so often to dig with his sifter for whatever treasure was registering on his earphones.

Steve looked at Cork, then gestured towards the beachcomber. "You know that guy?"

"No, but guys like him always come out after daybreak, particularly after a hot weekend or a major storm," Cork said. "They're looking for things like diamond rings lost by sunbathers or gold doubloons washed up from sunken Spanish galleons."

"Does that happen often?"

"About as often as you find dead mermaids," Cork said.

Steve thanked Cork for his help, asked him to stick around for the evidence collection team, and then marched over to the man with the metal detector.

The beachcomber had a deep tan, a scraggly beard, and long, matted hair that looked like a bird's nest. He wore four filthy shirts on top of one another and an oversized peacoat that hung from his wiry shoulders like a cape. His dirt-encrusted Top-Siders were held together with silver duct tape. His socks were mismatched, one black and one brown. He was totally focused on his task, his eyes locked on the dial of his detector, the sounds of the outside world dampened by his headphones. He didn't notice Steve until he swept his detector over the detective's feet.

The beachcomber looked up, startled, as if rudely awakened from a deep sleep.

Steve flashed his badge and motioned for the man to remove his headphones.

"Lieutenant Steve Sloan, LAPD. Have you been out here long?"

"Every morning," the man said in a voice that sounded like it was filtered through broken glass.

"I meant today."

"Since dawn," the man said. "Why?"

"I'm going to need to confiscate whatever you've found."

"It's mine," the man said, straightening up and puffing out his chest. "The Supreme Court ruled in *Benjamin v. Spruce* that property is deemed lost when it is unintentionally separated from the dominion of its owners. When items are accidentally dropped in any public place or thoroughfare, or anyplace where the inference can be made that such item was left there unknowingly, it is considered lost in a legal sense."

"You're a lawyer?" Steve asked incredulously.

"I spent fourteen years in the Disney legal affairs department before I was disbarred," the man said. He spit on the sand, then continued, "Furthermore, title to such items belongs to the finder against all the world except the true owner."

"So in other words," Steve said, "finders keepers, losers weepers."

"In a crude sense, yes," the man said.

"What does the Supreme Court say about taking evidence from the scene of a murder?"

The man frowned, reached into his jacket, and pulled out a crumpled and damp paper bag.

"I want an itemized receipt," he grumbled, shoving the bag into Steve's hands. "And I want everything back that isn't pertinent to your investigation and first dibs on anything that goes unclaimed after the trial."

"What about the paper bag? Would you like that back, too?"

Steve opened the bag and peered inside. Amidst the sand and loose change, there was a Hot Wheels car, a charm bracelet, a watch, an earring, a fork, a Saint Christopher medal, a fingernail clipper, a cell phone, a keychain, a fishing lure, a pen, a class ring, and a stick of gum still in its foil wrapping.

"What do you do with this stuff?" Steve asked.

"What any sane person would do." The beachcomber scratched at his soiled armpit. "I put it all on eBay."

*　　*　　*

Finding a corpse on the beach didn't slow Mark Sloan down. He still made it to Community General Hospital on time for his first appointment. Not that he'd been in any hurry to get there. It was a meeting he'd been dreading.

His patient was Dr. Dan Marlowe, a cardiologist at Community General. They'd done their internal medicine residencies together and were even neighbors for a while, back when their children were in diapers and their wives were still alive.

Dan was a big, gregarious, round-cheeked man whose hearty laugh, ready smile, and perpetual good cheer made him the natural choice at Christmas to play Santa Claus in the children's ward. He'd gladly donned the Santa suit and passed out gifts to the sick kids for nearly forty years.

Lately, Dan spoke with a hoarse voice that he blamed on too much laughter and lingering laryngitis. But being a doctor himself, he naturally put off seeing one. Mark finally nagged him into it, arguing it was probably a simple sinus or throat infection that could be quickly cured with the right antibiotics.

But it wasn't. Instead, Mark discovered something unexpected and much worse. The laryngitis was an alarm bell, one that rang far too late in Dan's case. The scratchy voice was caused by a tumor on the upper left lobe of his lung that had invaded his recurrent laryngeal nerve. Dan showed no other obvious symptoms of his dire affliction.

Dan insisted that Mark conduct all the follow-up tests and exams at another hospital so word wouldn't spread around Community General about his condition.

So now, rather than meeting in Mark's office or an exam room, they got together over coffee in the Community General cafeteria. They were both wearing their lab coats, stethoscopes slung around their necks, several files open between them. To anyone who saw them, they appeared to be just two doctors conferring on a case. There was nothing unusual about that. But this time the patient happened to be one of the doctors at the table.

The news Mark had to deliver was far from encouraging. The cancer had metastasized widely throughout Dan's body. Aggressive chemotherapy and surgery were the only options, but the prognosis wasn't good. Both men knew that. Dan was in his late sixties, and his cancer was advanced. At best, the treatment might add a year or two to his life, but not much more. His illness was a death sentence.

"This is probably sacrilegious for a doctor to say, but I'm not going to do a damn thing about it," Dan said. "It's a quality-of-life issue. What's the point of living another year or so if the extra time is going to be spent in misery?"

Mark had guessed that would be Dan's decision, and he couldn't really blame him. It was a choice Mark might have made himself had he been in the same position. But still, it saddened him.

"I understand," Mark said. "But there are still things we can do to relieve some of your discomfort."

"Nothing invasive and no drugs that are going to turn me into some kind of zombie," Dan said. "I want to continue showing up at this hospital as a doctor instead of a patient for as long as I can."

"You're going to keep working?"

"Of course," Dan said.

"Wouldn't you rather spend the time you have left traveling? Visiting with your grandchildren? Reading all those books you've always meant to get to someday?"

"Hell no. That would almost be as bad as the chemo," Dan said with one of his robust grins. "I love my job, Mark. I want to do it as long as I'm physically able. But don't worry, old friend. I'll find time to indulge myself and do some of the things that I've put off for too long."

It wasn't the first time Mark had told a patient that he was going to die, and the doctor knew it wouldn't be the last. He was continually amazed by the courage and serenity so many of his patients showed when faced with the certainty of their imminent death. Often it seemed to be their loved ones who felt the most fear, anxiety, and sadness over the news. This time Mark was one of them. He was losing an old, dear friend.

"Don't look so sad, Mark," Dan said. "I'd rather go like this than have a stroke, get hit by a car, or walk into an open manhole."

"I think I'd prefer the manhole."

"Nonsense," Dan said. "It's a luxury to know when you're going to die. It gives you a chance to put your life in order, to say all your good-byes."

"That's the thing," Mark said. "I'm lousy at good-byes."

Dan waved Mark's comment away. "Ah, we all have to go sometime. Few of us are privileged to do it on our own terms. I'm a lucky man."

They sat for a moment in silence, comfortable in each other's company. They had a history together that encompassed most of Mark's personal and professional life.

Mark knew his sadness wasn't for only Dan, but for all the friends and family he'd lost over the years. He'd reached an age at which more and more of his contemporaries were dying. It was as if his past was fading right before his eyes. Soon Mark would be the only one left who could say that what he'd experienced in his youth actually happened.

At that moment Mark realized that what troubled him wasn't just the loss of loved ones or the loneliness of becoming the only witness left to much of his own life.

It was fear.

Of what? Of surviving? Or of knowing that his own death might not be that far off?

But looking at Dan now, so clearly at peace, Mark wondered if there wasn't some benefit to knowing the end of your own story. Perhaps true peace came from seeing the whole picture, from being able to look upon the entirety of your life. Perhaps his fear came from the uncertainty about his own fate, of never being able to achieve that clarity.

"There aren't many of us left," Dan said. "This hospital has changed a lot since we first came in these doors."

"It's changed completely, thanks to me," Mark said. "I'm the reason a mad bomber blew the place up a few years ago."

"I don't mean the brick and mortar," Dan said. "I'm talking about the people, the technology, the practice of medicine. Look at us, Mark. We're still here. Imagine if our younger selves could see us now."

Looking past Dan, across the large cafeteria, Mark could almost see them.

CHAPTER THREE

Mark spent the rest of the morning attending a mind-numbing administrative meeting with the various hospital department heads, which actually wasn't such a bad thing. After finding a corpse on the beach and having an emotional discussion about a friend's imminent death, he needed a little numbing, to give his heart and mind a rest from the depressing events of the day. His eyes were open and he looked attentive, but sitting through the meeting was almost like sleeping, something he hadn't been getting enough of lately anyway.

Although the meeting felt endless, it did finally break up around noon. Mark headed down to the ER to see if his friend and protégé Dr. Jesse Travis wanted some company for lunch.

The ER was filled with patients, which was typical in the wake of a storm, when the number of accident-related injuries increased substantially. But the rain wasn't responsible for the crowded conditions. There were at least three dozen patients, some of them firemen and police officers, and they were all covered with hives.

Dr. Travis was scurrying around to treat the patients who were already there and deal with the steady stream of new arrivals. But if Jesse was overwhelmed, he didn't show it. If anything, he seemed to be enjoying himself, thriving on the urgency and activity. Jesse's boyish enthusiasm reminded Mark more than a little of himself in his twenties, or more accurately, of what he'd been told he was like by those few people who knew him back then.

Mark approached Jesse. "What happened?"

"See those two kids over there?" Jesse cocked his head towards two boys who looked to be about twelve years old, lying on adjacent gurneys, their legs elevated, IVs in their arms. They had red, swollen sores all over their faces, necks, and arms. "They saw a beehive in the eaves of their apartment building and thought it would be a lot of fun to throw rocks at it."

"Oh no," Mark said.

"Sixty thousand Africanized honeybees came swarming out," Jesse said. "Those two were stung a few hundred times before they dove in to the swimming pool. The swarm killed two dogs, attacked everybody in the building and on the street. They even stung the firefighters and paramedics who showed up. The firefighters doused the bees with fire-retardant foam and cordoned off the street until the exterminators got out there."

"Anyone seriously hurt?" Mark knew a healthy adult could endure a thousand stings, but just one sting could cause a hypersensitive person to have a potentially fatal anaphylactic reaction.

"We've have eight patients with massive angioedema but no evidence of cardiovascular problems," Jesse said. "I've got them on diphenylhydramine IV, epinephrine, and oral antihistamines. For everyone else, I've given them Benadryl, ice packs, and a recipe for a skin paste of meat tenderizer with a touch of garlic and seasoned salt."

"What's the garlic and salt for?"

"The steaks," Jesse said. "As long as you're going to be making the paste, you might as well marinate some meat for dinner."

"I'm surprised you didn't just prescribe lunch at Barbeque Bob's," Mark said.

. "That would be a conflict of interest, since Steve and I own the place."

"Looks like you've had an exciting morning," Mark said.

"Not as exciting as yours," Jesse replied. "It's not every day you go for a walk on the beach and trip over a dead mermaid."

"How did you hear about that?"

Jesse gave him a look. "It would be more amazing if I *hadn't* heard about it, don't you think? When a woman in a mermaid suit washes up on a beach with her throat slit, it's a big attention-getter. It's probably all over the Internet by now."

Mark felt a chill. How could he have missed it? He'd been so preoccupied with Dan Marlowe's health problems, he'd put the murder out of his mind for a few hours. But even at the scene, he'd been so caught up in the situation that he'd missed the gruesome point: The murderer wanted the killing to be noticed.

It was a message.

But to whom? And what did it mean?

"Are you okay?" Jesse asked.

Before Mark could reply, his beeper went off. He glanced at the readout to see who was summoning him. It was the pathology lab, also known as the adjunct county morgue. The answers to some of his questions were waiting for him on a stainless-steel autopsy table.

Dr. Amanda Bentley had seen lots of dead bodies, hundreds over the course of her career. She'd cut each of the bodies open and examined them in cold, clinical detail. But none of those autopsies prepared her for the mermaid. And none of them frightened her quite as much.

The first of the Sloans to arrive was Steve. He seemed surprised to find Amanda alone, the corpse of the dead red-haired woman laid out on the examination table in front of her, a sheet covering her eviscerated body.

"Where's my dad?" Steve asked.

"On his way," she said. "I called you first and gave you a half hour head start."

"What did I do to earn such special treatment?" Steve asked.

"You're the homicide detective. It's your case," she replied. "You should hear what I have to say before anyone else does."

"In other words, if Dad got here before me, he would have charmed you into telling him everything, and you didn't want to have to tell the same story twice."

"You should be a detective," Amanda said.

Steve studied her, suspicious. "There's something else you aren't telling me."

"There's a lot I'm not telling you," she said. "But I will, as soon as Mark gets here."

Mark Sloan bounded in at that exact moment, out of breath from running up the stairs.

"Steve," Mark said, "you got here awfully quick."

"You'll just have to run faster next time," Steve said.

Mark took a seat on a stool opposite Amanda and motioned towards the body laid out between them. "So, does she have a name?"

"Not yet." Steve stepped up to the end of the exam table and looked down at the dead woman's pale, expressionless face. "She doesn't match any missing-persons reports, and we came up with nothing when we ran her prints."

"What about the mermaid suit?" Amanda asked.

"It's a Halloween costume made in China and distributed worldwide for the last five years," Steve said. "They are sold by those itinerant, no-name Halloween stores that occupy vacant storefronts for a month or two before October 31 and then disappear the next day."

"So the costume is a dead end," Mark said. "The killer could have bought it anytime over the last five years just about anywhere in the world."

"We've got a good idea where she was dumped, though," Steve said. "Point Dume state beach. The evidence collection team is sifting through the sand right now. We've found a bunch of stuff, from charm bracelets to nipple rings, but nothing we've been able to trace back to anybody yet."

Mark glanced at Amanda. "Looks like the victim is still our best lead to whoever killed her."

Amanda took a deep breath and let it out slowly. Mark and Steve exchanged a look.

"What?" Amanda asked.

"You look upset," Mark said. "What's wrong?"

"She's what's wrong," Amanda said, tilting her head towards the dead woman. "She scares me."

"You've seen a lot worse," Steve said. "We all have."

"I'm not talking about the condition of the corpse," she said.

"You're talking about the message she sends," Mark said softly.

Steve looked at his father. "You mean with the mermaid costume?"

"There's more than that," Mark said, keeping his eyes on Amanda. "Isn't there?"

She nodded. "This is one I'm not going to forget very easily."

Amanda picked up a folder and reviewed her report, reading the salient facts aloud. "The victim is an unidentified Caucasian female, approximately seventeen to twenty years old. She's a brunette. Her hair was colored red shortly before or after she was killed."

"Which was when?" Steve asked.

"Last night, most likely between nine p.m. and midnight. The time she spent in the cold water makes it difficult for me to pinpoint a more precise time of death. But I can tell you she was dead before she went in the water."

"Was there any sign of sexual assault?" Steve asked.

"Not that I can tell," Amanda said. "But again, the immersion in the water, getting tossed around by the surf, could have removed any traces of semen."

"Any drugs or alcohol in her system?" Mark asked.

Amanda seemed to hesitate for an instant before she replied. "I found succinic acid in her blood and in her brain tissue."

Mark stared at her, beginning to understand why this case was going to haunt her, and perhaps him as well, for some time to come.

"Any residual traces of anesthesia?" he asked.

She shook her head.

"Hold on. Not everyone in this room went to medical school," Steve said. "I have no idea what any of this means, and I can tell from looking at your faces that it means a lot. Let's start with succinic acid—what is it?"

"It's a metabolized by-product of succinylcholine, a neuromuscular paralytic. It's usually administered through IV or injection to induce paralysis as part of general anesthesia and intubation," Mark said. "It's also used to control someone having continuous, violent seizures that are preventing the patient from breathing. The drug works almost immediately to relax the muscles and make it easier for the anesthesiologist to intubate the patient and place him on a ventilator."

"What happens if you're given this drug without anesthesia?" Steve asked.

"She would have been wide awake," Amanda said, "but completely paralyzed, unable to move or speak."

"Or breathe," Mark added. "If she wasn't immediately intubated and hooked up to a ventilator, she would have died of asphyxiation within a few minutes."

"You mean she didn't die from getting her throat slit?" Steve said.

"Yes and no," Amanda replied, her voice uneven. "The killer slashed open her trachea and her esophagus. It was a fatal wound. The angle of the incision indicates she was attacked from the front. She was facing her killer."

"I didn't see any defensive wounds," Steve said.

"That's because she doesn't have any," Amanda replied.

Steve looked at Amanda. "You're saying that while she was unable to breathe or move, this bastard looked her in the eye and cut her throat?"

She nodded.

"If she was going to die of asphyxiation anyway," Steve said, "why did he slit her throat, too?"

"To add to her agony," Mark said, his face tight. "And her terror."

They were silent for a long moment, all of them staring down at the unidentified woman in front of them and imagining the horror she must have experienced in the moments before her death.

"There's more," Amanda said, almost whispering.

Mark glanced up at her, shocked. What more could the killer possibly have done to this poor woman?

"When I opened her up, I found this in her stomach," Amanda said. "It was coated with bacon fat to make it easier to swallow."

She held up a sealed evidence bag that contained a tiny black object, rectangular with one clipped corner, that was about the size and thickness of a priority mail postage stamp.

It was a memory card, the kind used in a digital camera.

CHAPTER FOUR

Steve took the memory card back to the police lab to get it cleaned up and, if possible, extract any data that might be encoded on it.

Mark remained in the morgue, examining the corpse himself, going over every detail of Amanda's autopsy and reviewing all of the various test results. He wasn't sure what he was looking for, but something was nagging at him, something beyond the horror of what the killer had done to his victim.

Why did he dress her in a mermaid costume?

Why did he paralyze her and slit her throat?

Why did he dump her body in the ocean?

Whatever was on the memory card could hold some of the answers, but Mark couldn't shake the feeling that the questions added up to something else on their own. Even more troubling, in some strange way it felt familiar, as if somewhere deep inside he already knew the answers.

He'd never seen a dead woman dressed as a mermaid before, or anything like it. Was the murder symbolic of something else he'd heard about or encountered?

It was frustrating and infuriating.

While he conducted his examination, Amanda hardly acknowledged he was there, concentrating her attention on other autopsies. He didn't take it personally. He couldn't blame her for wanting to distance herself from the horror this dead woman represented.

Mark also knew Amanda wasn't offended by his re-examining the body and double-checking her conclusions. They'd been working together for too long, and respected each other too much, for any such resentment.

He found only one thing Amanda had missed—the puncture wound where the victim was given the lethal injection of succinylcholine. It was in her back, near her shoulder, suggesting that this was one attack the killer made from behind, taking the woman by surprise.

Jesse came in around four o'clock, at the end of his shift, eager to know the latest developments in the case. Mark was glad to fill him in because it gave him a chance to go over all the details for himself once more and get a fresh perspective at the same time.

"Whoever did this is one major sicko," Jesse said. "I don't know how he ever got a medical degree."

"What makes you think he has one?" Amanda asked.

"He had to get succinylcholine somewhere," Jesse said. "Which means he's either a doctor, a nurse, a paramedic, or a pharmacist."

"Or knows someone who is," Mark said. "Or he works in a hospital or pharmacy or in a nonmedical capacity that gives him access to drugs and the opportunity to steal them."

"What makes you think the killer is a *he*?" Amanda asked. "It could be a woman. She might have used succinylcholine because she didn't have the strength to subdue her victim any other way."

Amanda's phone rang and she answered it. She spoke for only a moment, then hung up.

"That was Steve," Amanda said. "They were able to pull a file off the memory card. It's a picture."

Amanda and Jesse got in their cars and followed Mark back to his beach house. There was no way either of them was going to miss whatever discoveries Steve had to share with his father. Mark didn't discourage them from coming. He had a feeling that soon he was going to need all the help he could get to solve this mystery.

While reexamining the body, Mark had come to a grim conclusion he didn't want to share, at least not yet. Whoever killed this woman took too much perverse delight in it to be satisfied with just one kill.

There would be more.

When Mark arrived at the beach house with Amanda and Jesse in tow, Steve didn't seem surprised. In fact, he seemed to be expecting them. He had a laptop on the kitchen table and four chairs already arranged at one end so they could all have a clear view of the screen.

"I've copied the file onto a CD," Steve said. "It's a photograph in JPEG format."

"What's it a picture of?" Jesse asked.

"That's the bizarre thing." Steve clicked a few keys, and the front page from an old issue of the *Los Angeles Times* appeared on-screen. The date on the masthead was Friday, February 9, 1962. The major headline was L.A. DECLARED DISASTER AREA AFTER SIX-DAY DOWNPOUR. TWENTY-ONE DEAD. Mark started to read the article.

> *Governor Brown has declared Los Angeles County a disaster area in the wake of six days of unrelenting rain, which has dropped three inches of water on the Southland and claimed 21 lives.*
>
> *Mudslides accounted for three deaths alone on Thursday in the San Fernando Valley, where two children and one woman were swept away when the rain-swelled Los Angeles River overflowed its banks.*
>
> *The children, Robert Reese, age 9, and his sister, Ginny Reese, age 12, were rescued by Los Angeles firefighters, but the woman drowned. The victim's*

identity is being withheld pending notification of next of kin.

A downed power line in Reseda is blamed for the death of a motorist, who was electrocuted stepping out of his car on Balboa Avenue. Arnold T. Tyler, 27, leaves behind a wife and two children, all of whom were inside the vehicle and witnessed his death.

Rising waters at two man-made lakes threatened to spill over dams and inundate the town of Palm-dale, and electricity in downtown Pasadena was knocked out for six hours when water submerged underground power lines.

Many sections of the county, particularly new subdivisions, were flooded, forcing evacuations of residents from their homes in Woodland Hills, En-cino, and Northridge.

A tree crushed a home in Westwood, while mud-slides in the Hollywood Hills swept three homes off their canyon perches.

Two schools in Culver City were closed when a six-inch high-pressure natural gas line was snapped in a sinkhole on Washington Boulevard.

Numerous city and county streets were closed to traffic due to the downpour.

Mark stopped reading midway through the article and took a seat at the table, while the others remained standing, huddled around the laptop. Suddenly, he could feel each day of the last forty years, as if they were bricks stacked on his shoulders.

He knew why the dead woman's hair was dyed red.

"What does that newspaper have to do with anything?" Jesse asked.

"Obviously it means something," Amanda said, "or the killer wouldn't have put it on a memory card and made his victim swallow it."

Mark knew why the dead woman was dressed as a mermaid.

"That newspaper was published forty years ago today," Steve said. "And it was raining then, too."

"Maybe that's not the story the killer wants us to see," Amanda said. "Maybe it's one of these other articles on the front page."

Mark knew why the killer slit the woman's throat.

"We're checking out each article," Steve said. "Starting with all the people whose names are mentioned in the stories."

"You think the victim or the killer is related to one of them?" Amanda asked.

"At this point I don't know what to think," Steve said, turning to his dad. "Do you?"

Mark looked up at his son and surprised him by nodding. "It's no coincidence that this body washed up in front of my house this morning. I was supposed to find her. She was killed for me."

Steve saw his father's ashen face and shaking hands and got very worried. His father had never looked so tired. So old. *So afraid.*

"Jesse?" Steve said, but the young doctor was already moving to Mark's side.

"Mark, are you all right?" Jesse asked, putting his hand to Mark's forehead. "Do you feel any dizziness or pain?"

"I'm fine," Mark said.

"You don't look it," Jesse said.

"Neither would you if you were responsible for the horrible things that were done to that poor, innocent woman," Mark said.

Jesse turned to Amanda. "Could you please get him a glass of water and a cold towel?"

She nodded and hurried to the kitchen.

"You didn't kill her, Dad," Steve said.

"Not directly," Mark replied. "But this newspaper

clipping proves it all has to do with me—and a series of events that began on this day in 1962."

Steve pulled out a chair from the table and sat down next to his father. "What happened, Dad?"

Amanda set the glass of water in front of Mark. He took a long sip, then faced his son.

"Forty-three years ago today, my life changed," Mark said. "I didn't know it at the time, but I was about to solve my first murder."

CHAPTER FIVE

1962

On the rare occasions when it rains in Southern California, it feels like the end of the world, certainly for a doctor struggling to keep up with all the people injured in the floods, mudslides, drownings, electrocutions, and countless car accidents.

I was a young GP on a rotation that had me doing time all over Community General. In February 1962, I was in the middle of a three-month stint in the emergency room. I was on call every other night, which on paper meant I was on for thirty-six hours and off for twelve. I was supposed to show up at the hospital at six thirty a.m. and leave the next day at seven p.m., then return twelve hours later and start all over again.

But that's not the way it really worked. I could never get out of the hospital before midnight. There were too many patients and too much paperwork, especially during a major rainstorm. So I actually worked at least forty hours at a stretch with about seven hours off.

In those seven short hours of freedom, I had to squeeze in one good meal, a shower, and some sleep, which you can manage if you're a single guy. It's not so easy when you're a newlywed with a wife, who naturally appreciates a little attention, and a newborn son, who wakes up every two hours, crying to be fed or have his diaper changed.

We were living in a two-bedroom, second-floor apartment on Armacost Avenue in West Los Angeles. The place was called the Tropic Sands and was built around a concrete courtyard and two palm trees planted in a sandbox. On sunny afternoons, residents scooted lounge chairs under the trees, sat in the shade, and used the sandbox as an ashtray. Our rent was sixty dollars a month and we were roller-skating distance from the hospital. I know, because when it wasn't raining, that's how I'd get to work.

In fact, a lot of people who worked at the hospital lived in the neighborhood. If a kid scraped his knee on the sidewalk, he could count on at least two doctors rushing out to treat him and someone from the accounting department making sure his parents got billed.

On that day in February, I straggled home around midnight, dead tired and completely drenched from the pouring rain. I made myself a sandwich and ate it as I stripped out of my wet clothes. I flopped into bed still chewing on my last bite, doing my best not to wake up Katherine, who was sleeping so peacefully on the other side. I was asleep as soon as my head hit the pillow.

It seemed like an instant later when the alarm jolted me awake again at five thirty a.m. I was alone in bed. Katherine was already up, and I could smell bacon sizzling in the pan. I threw off the sheets, put on a bathrobe, and lumbered into the living room, which was also our dining room, family room, and kitchen.

Katherine was sitting at our new dinette set, reading the newspaper. We got the set by trading in twenty-two books of Blue Chip stamps we'd saved up from grocery shopping. She was real excited about the table because it had a textured, laminated plastic top that looked like wood but was supposedly heat, stain, and scratch resistant. I say "supposedly" because I eventually decided to test that claim and managed to completely destroy the table.

She was freshly showered and wearing a pink bathrobe, an apron tied over it at the waist and neck. Her hair was wet, bound up in a towel using a technique that completely baffled me. I have no idea how it stayed in place.

I came up behind her and gave her a big kiss on the neck, where I knew she was especially ticklish. She smelled like a flower bed, and when she smiled it lit up her whole face. Her cheeks flushed, her nose crinkled, and her eyebrows arched in glee. I loved it and it only made me want to amuse her even more.

Katherine squirmed away from me, giving up her seat.

"Stop it," she said, still smiling.

I swiped her chair at the table and sat down. "I can't help myself," I said.

I fell in love with her the first time I saw her singing at the Blossom Room of the Roosevelt Hotel. The problem was she was engaged to someone else at the time. I couldn't help myself then either.

"That's your excuse for everything." She gave me a kiss on the cheek and went to take care of breakfast.

I looked at her standing there at the stove, the apron over her bathrobe, her hair wound up in that towel, her feet in those big fuzzy slippers, and it brought tears of happiness to my eyes. No woman on earth could possibly have been more beautiful than she was at that moment.

"You'll never guess what I found in bed this morning," she said, cracking some eggs in a bowl.

"An incredibly handsome young doctor with the body of a Greek god?"

"Half of a roast beef sandwich," she said.

"That was for you," I said. "In case you woke up in the middle of the night to feed Steve and wanted a snack."

"You're so thoughtful," she said. "Was it raining hard when you came home last night?"

"Noah waved at me from the ark," I said, beginning to browse the newspaper.

"I read in Hedda Hopper's column that Alfred Hitchcock believes the twist is responsible for all the rain we're having. He says it's a pagan rain dance."

"He must be joking," I said, though I wasn't entirely sure he was. Rock music was being blamed for everything from drug addiction to communism. Pretty soon, I was sure, they'd start prosecuting people just for listening to it.

That very week, a bookseller was being tried in Los Angeles for obscenity for selling Henry Miller's novel *Tropic of Cancer* in his Hollywood store. There was an article in the paper right in front of me that recounted a psychologist's testimony that the book was "the perverted, irrational babbling of an unhealthy mind." I don't know what that said about me, since I had a copy of *Tropic of Cancer* sitting on my nightstand.

While Katherine prepared bacon and eggs for us, I glanced at the headlines. A hundred and twenty people had to flee their homes when the LA River overflowed and flooded the streets. The U.S. Navy was testing its first nuclear-powered ship. Mrs. Nelson Rockefeller had moved to Nevada to begin her six weeks of compulsory residence before filing for divorce from the governor of New York. A landslide on the Pacific Coast Highway swept several cars out of traffic and onto the beach. Construction workers were rushing to finish the Space Needle in time for the Seattle World's Fair. And astronaut John Glenn was preparing to take off and orbit the earth in a space capsule, weather permitting.

I noticed Katherine had bent the corner down on an advertisement for new homes in the valley. She must have been waiting for me to get to it because no sooner had I arrived at the page than she placed my breakfast in front of me and said, "Did you read about the beautiful ranch-style homes they're building in Encino?" She went back into the kitchen area for the coffeepot. "All the homes have three bedrooms, two baths, sliding glass doors, and thermostatic heating."

"They start at eighteen thousand," I said. "We can't afford that."

"Not yet," she said, pouring me a cup of coffee. "But that doesn't mean we shouldn't start thinking about it."

"Dreaming is more like it," I said.

"Dreams have a way of coming true." She set the coffeepot down on her new heat-resistant dinette table and gave me a big kiss. "Look at the two of us."

That's when Steve started crying. It wasn't something you could ignore. I couldn't believe a human being, especially one so small, could make a screech as earsplitting as that. It sounded like some enraged cheetah on a megaphone.

Katherine sighed, gave me another kiss, and went back to the kitchen. "Would you mind seeing to Steve? I'll get his milk ready."

I shoved a piece of bacon in my mouth and went to his room. Steve was in his crib, wailing. He was a chubby little baby. We affectionately called him the Tank. I picked him up and took him to the changing table.

Nothing in medical school had prepared me for changing Steve's diapers. It was like some six-hundred-pound grizzly bear had been wearing them instead of my son. Every time I had to do it, I found myself longing for gloves, oxygen, and a nurse to swab my forehead.

Somehow I managed. He stopped crying and gave me a smile he'd obviously inherited from his mother. I couldn't resist tickling him either. He giggled and kicked and squirmed with delight. I carried him into the kitchen and gave him to Katherine, who had a bottle ready.

And that was when I saw the time. It was already after six. I couldn't possibly eat, shower, get dressed, and make it to the hospital on time. And I couldn't be late—not again. Not unless I wanted to face the wrath of Dr. Alistair Whittington.

Have you ever tried eating scrambled eggs while taking a shower? Let me tell you, it's not easy. But I'm proud to say I'm one of the few people who has mastered the art.

You can tell a lot about a person by the kind of car he drives. I was driving a two-door 1959 Chevrolet Biscayne, which I bought used with a loan from Katherine's parents. It had two gigantic horizontal rear fins that looked like mischievously arched eyebrows over a pair of teardrop-shaped taillights. The combined effect was like a big steel-and-chrome happy face.

By comparison, the car I almost smashed into as I sped, tires squealing, into a parking space at the hospital was a brand-new 1962 Chrysler Imperial Crown Southampton. In name alone, it perfectly summed up the personality and bearing of the man who owned it, Dr. Alistair Whittington, who had been recruited from England by the trustees to run the hospital and its nursing school.

The Imperial was elegant and imposing, with an aggressive face, stylish detailing, and enormous power. The same could be said of Whittington, who stood glaring at me from under his pearl-handled umbrella as I emerged from my car. It was the same umbrella he deployed on sunny days for his midday "constitutional."

He wore a dark Trilby hat, a single-breasted jacket, a white Turnbull and Asser tailored shirt, red-and-black-striped Oxford University tie, a four-pocket vest, and dark, crisply pleated pants neatly cuffed above polished shell cordovan shoes. Dr. Whittington exuded class and authority. I imagined he exuded it even when sitting on the toilet. He remained resolutely British at all times and in everything he did, refusing to bow to California's casual lifestyle or American customs.

"Good morning, Dr. Whittington," I said as I opened my umbrella, which had two broken spokes and sagged on one side. Somehow I turned into a hapless clown whenever he was around.

He looked at me with undisguised contempt. Then again, it was hard to say, since he seemed to regard everything about America and Americans with contempt. Or maybe it was just everything about me.

"Are you familiar with Oscar Wilde, Dr. Sloan?" he asked with a heavy, upper-class British accent.

"'I have nothing to declare except my genius,'" I said. Then I caught the glower on his face.

"Is that so?" Dr. Whittington said. I wanted to disappear.

"I didn't mean I'm a genius, of course," I stammered.

"I should hope not," he said.

"I was quoting something Oscar Wilde said to show that I was familiar with him, when I suppose I just should have said yes."

"A lesson you should take to heart more often. Oscar Wilde said, 'A well-tied tie is the first serious step in life.'" Whittington cleared his throat. "I do wish you'd take that step."

I looked down at my tie. It looked tied to me, though not as tightly and efficiently as Dr. Whittington's knot. But when I checked out my tie, I also saw my feet and, with rising embarrassment, realized that he'd seen them, too.

"Nice to see that your shoes match for a change," Whittington said. "Perhaps someday you will accomplish the same with your stockings."

In my rush to get out of the house, I'd put on two different socks. One white. One black. And of course he'd noticed. He noticed everything I did wrong.

"I suppose I should be grateful that at least you aren't wearing roller skates," he said.

"I only roller-skate to work when it's sunny," I said, as we started walking toward the entrance to the hospital. "But it's interesting you should mention that, sir. I've been thinking I could accomplish more if I wore them in the hospital. We all could. Imagine how much more quickly we could get around if we were all on wheels."

He stopped and looked at me incredulously. "You'd like me to imagine a hospital full of roller-skating doctors?"

When he said it that way, it didn't sound quite the way I'd intended it. Before I could reply, he shook his head and marched on.

"You terrify me, Dr. Sloan," he said. "I fear that someday you're going to destroy this hospital. I just hope I'm not here to see it."

I didn't know it then, but he was right on both counts.

CHAPTER SIX

I fully expected Dr. Whittington to walk off without saying another word to me, but as we stepped into the emergency room, he did something surprising. He stopped, reached into his jacket pocket, and handed me an envelope.

"I'm having a little informal mixer at my home this Saturday," he said. "I hope you and your wife will come. And do try to wear matching socks."

He continued on, leaving me standing there in shock.

"Don't you just love it? We finally get a day off and we have to spend it with him," Dan Marlowe said, putting his arm around my shoulder. He looked pretty much the same then as he does now, only with a full head of hair and not a hint of gray.

"But he hates me," I said.

"He doesn't hate you, Mark," Dan said. "Whittington hates all of us."

I went to the doctors' locker room to change out of my wet clothes and swap my busted umbrella for my stethoscope. I was rooting around for an extra white or black sock when I noticed another colleague of mine, Dr. Chet Arnold, sitting on a bench snoring, with his forehead against his locker.

Chet was at the end of his shift and was so tired he'd fallen asleep before he could even open his locker. I thought I had it bad, but he had it worse. He had a wife and two toddlers at home.

The nurses called him Troy because he looked like Troy Donahue and had a movie star's natural charisma, but his bedside manner still put all his patients to sleep. He was an anesthesiologist.

I gently nudged him awake and he jerked as if electrocuted.

"Oh hell," he said. "I'm still here."

"Where did you think you were?" I asked.

"In my car, driving home," he said. "I was almost at my front door when you woke me up. I could practically smell my wife's pot roast."

"Now you have something to look forward to," I said. "Speaking of which, did you get invited to Dr. Whittington's party?"

Chet nodded and opened his locker. "You're looking forward to that?"

"Maybe he's more relaxed in a casual setting," I said.

"I doubt it," Chet said, taking off his lab coat and his shirt. "I think he's just lonely. His wife and kid have been visiting family in London for weeks."

My locker was a disorganized mess overflowing with files, books, dirty clothes, roller skates, newspapers, two lab coats, some magic tricks I was practicing, and a few sack lunches I'd never gotten around to eating.

Chet's locker was the model of organization. He had two or three sets of shirts and pants, a selection of ties, and several pairs of socks in assorted colors, all folded and rolled into neat rectangles for easy stacking.

"You mind if I borrow a pair of socks?" I motioned to my feet. "Either black or white will do."

He glanced at my mismatched socks and broke out in a big grin, then tossed me two pairs, one white and one black.

"Why don't you just poke Whittington in the eye when you see him?" Chet asked. "You know whatever you do is going to have the same effect anyway."

I took one of the white socks, swapped it for my black one, and was just tying up my shoe when there was an urgent pounding on the door. Before either one of us could reply, Alice Blevins threw open the door. I was surprised she'd bothered to knock. The last thing she cared about was the privacy or modesty of a bunch of pampered doctors. She was the head nurse and had served in a mobile army surgical hospital during the Korean War. Nothing rattled her except, perhaps, having to trade her camouflage fatigues for a dainty nurse's cap and apron.

"Incoming," she said.

The pounding rain created a swath of destruction in the San Fernando Valley. The Los Angeles River overflowed, washing two children, a brother and sister, off the banks and into the raging current of mud, plants, and debris. The children were carried two and a half miles before being rescued by firefighters, who dangled from the Zelzah Avenue bridge on ropes. It was during the rescue that the firefighters stumbled on another victim, a young woman caught up in some branches snagged around the bridge pilings.

The children arrived first. The nine-year-old boy was unconscious and suffering from hypothermia. A firefighter gave him mouth-to-mouth all the way to the hospital. Dan took the boy from the gurney, draped him over his knee, and smacked him twice on the back, very hard. The boy coughed up water, and kept coughing it up, before starting to breathe on his own. Dan rushed the child into the exam room, where hot blankets were waiting. The kid was lucky to be alive, and so was his sister, a twelve-year-old girl who came in conscious but shivering, her left arm dangling awkwardly at her side. She was shivering so hard you could almost miss how much pain she was in.

She had a dislocated shoulder, and I knew the sooner we popped that arm back into place the better, or serious complications could result. I also knew it would be painful and I dreaded hurting the child, but there was no other way.

The girl was wheeled on a gurney into the exam room. I gestured for Alice to join me and to draw the curtain.

"I'm Dr. Mark Sloan," I told her. "What's your name?"

"Ginny Reese," she stammered, freezing, clutching the firefighter's blanket around herself with her good arm.

"You've dislocated your shoulder, Ginny. I have to put it back."

"Is it going to hurt?" she asked.

"Yes," I said. A lot of doctors would have soft-pedaled that, but I was a firm believer, even with the limited experience I had then, in being honest with all my patients, regardless of their age.

"Okay," Ginny said. "Let's get it over with."

I smiled at Alice. "She's almost as tough as you."

Alice shook her head. "I bet she's a lot tougher. Aren't you, Ginny?"

"I didn't save my brother," she said.

"I thought you were both swept up by the river," I said. "You're telling me you went in after him?"

"I'm his older sister," she said.

I wanted to hug her, but I knew how much it would hurt if I did. So instead I stroked her head.

"You're a terrific older sister," I said. "And he's just fine. He probably would have given up if it wasn't for you."

"You think so?" she asked.

"Positive," I said. "Okay, I need you to sit on the edge of the bed. Can you do that for me?"

Ginny did what I asked.

"Here's what's going to happen, Ginny. I'm going to take your arm, turn my back to you, and lift you up as if I wanted to give you a piggyback ride. This will pull your arm forward and slip it back into the shoulder socket."

I gave her a minute to think about what I'd said. When it comes to hurting children, some doctors like to amuse, trick, or distract them from the pain they are about to experience. The theory being, I suppose, that telling children what's going to happen will terrify them, that whatever you're going to do will be over before they know it anyway.

They always know it. And then the kids end up resenting the deception and distrusting doctors, an attitude that continues into adulthood. I believe that half of fear is uncertainty and that if a child, or any other patient, knows what's coming and has a chance to prepare for it emotionally, it also deadens the pain.

"Are you ready, Ginny?"

She nodded.

I took her dislocated arm, bent my body forward, and lifted her up on my back. She screamed and I heard the pop of the humeral head slipping back into place.

Tears were rolling down her cheeks when I set her back on the gurney, but she wasn't crying. "I'm sorry I screamed."

"Of course you screamed," I said. "If it was me, I would have screamed even louder."

That's when the firefighters came in with the third victim on a gurney, the woman they'd found in the river under the bridge. I hurried out to meet them, but Dan got to her first, placing a stethoscope on her chest.

The woman was wearing a raincoat, a white blouse, and a businesslike black skirt with garter stockings. The clothes were disheveled and torn from her journey in the roiling water. Her shoes were gone. Her entire body was caked with dirt, her face scratched. Her nose and mouth were full of mud. She'd clearly drowned. Our job now was to make the obvious official.

Dan shook his head sadly and glanced at the clock on the wall. "Time of death, eight forty-eight a.m."

I stood beside him and looked at her. She was an unnatural redhead. The hair color had run and stained her blouse. She smelled of mud, rot, and fresh flowers.

I felt an inexplicable, sudden stab of fear. I took a big step back from the gurney and collided with a firefighter, who stood dripping behind me.

"Haven't you ever seen a dead body before?" the firefighter asked.

"Too many times," I said. I didn't think I'd ever get used to the death. It was an inescapable part of my job and I saw it every day.

It wasn't the corpse that frightened me. It was something else. But what?

"Do you know who she is?" I asked.

The firefighter shook his head. "The police are looking for her purse along the riverbank. All we found in her pockets were these."

He showed me a compact, a lipstick applicator, and a shiny new key all by itself on a rabbit-foot chain.

Dan looked at the belongings, too. "We've made a major discovery here today, Mark."

"What's that?" I asked.

"A rabbit's foot definitely doesn't bring good luck," he said and walked away.

I glanced back at the dead woman one last time and felt the oddest tingle. It wasn't fear. And it wasn't a physical sensation either. Something was flitting across my consciousness, tickling my mind. It was like a burst of static on a television screen, only I felt it rather than saw it.

Back then, I didn't know what the feeling meant, so I simply ignored it. I've learned never to ignore it now.

Alice brought over two orderlies, and they draped a blanket over the woman's corpse and wheeled it down to the morgue in the basement.

CHAPTER SEVEN

I went to the cafeteria for lunch, where I was served the "doctor's special," which was chopped beef, mashed potatoes, cubed carrots, a cup of chocolate pudding, and a tiny carton of cold milk. It made me long for the gourmet pleasures of a TV dinner.

Dr. Bart Spicer was sitting alone at a table, smoking a cigarette and leafing through an issue of *Life* magazine with astronaut John Glenn on the cover, wearing a space helmet. The cover read: THE MAKING OF A BRAVE MAN.

I took a seat across from Bart, who acknowledged me with a nod and a perfect smoke ring. "I was just reading about John Glenn. They call him 'A Man Marked to Do Great Things.' They say it was clear from the day he was born. What do you think of that?"

"It takes guts to fly into space and attempt to orbit the earth," I said.

"It takes guts just to get out of bed in the morning." He snubbed out his cigarette in the remains of his mashed potatoes. "You want to know who's a great man?"

"Sure," I said.

Bart opened up the magazine to an advertisement for the Admiral Multiplex FM stereophonic radio and high fidelity phonograph in a French provincial cabinet. "The guy who has to sell four of five of these a week or he loses his job. But you're never gonna see that guy's mug on the cover of *Life* magazine."

"Probably not," I said.

I liked Bart. Having lunch with him was like listening to the radio. He had opinions about everything and liked to express them. You could participate in the conversation as much or as little as you wanted. He'd simply go on talking without you.

Bart was a farm boy from Kansas, the first in his family to go to medical school. Actually, the first to go anywhere after high school except back to the plow. He and his wife, Mary, lived on our street and had a baby girl only a few months older than Steve.

"I'm going to be on the cover of *Life* magazine," Bart said casually.

"For orbiting the earth or selling radios?" I asked.

"It's not actually going to be my face that you see," he said. "It's going to be all the beautiful people I make more beautiful with my scalpel. You know why John Glenn is wearing a helmet in this picture?"

"Because he's an astronaut?"

"To distract people from his face. If I had that mug, I'd be wearing a mask," Bart said. "He should've come to see me."

"You aren't a plastic surgeon yet," I said.

Bart shrugged. "He couldn't look worse than he does now."

He looked past me and broke into a broad grin. "It's raining outside, but here comes a ray of sunshine."

I turned to see which nurse he was flirting with and saw Katherine coming in, carrying Steve. It was a wonderful surprise. I got up and gave them both a kiss, taking Steve from her arms. She sat down at the table.

"Bart, you are an awful flirt," she said.

"How's my big boy?" I said, tossing Steve up into the air and catching him again. It always made Katherine nervous, but I was a good catch and Steve loved it, shrieking with glee.

"What brings you here, honey?" I asked her.

"Me, of course," Bart said, kissing her cheek.

Katherine smiled. "Isn't this chopped-beef-and-mashed-potato day? We couldn't miss that. And we certainly can't go a whole day without seeing Mark."

"Now you've hurt my feelings," Bart said.

"I'm glad you came. I have some news. Dr. Whittington has invited us to a party on Saturday." I showed Katherine the invitation and gave Steve another toss in the air. "We need to find a babysitter quick."

"No problem," Bart said. "We've already lined one up. You can drop Steve at our place and the four of us can go to the party together."

"Are you sure Mary won't mind?" Katherine asked.

"Why should she?" Bart replied. "As long as she's out of the house having a good time, I could bring a walrus home and she wouldn't mind."

I held Steve up high and smiled at him. "Are you a walrus? Is that what you are?"

He giggled uproariously and then vomited all over me. My shirt and lab coat were covered. Bart burst out laughing and Katherine joined him. Even Steve thought it was funny, giggling so much I thought he might vomit on me again just for the fun of it. I was the only one not laughing because I was the only one who knew I was wearing my last clean shirt and lab coat.

I handed Steve back to Katherine, picked up a napkin, and began the hopeless task of cleaning myself off.

"That will teach you to call Steve a walrus," Katherine said. "He's very sensitive."

"So I've discovered." I went over to Katherine. "Thank you so much for coming."

"Do you really mean it?"

"Of course I do," I said.

"Even after what Steve did?" she said.

"A small price to pay for the chance to spend some time with you," I said.

Katherine glanced at Bart. "You're a good influence on him."

"I'm a good influence on everybody," he said.

"I better go clean up before Dr. Whittington sees me," I leaned down to kiss Katherine. I could still smell the faintest hint of fresh flowers.

Suddenly I felt a jolt of fear, the same flutter in my chest I'd experienced when I saw the dead woman who was pulled from the Los Angeles River.

"What is it?" Katherine asked, studying my face. "What's wrong?"

The fear passed quickly, but that nagging sensation, that mental itch, returned. I sniffed Katherine again.

"What is that smell?" I asked.

"Vomit," she said.

"I mean on you," I said. "The flowers?"

"It's probably my bath oil," she said. "Why?"

I thought back to the dead woman, but the image that came to me wasn't her entire body laid out on the gurney. It wasn't even her face. It was little, seemingly inconsequential details. The tan line around her wrist. Her pierced ears. The seam of her stockings. I was remembering things I didn't realize I'd even seen.

I knew why I was jerked back when I saw the dead woman.

She smelled like my wife.

I was beginning to understand what that nagging feeling meant and why I'd felt afraid. But there was only one way to find out if I was right.

I reassured Katherine that everything was fine, then hurried to the locker room, washed up, and changed into a pair of surgical scrubs before making my way down to the morgue.

The woman's body was on a gurney in the cold room

with a dozen other corpses, patients of all ages who had died of all kinds of ailments. Most of the bodies had been stripped and cleaned and were ready to be picked up by morticians. But the woman from the river was exactly as we had left her, still in her muddy clothes, waiting to be claimed by the medical examiner for her autopsy.

I wheeled her out of the cold room and into the light of the pathology lab.

She wasn't a corpse anymore. She was a puzzle.

I put on a pair of gloves and sniffed her. Although she was covered with mud, the smell of bath oil was strong. Her blouse must have been soaked with it; the river water hadn't managed to overcome the scent.

She was tan and fit, with perfect proportions, long legs, and an even tan. She spent a lot of time outdoors, probably at the beach. She was a true California girl, though I couldn't figure out why she'd chosen to dye her hair red instead of blond.

I looked at her wrists, her fingers, and her ears.

I lifted her skirt and examined the garter belt, the straps stretched over her panties to her nylon stockings, the seams running up the sides of her legs from her heels to the middle of her thighs.

I knew at that moment with chilling certainty what it all meant, what my subconscious had been trying to tell me. And yet it only intensified my curiosity.

I rolled her on her side, pulled her blouse up to her shoulders, and was in the midst of scrutinizing her bra when someone walked in.

"What the hell do you think you're doing?" the man demanded.

I turned and got my first look at Dr. Jay Barbette, the medical examiner, standing in the doorway in his lab coat, flanked by two of his morgue attendants.

Barbette was a tall man in his sixties with a bushy gray mustache, tousled hair, and a tiny pair of glasses that seemed far too small for his bulbous nose and his round face, which, at that moment, was flushed with outrage.

"I'm Dr. Mark Sloan," I said. "She was one of my patients."

"Before or after she drowned in the LA River?"

"That's a difficult question to answer," I said.

"Why is that?"

"Because I never saw her before today," I said. "And she didn't drown in the river."

"Didn't the firefighters find her in the river?"

"Yes, they did," I said.

Barbette came over, stood beside me, and looked at the body. "She definitely drowned. I can see that already."

"I agree," I said.

"I'm so relieved to hear that," he said, rubbing his temples. "Son, you're giving me a headache. You better make your point and make it quick, or I'm going to ask my friends here to drag you out and restrain you until the police can get here."

I smiled at Dr. Barbette's two brawny assistants. "That won't be necessary."

"I'll be the judge of that," Barbette said.

"I believe she drowned in her bathtub and her body was dumped in the river."

He looked at me incredulously. "You do."

"She smells like fresh flowers," I said.

"Excuse me?"

"Sniff her," I said.

"Are you some kind of pervert?"

"Her blouse is soaked in bath oil," I said. "It's like she put her clothes on without drying off first."

"You're saying she drowned in her bathtub simply because she didn't adequately towel herself this morning?"

"That's not all, Dr. Barbette. Her ears are pierced and she has tan lines where she usually wears a watch and several rings," I said. "But she isn't wearing any jewelry."

"She fell into a raging river," he said. "Didn't it occur

to you that her jewelry might have been swept away in the current?"

"Yes, but that doesn't explain the seams on her stockings."

"The seams?" he asked.

"They should be going up the back of her legs," I said, pointing it out with my finger. "And the garter belt straps are on top of her panties, not underneath them."

"What does that have to do with where she drowned?" he said, his voice rising with impatience.

"No woman would go out in public with the seams showing in front, and she certainly wouldn't put the straps over her panties. That's how garter belts are modeled, but that's not how real women wear them."

"I suppose you're an expert on 'real' women," he said.

"I'm married to one," I said. "I know if my wife had to go to the bathroom, she wouldn't want to have to take off her garter belt and stockings to do it."

Barbette turned and studied the dead woman again, then glanced back at me. When he spoke, the impatience in his voice was gone.

"But someone dressing her might make that mistake," he said. "Someone in a hurry."

"A man," I said. "A woman would know better."

Barbette nodded, a thoughtful expression on his face, then turned to his two attendants. "Gentlemen, why don't you go get us a couple cups of coffee? Hot as possible, please. How do you take yours, Doctor . . . ?"

"Sloan," I said. "Mark Sloan. Black, with two spoonfuls of sugar."

"Same for me," Barbette said.

The two attendants seemed confused by the sudden turn of events, but no more so than me. They left. As soon as they were gone, Barbette gestured to the woman again.

"Why were you turning her on her side when I came in?" he asked.

"I was looking at her bra. It's too tight." I pointed to

the clasps. "See these two loops? They're scuffed and worn. This is where she usually hooked the clasps, not where they are now. Whoever dressed her didn't know that either. He wasn't worried about her comfort, and she wasn't alive to tell him it hurt."

Barbette adjusted his glasses and scratched his head, mulling something over before he spoke.

"Have you ever observed a forensic autopsy before, Dr. Sloan?"

"No," I said.

"I'd like you to come downtown with me and observe this one," he said.

I was thrilled by the invitation, of course, but I couldn't possibly accept—not unless I wanted to get fired.

"I wish I could," I said, "but I'm on call. In fact, I'd better get back to the ER before Dr. Whittington notices I'm not there."

"You let me handle Whittington," Barbette said.

CHAPTER EIGHT

Whatever Dr. Barbette told Dr. Whittington, it worked. I accompanied Dr. Barbette downtown to the county morgue, where I didn't just watch the autopsy; he actually let me assist.

I didn't know it then, but it was the first of many autopsies I would help him perform over the years. He took me on as an unofficial apprentice, teaching me everything he knew about forensics and the secrets a corpse could share. I knew he was grooming me to take his place one day, but I couldn't give up treating patients. I wanted to use medicine to make people's lives better, not simply as a tool to solve the mysteries of the dead. As it turned out, I ended up finding a way to do both.

But on that rainy day more than forty years ago, it was all new to me. I watched closely as he went about his work, dissecting the body, removing the vital organs, and collecting fluid, tissue, and blood samples.

As he did it all, he talked me through every step in the process. He also explained, in detail, exactly how a person drowns in a river.

You can't hold your breath forever. Reflexively, you will inhale, drawing water and whatever particles it contains deep into your sinuses and lungs, causing you to cough.

The coughing triggers another inhalation reflex, which

sucks even more water and mud into your lungs. The struggle to survive, and the loss of air supply, rapidly consumes the oxygen in your blood. Within a minute or two, you lose consciousness and your life.

If a person is dead before entering the water, dirt and debris will fill the mouth and pharynx, but it won't enter the lungs for several days, drawn into the vacancy created by the gradual escape of air from the body.

The woman who was pulled from the Los Angeles River wasn't in the water, in Barbette's opinion, for more than an hour or two. Her mouth was full of mud, but there wasn't any debris in her lungs.

Her lungs *were* filled with water, however.

Bathwater. With a heavy concentration of soap and hair dye.

"This woman was murdered," Barbette declared, taking off his glasses and wiping them clean with a towel.

I'd come to the same conclusion on my own before Dr. Barbette walked in on me at Community General, but hearing him say it made it real.

I should have been saddened by this woman's death. I should have been horrified by the way in which she died. I should have been afraid of the man who'd done it.

I did feel those things. But I also felt something else. Something stronger. There isn't a word for it. I can only describe the sensation.

When you're fishing, there's a tingle you get when you feel that first little hit on your line.

Hello.

A charge goes through your whole body. All your attention focuses on the tip of your pole and the tension on the line as you wait for another tap.

At that instant, there's nothing else except you and whatever is down there in the dark depths, waiting to be caught. You can almost feel the fish, sense him swimming around your baited hook, waiting to strike.

It's exciting. It's exhilarating. And it's addictive.

Well, that's what I felt. Only much, much stronger. I felt the presence of her killer. I couldn't see him, but I knew he was out there in the storm, hidden in the shadows.

I'd felt his tap.

"Her killer dressed her and dumped her body in the LA River in the middle of a downpour to make it look like an accident," Dr. Barbette said with a frown. "Damn near got away with it, too."

"You would have caught him," I said.

Barbette shook his head and put on his glasses. "No, Dr. Sloan, I wouldn't have. The facts surrounding this woman's death seemed obvious. I hate to admit this, but I wouldn't have investigated any further. No one would ever have known she was murdered if not for you."

"It was just dumb luck on my part," I said.

"It's more than that," Barbette said. "It's instinct. You're a born detective. It's a gift. You should embrace it."

I thought about what Dr. Barbette said, and it troubled me as I drove back to Community General in the pouring rain.

You're a born detective.

It was a legacy I'd been running from since I was ten years old, since the morning my father, a homicide detective, went to work and decided never to come home again. A few months later, he sent us a postcard from New York. All it said was "I'm sorry."

The other cops on the force felt real bad about what had happened and adopted us, making us part of their families. The men would do handyman stuff around the house, making sure we had a solid roof over our heads and that Mom had a car that was always running smooth. And the wives, they'd babysit us, cook us meals, and mend our clothes, easing Mom's burden while she looked for work.

Mom finally found herself a job as a secretary at our grade school, rising up through the bureaucracy until she eventually became a senior administrator in the Los Angeles Unified School District.

But even after she got settled, those police officers and their families never stopped looking out for us. The local police station was like a second home to me. They hated what my father had done, but at the same time, they didn't want to tear him down in my eyes. They kept telling me what a great detective he was and about all the murders he'd solved.

James Sloan, they said, saw clues nobody else could see. He had a sixth sense about crime. He just knew when someone was guilty. And then, with dogged determination, he would set out to prove what his nearly infallible instincts had already told him.

I used to wonder if he detected guilt so well in others because there was so much in him. How long was he thinking about leaving us before he actually did it? What clues did we miss?

I don't know whether it was because of my dad, or all the time I spent with police officers, but I was fascinated by the puzzle-solving aspect of detective work, the slow and steady accumulation of information. I learned that gathering facts wasn't enough to solve a mystery; finding the solution ultimately came down to intuition, inspiration, and dumb luck. It was an art. As much as I wanted to master it for myself, I also wanted nothing to do with it.

My grandfather was a cop and so was my father. Becoming one myself meant following my father's example, which I would never do. The only way to get back at him for what he did to us was to deny him any influence in my life, to treat him as if he'd never existed. So I found another calling, another way to solve mysteries and help people.

Medicine isn't unlike police work. The crimes are pain, suffering, and death. The perpetrators are diseases, traumas, and viruses. The mystery is identifying the ailment that afflicts your patient. The solution is the diagnosis and treatment.

I discovered that solving the mysteries of medicine is as much about education and experience as it's about intuition and imagination. My years hanging around detectives were the perfect preparation for becoming a doctor.

The cops who became our extended family were proud of me when I was accepted to medical school, but they were disappointed I didn't join their sons at the police academy.

I got a unique satisfaction from being a doctor that I could never have as a police officer, something only I could appreciate. The first time someone called me "Dr. Sloan," and for years afterwards, it reassured me that I'd become a very different man from my father.

When I married Katherine, I made a vow to myself that I would always be there for her and for my children, a promise my father either never made or didn't keep. I was determined that whatever made my father the man he was, it wouldn't do the same to me. Until that dead woman was brought into our ER, I thought I'd succeeded.

I couldn't get Dr. Barbette's words out of my head.

You're a born detective.

I'd thought of myself as many things. A son. A brother. A father. A husband. A doctor. The one thing I was certain that I wasn't, that I tried so hard not to be, was a detective. A man like James Marcus Sloan.

I hadn't set out to investigate anything. But when I looked at that dead woman, it triggered something in me. I saw details without being aware I was seeing them. Or maybe I just didn't want to see them.

It didn't matter. My mind worked on it anyway, nagging me until I consciously acknowledged what was right in front of my face.

She had been murdered.

I knew it even before I could prove it. *Instinctively.* Because I was a born detective. Because I was my father's son.

Did I feel that pang of fear when I first saw that woman because I sensed the presence of a killer? Or was it because I sensed the presence of my father in me?

And yet I couldn't deny the exhilaration I felt at uncovering the murder or the strong, almost gravitational pull I was feeling to find out who was responsible.

You're a born detective.

If that was true, I was more like my father than I had ever known. I couldn't help wondering if that meant I was destined to leave my wife and abandon my son, too.

CHAPTER NINE

The rest of my shift was a blur of activity, one trauma patient after another, punctuated by thunderclaps and temporary power outages. For nurse Alice Blevins, it was like being back in her M.A.S.H. unit, feeling the rumble of mortars landing on the battlefield. She told me she hadn't seen this many wounded since Korea. I hadn't known raindrops could be as deadly as bullets, but evidence of it was all around me.

I was glad for the activity. It took my mind off the woman's murder and the conflicting feelings it provoked in me. But as soon as my shift was over, I called Dr. Barbette and asked him if the police had identified the dead woman yet. They had. Her name was Sally Pruitt, she was nineteen years old, and she lived with her parents, Joan and Vernon, in the San Fernando Valley.

I bombarded him with questions about Sally and the circumstances of her death. Did she have a boyfriend? When was the last time her parents had seen her? Did the murder happen at home? If not, where? What happened to her jewelry?

But Dr. Barbette didn't know any of the answers, nor did he care. He told me it was up to the homicide detectives now. His job was over.

It should have been over for me, too.

Despite the chaos, I somehow managed to leave the

hospital the moment my shift was officially over. I got home in time to give Steve a bath, put him to bed, and have a nice dinner with Katherine.

I told her all about Sally Pruitt and how I figured out she didn't die in the river but was murdered in a bathtub. I told her about meeting Dr. Barbette and assisting in the autopsy. I told her what he said to me and my fears about what it could mean.

By the time I was done telling her all those things, we'd long since finished dinner and were snuggling on the couch, Katherine's arms around me, her head against my chest.

"Dr. Barbette is right," she said. "You *are* a born detective. Don't tell me you haven't known it all your life."

"I haven't," I said.

"I have," she said.

"You *have*?" I asked, stunned.

"Oh come on, Mark. It's been obvious since the day I met you. You see things others don't. You know you do."

"I do not," I said.

"What about that thing you do at parties to entertain the guests?" she said.

"I don't know what you're talking about."

"The thing where you pick out someone you've never met and tell everybody all about him based on his clothes, mannerisms, and physical features."

"That?" I said.

"Yes, *that*," she said.

"It's just a game," I said. "Everybody does it."

"*Nobody* else does it," she said, "with the possible exception of Sherlock Holmes."

"He's a fictional character."

"I rest my case," she replied.

"I don't like playing that game anyway."

"You say you don't, but you do," she said. "You love it. Until tonight, I never knew why you were always so reluctant to do it. Now I know. It's because you're afraid of your natural talents, afraid it means you're going to become your father."

"Exactly," I said.

"Hogwash," she snorted. "I've never heard anything so ridiculous in my life."

"Children of alcoholics often become alcoholics themselves, even though they've seen the physical and emotional damage that it does," I said. "Heredity is a powerful force."

"It's true. You have a lot of your father in you. There's nothing you can do about that. Instead of running from it, accept it. Embrace those qualities that can work for you and make your life better. You don't have to worry about ever becoming your father."

"Why not?"

"Because you have me and I won't let you get away with it," she said, giving me a squeeze. "But you also have something else he didn't have."

"What's that?"

"Your mother—one of the most caring, giving, and nurturing women I've ever known. She was a fighter who raised three kids on her own," Katherine said. "What your dad lacked in character she made up for many times over. She's as much a part of you as he is, maybe more."

I didn't know if she was right, but it made me feel a lot better. I kissed her and we sat for a while in silence, listening to the patter of raindrops on the roof and the wind whipping against the windows.

"So what are you going to do now?" she asked.

"I was thinking about kissing you some more," I said.

"I meant about Sally Pruitt."

"I've done all I can do," I said. "I'm a good doctor, but even I can't raise the dead."

I woke up late Saturday morning to big news. U-2 pilot Francis Gary Powers had been released after two years in captivity in a Soviet prison, swapped for Russian spy

Rudolf Abel on a bridge between West Berlin and East Germany. More rains were expected, extending by at least another two days the heaviest rainstorm in Southern California in nearly a decade. And Harry Trumble was sitting at our kitchen table, eating pancakes and eggs.

Harry Trumble was the son of one of the policemen who had looked out for our family after Dad abandoned us. Harry and I grew up together, and our friendship lasted even after I became a doctor and he became a uniformed police officer. We remained friends right up until his fiancée and I fell in love with each other.

The last time I had spoken to Harry was three years earlier after we were pulled off each other in the middle of a fistfight outside the Blossom Room at the Roosevelt Hotel. You can guess what that fight was about.

Harry had changed since then. He was heavier, with hunched shoulders, a long face, and bloodshot eyes. There was a half-smoked Camel pinched at the edge of his wry smile. He wore a suit and tie. His wet hat was on the empty seat beside him.

I was wearing my bathrobe over my pajamas and felt a little silly dressed like that in front of him, even though I was in my own house.

"Kat's in your kid's room, changing his diaper," Harry said.

Nobody ever called her Kat but him. He was telling me he still owned a part of her and always would. I took a seat opposite him at the table. "How long have you been here?"

"Since about eight," Harry said. "She didn't want to wake you, seeing as how it's your day off, so she cooked me breakfast. You know, this is the first breakfast she's ever made me. She's a hell of a cook, Mark."

I nodded. "Congratulations on making detective, Harry."

His eyes widened. "I didn't know you kept up on personnel changes at the department."

"I don't," I said. Most of the police officers I knew had stopped socializing with me after Katherine dumped

Harry for me. "But here you are, wearing a brand-new suit, coming by to see me for the first time in years, the day after I discover a murder. I'm guessing it's your first homicide case and you're pretty nervous about it."

He took a drag on his cigarette and blew a stream of smoke into the air. "Why do you guess that?"

"Because this has to be even more uncomfortable for you than it is for me," I said. "And you wouldn't be putting yourself through it if you didn't have a lot at stake."

He flicked some ashes onto his plate. "You're still good at that party game of yours, Mark. But we aren't at a party."

He stood and picked up his hat. "And the murder of this girl, it's not a game. I came by to tell you to stay out of it."

"What makes you think I'd get involved?" I asked.

Before he could answer, Katherine emerged from Steve's room with the baby in her arms. She wore a turtleneck sweater and Capri pants and had a big, forced smile on her face.

"Good morning, Mark," she said. "Look who's here, it's Harry."

"I see," I said.

"Isn't this a wonderful surprise?" she said. "We've spent the last hour catching up."

"That's terrific," I said.

"Sit down, Harry," Katherine said. "We can visit some more while Mark eats."

"I wish I could, Kat," Harry said, making funny faces at Steve and getting rewarded with a big smile. "But I've got to get to work. Thanks for breakfast."

"Come back again soon," Katherine said. "I mean it."

She didn't mean it. Harry nodded, knowing it, too. He glanced at me, his gaze putting an exclamation point on his earlier warning, then put on his hat and left. As soon as he was gone, Katherine handed the baby to me and left the room. I knew she was crying.

I waited a few minutes, bouncing Steve on my knee and letting him chew on my finger. Then I put him in his playpen and went into the bedroom.

Katherine was sitting on the edge of the bed, a tissue balled up in her hand.

"You okay?" I asked, sitting beside her.

She nodded. "When I opened the door and saw Harry, I almost fainted with surprise. He looks ten years older. Did I do that to him? Did we?"

I shrugged. I honestly didn't know. Even when he was a kid, Harry had that weary, basset-hound expression on his face.

"We talked for an hour," she said. "He hasn't got anyone, you know."

"You asked?"

She shook her head. "He made sure I knew without actually telling me straight out. We mostly talked about the friends we had in common, what's happened to them since . . ."

Katherine's voice trailed off.

"Since you broke his heart and I betrayed him," I said, finishing her sentence.

"It wouldn't have worked out with Harry anyway," Katherine said. "He was married to his badge. I was just his mistress. His little 'Kitty-Kat.' "

"But you still feel guilty," I said.

"No," she said, taking my hand and resting her head on my shoulder. "I love you, Mark. I love the family we've made together. I wouldn't trade this for anything. But when Harry looked at me and Steve, I knew what he was seeing."

"What might have been," I said. "The life he doesn't have."

"A life I'm not sure he ever really wanted," she said. "Even so, he seemed so sad."

"It's okay to still care about him," I said, giving her hand a squeeze. "I do, too."

CHAPTER TEN

It was wet and dreary outside, so we spent the morning in the apartment, playing with Steve and doing all the domestic tasks that had piled up during the week, like paying bills, cleaning up the house, and putting our Blue Chip stamps into savings books.

We got one Blue Chip stamp for every dime we spent at participating supermarkets, drugstores, and gas stations. During the week we'd drop the loose stamps we accumulated into a big bowl on the kitchen counter, and then every Saturday we'd put them in the book. We were saving up for a Murray Ohio Super Deluxe Fire Truck for Steve to drive around in the courtyard. The truck was bright red and had pedals, ladders, whitewall tires, and a big silver bell. It cost ten books, which was about ten thousand stamps.

When we finished emptying the stamp bowl, Katherine made us grilled cheese sandwiches by wrapping them in aluminum foil and running the iron over them. It was how her mother taught her to do it. She sang while she worked, which always brought back memories of her performing at the Blossom Room. If she minded trading the stage for an ironing board, she never said so.

Steve started wailing around noon. We put him down in his crib for a nap, but that only made him cry louder. When he was like that, there was only one way he'd sleep. We had to take a drive.

So we bundled him up in his little rain slicker, put on our raincoats, and got into the Chevy. Five minutes after I started driving, Steve was asleep. The only problem was that if we stopped for more than a minute or two, he'd wake up again.

We headed over Sepulveda Pass into the valley, as we often did on what we called our "nap expeditions." It gave Katherine an excuse to cruise by the many new neighborhoods and housing developments. Usually, once we'd decided Steve had slept long enough, we'd stop and visit a few of the furnished model homes, buy some produce at one of the fruit and vegetable stands, and head back home in time for dinner.

The valley was one massive grading project, countless citrus and walnut orchards plowed under and replanted with neat rows of new homes. The construction had left the ground naked, and the steady downpour of the past week had turned the subdivisions into massive mud puddles and the streets into brown streams that spilled over the hundreds of sandbag dams meant to contain them.

So we gave up on exploring the new subdivisions and daydreaming about the house we hoped to own someday. Instead, I drove towards the slightly more established neighborhoods where some lawns and trees had taken root. These were homes built in the postwar boom of the early fifties, catering to veterans on the GI Bill. The homes were one-story, two-bedroom, assembly-line stucco boxes designed to get the most square footage out of the fewest dollars and the cheapest materials.

Vernon and Joan Pruitt lived in a house that faced a mirror reflection of itself across the street. Everybody in the Van Nuys housing tract had the same floor plan, only flip-flopped and alternating with every other house. Even the landscaping and the automobiles in the carports looked similar. It was dizzying. If it hadn't been for the addresses painted on the curbs and repeated in large numbers atop the carports, I never would have found the right house.

I'd looked up the Pruitts' address before leaving the hospital the night before, telling myself I was doing it in case I needed the information to fill out paperwork on Sally Pruitt.

As luck would have it, our Saturday "nap expedition" just happened to take us past the Pruitts' home.

At least that's how I explained it to Katherine as I slowed to a stop in front of the house.

I braced myself for an argument, but I didn't get one. Instead, she told me to get out of the car quickly before Steve noticed we weren't moving and woke up. She slid over into the driver's seat and said she'd drive around the block a few times.

I pulled the collar up on my coat, held it tight around my neck, and ran through the rain to the protection of the Pruitts' covered front porch. I rang the bell.

Vernon Pruitt opened the door immediately, giving me no chance at all to figure out what I was going to say. He was a big, barrel-chested man with a crew cut, wearing a two-tone bowling shirt and slacks.

"Mr. Pruitt?" I asked.

"Yeah?"

"I'm Dr. Mark Sloan." I offered him my hand. "I was on call in the ER at Community General when your daughter was brought in."

I figured I'd say as little as possible and let him fill in the missing information with assumptions of his own. It was easier than trying to come up with a convincing lie, though if I had thought of one, I'd have used it.

He nodded and let me in.

The house was not much larger than our apartment and decorated with contemporary furniture. I could see across the living room into the kitchen, where Mrs. Pruitt was ironing clothes, pausing every so often to wipe away tears. She wore a flowered apron over a skirt and a bright pink blouse.

"I'm deeply sorry for your loss," I said, loud enough for his wife to hear as well.

"It was my understanding that my daughter was already dead by the time she was brought to the hospital," Mr. Pruitt said. "That she had been dead for some time."

I heard Mrs. Pruitt sniffle and attack her ironing with renewed fervor. I stalled for a moment, trying to think of what to say.

"Yes," I said, "but at the time she was still unidentified, so we didn't have the necessary information to fill out her forms."

"You mean like her name, address, date of birth, the names of her nearest relatives," he replied.

"Exactly," I said. "That's why I'm here."

I realized how lame the lie was the instant it escaped from my mouth. And so did he.

"If you're here," Mr. Pruitt said, "you must already have that information."

I swallowed hard and felt myself flushing with guilt. I had no legitimate reason to be intruding on their grief except my own curiosity. And the more I tried to obfuscate the facts, the deeper trouble I was going to get into.

"The truth is, Mr. Pruitt, I wasn't convinced your daughter drowned in the river, so I started investigating and discovered that she didn't," I said. "Now I don't think I can stop."

"Stop what?" he asked.

"Thinking about her," I said. "I need to know what really happened to her and who is responsible for it. I won't be at peace until I do."

I surprised myself with that answer. I must have surprised him, too, because he finally motioned me to a seat.

"What would you like to know, Dr. Sloan?"

"Anything," I said. "Everything. I really don't know what I'm looking for."

"I'll tell you what I told the police," Mr. Pruitt said. "She didn't come home Thursday night. I wish I could say that was unusual, but it wasn't. She's a woman now. She has her own life and makes her own choices."

I noticed he was still using the present tense. I wondered how long it took after people died before they became part of the past.

"Did she tell you where she was going?"

He replied by shaking his head.

"How did she get around?" I asked. "Did she have a car?"

"She gets rides from friends or takes the bus," he said. "Sometimes I'll drop her off places if it's on my way."

"Did she have a boyfriend or anyone special she was seeing?"

"Sally and I don't talk about her love life," he said. "It only leads to arguments. I don't believe in sex before marriage."

"So if her lifestyle didn't meet with your approval, why was she still living at home?" I asked. "It couldn't have been easy for either one of you."

"She's saving up for nursing school," he said. "It costs five hundred dollars a semester, and with the paycheck I get working out at the GM plant, we can't afford it."

"What was she doing to earn money?"

"Waitressing, babysitting, doing some laundry and housecleaning around the neighborhood."

Mrs. Pruitt came out of the kitchen, carrying a basket full of freshly folded and ironed clothes. I loved the smell of warm linen.

"Sounds like she was working hard," I said.

"Every little bit helps," Mr. Pruitt said. "She was determined to get that degree. She didn't want to work an assembly line like her parents."

"Sally never crawled," Mrs. Pruitt said softly. "Not once."

I turned to look at her. She set the basket down on the coffee table and took a seat beside me.

"She went straight to walking," she said. "Of course she couldn't do it on her own right away, we had to hold her hand. She didn't like that. She'd fight for us to let go and then she'd fall. We'd pick her up, she'd take a few steps, then shake her hand free and fall all over again."

Her pain was palpable. Feeling uncomfortable, I shifted my gaze to her laundry basket. Mrs. Pruitt had fit an incredible amount of clothing into it. The blouses were folded in squares, the socks in rectangles, the bras into single cups. Everything was starched and ironed. And all of it was clothing for a young woman. All of it was Sally's.

"She was in such a hurry to grow up," Mrs. Pruitt said, tears running down her cheeks. She took a handkerchief from her apron pocket and dabbed at her face.

"Maybe you should put Sally's clothes away," Mr. Pruitt said. "Before they get wrinkled in that basket."

She rose to her feet and picked up the basket, pausing to look down at me.

"The pediatrician told us if she didn't crawl she'd have all kinds of physical and mental problems later in life," Mrs. Pruitt said. "Do you think that's true? That something was wrong with her?"

"No, ma'am," I said.

She nodded and walked slowly down the hall. Mr. Pruitt quickly swatted a tear off his cheek with his finger, as if it was a bug crawling on his face.

"Is there anything else, Dr. Sloan?" he asked, clearing his throat.

"She had a key in her pocket," I said. "It was attached to a rabbit's foot. Do you have any idea what the key was for?"

He shook his head. We sat for a moment in silence as I tried to think of something else to ask him. I couldn't think of anything, so I got up.

"Thank you, Mr. Pruitt, for taking the time to talk with me," I said. "I'm sorry if it was an intrusion."

Mr. Pruitt rose to his feet. "You mind if I ask you a question?"

"Of course not," I said.

"Are you going to find the man who did this to my daughter?"

"I'm going to try," I said.

Mr. Pruitt studied my face for a long time, then held his hand out to me. We shook, but he didn't let go, holding my hand in his firm grasp.

"You're a doctor, so you know how to save lives. But I'm sure you know how to take them, too." Mr. Pruitt looked into my eyes. "If you find the bastard who did this to my daughter, kill him."

"I can't do that," I said.

"Try," he said.

CHAPTER ELEVEN

We made it back home with barely enough time to get changed for Dr. Whittington's party. As I dressed, I thought about my conversation with Vernon and Joan Pruitt. I played back everything they said and everything I said, too. The only thing I'd really learned from them was about myself. It was the first time I admitted to myself, or anybody else, that I intended to solve Sally Pruitt's murder.

I had no right, no authority, and certainly no skill. My only connection to the victim was looking at her corpse. Perhaps that was enough.

There were a lot of obstacles to conducting my own investigation. For one thing, I wasn't a cop, so no one had any reason to talk to me. I was working thirty-six hours at a stretch at Community General, so finding the time to devote to the case wouldn't be easy. And eventually Harry Trumble was going to find out what I was doing and make it hard, if not impossible, for me to continue.

I was in the middle of putting on my tie when Katherine swatted my hands away, undid what I'd done, and retied it for me. She looked wonderful in a sleeveless black cocktail dress that stopped just above the knees of her slim dancer's legs, which she retained even though the only dancing she'd done lately was around baby toys on the floor.

Katherine hadn't asked me anything about my conversation with the Pruitts after she picked me up outside their house. We were quiet during the ride back to our apartment. It wasn't one of those uncomfortable or angry silences either. She was giving me time to sort out my thoughts, and I had.

"I'm going to find the man who killed Sally Pruitt," I said.

"I know," she said, straightening my tie.

"Is that okay with you?"

"As long as you don't get killed doing it."

I gently tipped her chin up towards my face and kissed her. "Don't you want to know why I'm doing it?"

"I already do," she said. "I've known it from the moment you told me what happened to her."

She kissed me back, then gave me a gentle shove. "Come on, Mark, let's go. You don't want to disappoint Dr. Whittington by being late."

"He's used to it," I said.

It was drizzling lightly outside when Katherine and I, carrying Steve in my arms, walked across the rain-slicked street to the Armacost Sands, the sixteen-unit apartment building where Bart and Mary Spicer lived. The name of their building was written diagonally across the front in plywood script and punctuated with a starburst lamp. The building was a rectangular stucco box much like our own, disguised with enormous wooden fins that made the tenants feel as if they were living in the trunk of a 1959 Cadillac.

Mary Spicer met us at the door of their ground-floor apartment to show off her brand-new bouffant hairdo. She wore a dark red wool bouclé dress and a matching single-breasted jacket with enormous buttons, doing her best to emulate the first lady, Jacqueline Kennedy.

Behind her, Bart looked more like John Cassavetes than John F. Kennedy, wearing pleated slacks, a blazer, and a narrow black tie, a thin cigarette dangling from his lips.

"You look beautiful," Katherine said to Mary. "Where did you get that wonderful dress?"

"The Back Room at Loehmann's," Mary said. "I've been waiting for months for the perfect opportunity to wear it. I was beginning to think it would never come."

I carried Steve into the apartment, setting him down on the floor to play beside the Spicers' daughter, Tina, who was a little over a year old. There were building blocks and big stuffed animals all around them. Steve grabbed the first block he could find and tried to cram it into his mouth.

"Mark, this is Joanna Pate," Bart said, leading over a perky young girl in her late teens. She had long black hair and a book bag over her shoulder. "She'll be keeping an eye on the kids while we're gone. Joanna, this is Dr. Sloan."

I offered her my hand. "Pleased to meet you, Joanna."

"Don't worry about Steve, Dr. Sloan," she said. "I'm the oldest of three kids, so I'm used to taking care of children. Is there anything special I should know about your son?"

"Whatever is within reach, he'll put in his mouth," I said, glancing at Steve, who was still gnawing on the block, covering it with drool.

"My brother is still like that," she said. "And he's fourteen."

She smiled and I liked her immediately. I was sure Steve would be in fine hands. Katherine needed a bit more convincing.

Katherine introduced herself to Joanna and handed her a handwritten list of dos and don'ts that was so long it should have come with an index. At the end of the manuscript, she'd included phone numbers for Dr. Whittington's home, Community General, the police, the fire department, my in-laws, and six or seven friends in the neighborhood. I was going to ask her why she'd left out the numbers for the FBI, the Pentagon, and the Civil Defense Authority, but I didn't think she'd see the humor.

As we walked across the street to my Chevy, Mary assured Katherine, who was still clearly nervous about leaving Steve behind, that Joanna had been babysitting for other doctors in the neighborhood and came highly recommended.

I reminded Katherine that we weren't going to be gone long and we weren't going far. Dr. Whittington lived in Brentwood, only about five miles north of us, along the southern slopes of the Santa Monica Mountains.

Considering Dr. Whittington's proper Empire mentality, I fully expected his home to be an imposing, timbered English Tudor mansion surrounded by tall trees—his little bit of England in the Colonies. So I was surprised to discover that he lived in a free-flowing, ultra-contemporary home that epitomized the California lifestyle of sunlight, barbeques, and outdoor patio living. The front of the house was dominated by floor-to-ceiling windows, a slanted roof, and walls of thin, horizontally shaved stone.

There were already several cars parked out front, a field of sharp fins and rocket taillights that made it feel like I was parking on a landing strip instead of a driveway.

Dr. Whittington greeted us at the door. His house defied my expectations, but he didn't. He wore dark suit pants, a cashmere V-neck sweater over a white shirt, and a navy-colored jacket, all topped off with a gray silk cravat. He looked out of place in the doorway of his own house and I got the sense that he was aware of it, too.

"Dr. Sloan, I'm so pleased you could come," he said, smiling warmly, something I'd never seen him do before. "This must be your lovely wife, Katherine."

He took her hand and kissed it. I don't know what astonished me more, the fact that he knew her name or that he'd kissed her hand. Katherine blushed, flattered.

"Mark talks so much about you," she said. "He's a great admirer of yours, Dr. Whittington."

"Your husband has a bright future in medicine," Dr. Whittington said.

Did he really think that? I wondered. If so, he'd done an incredible job of hiding it. I wanted more details. Before I got a chance to ask, he shifted his attention to Bart and Mary Spicer and we slipped past him into the house.

"He doesn't seem so bad," Katherine whispered to me.

There were a dozen or so couples there, all doctors from the hospital and their wives. I was among the youngest and most inexperienced of the doctors in the room, which was open and airy and offered a view of the immaculately manicured lawn. The backyard was rimmed by perfectly sculpted hedges and trees illuminated by lights placed strategically for dramatic effect.

All of the living room furniture was designed with sharp, aerodynamic angles and upholstered in vibrant colors. The side tables were shaped like boomerangs. The lamps were flying saucers, glowing with atomic energy. I got the feeling that if I didn't sit down soon, the furniture would leave without me and break the sound barrier on its way.

We immediately gravitated towards big Dan Marlowe and his petite wife, Irene, who were helping themselves to the cucumber sandwiches, scones, and tea spread out on platters at one of the palette-shaped coffee tables. Irene wasn't actually any more petite than I was, but a linebacker would look small beside Dan, who had one of his meaty paws around her thin waist.

"I asked one of the servers for a cup of coffee," Dan said. "You would have thought I was asking for a cup of crude oil."

"It's tea or nothing," Irene said. She wore a lime green short-sleeved dress and a pillbox hat tipped at a jaunty angle. The way she held her teacup, it looked as if she was modeling it rather than drinking from it.

"I love tea," Katherine said, pouring herself a cup. "I bet it's imported from England."

I gobbled down a few of the sandwiches and turned to Dan. "Dr. Whittington just told me I had a bright future."

"It's amazing what a difference a well-knotted tie can make," Dan said.

"And matching socks," said Chet Arnold as he drifted over with his wife, Gladys, who was staring in horror at Irene. They were wearing identical dresses and hats.

I didn't see the problem. Chet, Dan, and I were dressed almost alike and it didn't bother us. But Gladys and Irene obviously saw it differently. They were still staring at each other, mouths gaping open.

"This is so embarrassing," Gladys muttered. "We really should call each other before these gatherings."

"I think you both look wonderful," I said, trying to de-fuse the awkward moment.

Gladys and Irene glared at me. Irene tugged at Dan's sleeve and gestured across the room.

"Oh, look, it's the Pattersons," she said. "We haven't seen them in ages."

"I see Dick Patterson every day," Dan said.

"Well, I don't," Irene said. "Excuse us."

She practically dragged her husband away, which, considering his bulk, wasn't an easy feat. Irene wanted to put as much distance between herself and the other dress as possible.

Katherine put her arm around me and gave me a squeeze. I knew she was amused. She didn't care much about fashion and wouldn't have been bothered if every woman there was wearing the same outfit as hers.

"I need a drink," Gladys said. "Isn't there anything a bit stronger here than tea?"

"Not that I've seen," said Bart Spicer as he and his wife, Mary, joined us. "Nice dress, Gladys."

Chet groaned and Gladys looked like she might be sick. She was as green as her dress.

"Does Dr. Whittington live in this big house all by himself?" Katherine asked, quickly changing the subject.

"He's got a wife and a nine-year-old son," Bart said. "I hear they went back to London for a while."

Katherine glanced around the room. "Must be a long while. There aren't any flowers in the house and not a single toy outside. It doesn't feel lived in at all, certainly not by a family with kids. It's almost like a model home."

"Now who's playing detective?" I chided her.

Dr. Whittington strode into the center of the room and rang a tiny bell to get everyone's attention.

"I want to thank you all for coming this evening," he said. "It's not often I get the opportunity to enjoy the convivial company of my esteemed colleagues outside of the hospital."

I glanced at Dan and Bart, who, judging by the expressions on their faces, were as confused by Dr. Whittington's remarks as I was. He'd never expressed any interest in my convivial company before. If anything, he could barely stand my company at all.

"It's because I care about you, and the well-being of your families and our way of life, that I invited you here this evening," he said. "I want to help each and every one of you protect youselves and your loved ones from the Red threat."

As he said this, two men came out of an adjoining room wheeling a movie projector while another man brought out a screen, which he began erecting behind Dr. Whittington.

"It's only a matter of time before the Soviets drop a hydrogen bomb, and it could be right here in Los Angeles," Dr. Whittington said. "That's why it's essential that every family have their own bomb shelter, one designed to protect you from the devastating effects of nuclear fallout."

For the next ten minutes, Dr. Whittington lectured us about the likelihood of an imminent, full-scale nuclear attack. Even if the bomb wasn't dropped on our heads, he assured us, the fallout from an explosion nearby would decimate us unless we sought refuge in a reinforced concrete bunker and slammed a half-inch-thick steel door shut behind us.

He then introduced us to Carl Stokes, a man with eyes that sparkled so intensely and teeth that were so blindingly white, I wondered if he wasn't radioactive already. Carl was a sales representative from Safe Haven, Incorporated, the leading builder of suburban bomb shelters.

At least now I understood why I'd been invited to Dr. Whittington's home. It wasn't because he wanted to socialize with me. It was because he wanted to sell me something. But it was too late to leave now, even though I felt Katherine gently nudging me in the direction of the door. If I fled now, I'd only incur Dr. Whittington's wrath later, and there was no bunker I could hide in to protect me from that.

Carl told us that a bomb shelter would become as common and essential a feature in the home as the kitchen. And it wouldn't be saved just for nuclear attacks.

"Think of it as an extension of your family room," Carl suggested. "With colorful wallpaper, comfortable chairs, board games, toys, a record player, and a battery-powered radio. A welcome refuge not only from radiation but from the stress of everyday life."

The refuge should also contain portable toilets, candles, bunk beds, books, magazines, and enough cigarettes, canned food, powdered milk, liquor, and water to last a family of four for two weeks.

We were then shown a twenty-minute movie that began with mushroom clouds, footage of devastated cities, and depictions of hordes of decaying people, staggering through the streets, tripping over corpses. The movie then dramatized what might happen if the bomb was dropped on a typical American suburb. The families with bomb shelters in their basements or in their backyards survived, casually playing board games and joyfully eating canned foods, while their foolish neighbors who didn't have shelters fought one another for scraps of irradiated garbage and died horrible, drooling deaths.

"Oh, how they wish they'd recognized the importance

of building a bomb shelter," the narrator, who was also Carl, intoned gravely.

The movie discussed the need of hiding your bomb shelter from your neighbors, lest they want to take refuge in it during a nuclear attack.

"Tell them it's a wine cellar," Carl suggested, "or a new rumpus room for the kids!"

But if neighbors did discover your shelter, it was your moral obligation in the event of a nuclear attack to keep them out, with lethal force if necessary, so they wouldn't imperil your family's safety by using your provisions. The moral thing, we were told, was not to let a neighbor into your shelter but to encourage him, before the bomb was dropped, to build his own.

Following the movie, colorful brochures were handed out inviting us to arrange an appointment to visit the model home and shelter in a valley housing tract. Bomb shelters weren't just good for our lives, they were also good for our money. Carl told us the bomb shelter industry itself was a great investment opportunity. The industry could gross as much as twenty billion dollars in the next five years, assuming a nuclear war didn't break out first.

That explained why Dr. Whittington had invited us all there. He wasn't concerned about our survival. He was an investor.

When Carl was finished with his presentation, cake and tea were served. Somehow nobody seemed to be in much of a party mood, though.

We didn't stay for dessert. We thanked Dr. Whittington for a lovely evening of convivial company and nuclear holocaust and left as fast as we could.

CHAPTER TWELVE

We rarely had a free night and a babysitter, so we were determined take advantage of the opportunity. We went to a steakhouse on Wilshire Boulevard for a late dinner with the Spicers and the Arnolds.

Naturally, the big topic of conversation was Dr. Whittington's disastrous party. We were all living in apartments. What made him think we were in the market for bomb shelters?

"Carl made the bomb shelter sound so homey and attractive, who needs a house?" Katherine said. "We could build a bomb shelter for one third of the price."

We laughed about that for a while, then we started talking about the difficulties of saving up for a house, sharing anecdotes about our kids, and complaining about our hours at the hospital.

Once we got on the subject of Community General, the three of us doctors at the table all remembered we had long shifts the next morning and that it was probably best to get home.

It was pouring rain when we parked in front of the Armacost Sands to drop off the Spicers and pick up Steve. The children were asleep in Tina's playpen and the babysitter, Joanna, was sitting at the kitchen table, hunched over some open textbooks, taking notes and studying. One of the books was very familiar to me. It was the tenth edition of the *Merck Manual of Diagnosis and Therapy*, the bible of medical professionals and students.

I asked Bart how much I could contribute towards paying the babysitter, but he wouldn't take any money from me. Instead, since his car was in the shop, he asked me to drive Joanna home so she wouldn't have to take the bus. I was glad to. I wasn't going to leave the poor girl out alone in the rain, waiting for the bus to show up.

Steve didn't even stir as Katherine lifted him out of the playpen and dressed him in his raincoat. He was deep asleep.

"They played hard," Joanna explained. "He may sleep until Tuesday."

"I wish," Katherine said, then whispered to me, "Be sure to get her number, Mark. We could use a good babysitter."

Joanna Pate told me that she shared an apartment in Santa Monica with another nineteen-year-old girl she'd met during her senior year at Fairfax High School. Her friend wanted to be a stewardess but was waiting tables now at Norm's.

Ordinarily, it wouldn't have taken me more than a few minutes to drive Joanna home. But it was a dark, foggy night and the rain was coming down hard. I drove very slowly. I didn't want to become a patient in my own ER.

She sat beside me in the front seat, her book bag at her feet. "How was the party?"

"It wasn't quite what we expected," I said.

"I'm not surprised," she said. "Dr. Whittington doesn't strike me as a real festive guy."

"You know Dr. Whittington?"

"Sure. He runs the nursing school at Community General and controls admissions," she said. "I'm studying to be a nurse. I babysit to help pay for my tuition."

I felt a chill go down my back and it wasn't because I was cold. Sally Pruitt was also babysitting to earn money for nursing school. Could they have known each other? I wanted to ask right away, but instead I forced myself to relax, to take it slowly.

"How did you meet Dr. Spicer?" I asked, trying hard to sound casual.

"Almost all the doctors at Community General are married and work long hours," she said. "Their wives are stuck at home all day with the kids. They're both tired and irritable and need a break. So we got this idea. A few of us girls got together and started approaching anyone with a wedding ring and asking them if they needed a babysitter. And they all did. We had more work than we ever imagined."

"Doctors are paying you to go to nursing school," I said.

"I never thought of it that way," she said. "I like it."

"Are you sure you don't want to go to business school instead? It sounds to me like you have a natural talent for marketing and sales."

"My dad is a salesman," she said. "I guess a little of it rubbed off on me."

"I know somebody else who babysits to make money for nursing school," I said. "Have you ever met Sally Pruitt?"

"Yes, I knew Sally," Joanna said softly. "I have some bad news. She's—"

"Dead," I said. "I know."

"Were you a friend of the family?"

"I didn't actually know her. It was a poor choice of words." I shifted uneasily in my seat. "I was on call in the ER when she was brought in."

"You missed knowing a really special person," Joanna said, beginning to cry. "She was so sweet, so kind. All she wanted was to be a nurse."

Her shoulders started to heave. I felt guilty for making her so sad, and yet at the same time I wanted to ask her more.

I pulled the car over to the curb in front of her building and let the motor run.

"I just can't believe she's gone," she said, turning herself against me and pressing her face to my chest. I patted her head and felt her tears moisten my shirt. "It was such a horrible accident. This damn storm is a nightmare."

"Did you know her well?" I asked.

"No." Her voice was muffled, her face against me, her shoulders shaking. "But now I wish I had. I just saw her around. She wasn't a student yet. She was hoping Dr. Whittington would admit her next term. One of the girls met her at the admissions office, got to know her, and put her name on the list."

"What list?"

"Of students willing to babysit," Joanna said. "Why do you want to know these things about her?"

"I suppose it's because of the way I met her," I said. "I only knew Sally as a corpse. I'd prefer to know her as a person."

If Joanna didn't know that Sally was murdered in a bathtub, I wasn't going to be the one to tell her. I certainly wasn't going to admit I was bumbling around trying to find her killer.

"It's just so sad," she said, sniffling. I patted her back reassuringly.

"Do you remember who the girl was who met Sally and put her on the list? I'd like to talk with her."

Joanna started to shake again and held me tight, crying even harder. I stroked her hair, trying to calm her down, rocking her the way I would Steve. What did I say? What had I done?

"What's wrong?" I asked.

"She's dead," Joanna said.

"Who is?"

"Muriel Thayer," she sobbed. "She died, too. In a car accident."

Another dead girl. Another dead babysitter. Another dead aspiring nurse.

I felt my heart start to race and hoped that Joanna, her head against my chest, couldn't feel it, too.

"When did this happen?" I asked, trying to keep my voice even and not betray the excitement I was feeling.

"Last week, when the rains started," Joanna said. "She drove her car off a cliff along Mulholland Highway."

Someone had gone to a lot of trouble to make Sally Pruitt's murder look like a storm-related accident. What if Muriel Thayer's death wasn't an accident either?

It meant there was a killer on the loose murdering young women and using the storm to cover his crimes.

Then again, perhaps Muriel Thayer's death really was an accident. The fact that Muriel was a nursing student and a babysitter and died the same week that Sally Pruitt was murdered could simply be a coincidence.

But I knew it wasn't.

I could feel it.

Proving what I felt was another matter altogether, and I had no idea where to begin.

"It hurts so much," Joanna said, lifting her head and looking at me with wide, wet eyes. I wiped a tear from her cheek.

"I know," I said.

"Make it go away," she said huskily, and then she kissed me. It wasn't the gentle, affectionate kiss of a child. There was a hunger, an adult need. She put her whole body into it, reaching a hand behind my neck to draw me to her. I responded instinctively, kissing her back, until I felt the tip of her tongue brushing my lips.

I took her by the shoulders and gently pushed her away. She looked into my eyes, searching them for something. "Isn't that what you wanted?"

"No, it isn't," I said.

"But you were holding me," she said. "Caressing me."

"I only wanted to comfort you," I said.

"That's all I want to do," she said softly.

"Not in the same way."

Joanna shook her head. "I felt your heart." She placed her hand on my chest. "I still can."

She took my hand and held it between her breasts. "Feel mine."

I could feel it, pounding urgently, her breathing hard.

I took my hand from her. I wanted to tell her she was wrong, that my heart wasn't racing over her. But now I wasn't sure. I couldn't deny that I was attracted to her. Any man would be. She was warm and soft and beautiful. But I loved my wife, and the thought of making love to Joanna had never entered my mind.

Until she kissed me.

For an instant, when her body was against mine, when I could feel her warmth and her aching need, the temptation was there. It would have been so easy to give in to it, to lose myself in her. But just as quickly the temptation was gone, replaced by shock and embarrassment.

"I'm sorry if you misunderstood," I said.

"Did I?" she asked.

If I'd offended or embarrassed her with my rejection, she wasn't showing it.

"It's getting late," I said. "I need to get home to my family, to my wife."

I underscored those last three words, hoping they'd make an impression on her.

"Will you walk me to the door?" she asked.

Ordinarily, I would have without thinking twice about it, but not now. Not after her kiss.

"I'll watch you from here," I said.

She gathered up her bag, studied my face for a long moment, then kissed me on the cheek and got out into the rain.

When I got home, Katherine was sitting up in bed in her nightgown, reading *Life* magazine, the same issue

Bart had been looking at the other day in the cafeteria. I could still feel the moisture from Joanna's tears on my chest.

During the short drive back, I had debated whether or not to tell Katherine what had happened. I still hadn't decided.

"How would you like to drive a brand-new Chrysler Imperial?" Katherine said.

"Is Dr. Whittington looking for a driver?"

"You can have one of your own," she said. "For free. Chrysler is going to be calling you."

"They will?" I asked. "Why?"

"Because you're a handsome young doctor." She opened the magazine up and held it in front of her for me to see. I sat on the edge of the bed beside her and took a look.

It was a full-page advertisement featuring a square-jawed doctor in a suit, holding his medical bag and admiring a gleaming black 1962 Imperial Crown Four-Door Southampton.

Below the photo, the advertising copy read:

> *To America's Doctors: We're inviting you to enjoy the personal use of a new Imperial for three days. Soon you will receive a phone call to schedule the delivery of a brand-new car to your door with absolutely no obligation. All we want is for you to make a thorough diagnosis of the Imperial's superior handling, astounding road performance, faultless smoothness, and breathtaking elegance.*

"I'll go wait by the phone," I said. "You can take over for me in the morning."

I started to get up but she pulled me back onto the bed, crawled on top of me and pinned me down playfully.

"It's a beautiful car. I think it's going to look great parked outside of our new bomb shelter," Katherine said.

"When they call, tell them to deliver it right away. We can drive around Beverly Hills and pretend we're rich."

"Would you like that?"

"I'd love that. It will be fun," she said. "Speaking of calls, did you ask the babysitter for her number?"

"I forgot," I said, which was true. "Sorry."

"Not good enough," Katherine said with a wicked smile.

I suppose I could have told her at that moment about Joanna, but then my wife started to kiss me, and I decided that perhaps it wasn't the best time to talk about necking with another woman.

CHAPTER THIRTEEN

I managed to beat Dr. Whittington to the hospital, which disappointed me, because I'd never looked better. My socks matched, my tie was tightly knotted, and I wasn't late.

I'd made it to the hospital with time to spare because I woke up long before my alarm rang. I'd slept fitfully, tormented by guilt about what had happened with Joanna Pate.

I didn't kiss her, she kissed me. What bothered me was that I liked it. I felt as if I'd cheated on Katherine. Somehow, not telling Katherine about it made it seem even more wrong.

When I wasn't replaying the encounter with Joanna over and over in my mind, I thought about what she'd told me before the kiss and what it might mean.

A week ago, the dark clouds moved over the city, bringing rain and thunder, lightning and death. Two nursing students had died. One of them was murdered.

Was Sally Pruitt actually the *second* victim? If so, were there others we didn't know about?

As long as the storm lasted, I knew, there would be more mudslides and flooding, more fallen trees and car accidents.

And more murders.

I was still worrying about that as I walked into the ER,

which was in chaos. The roof of an apartment building had collapsed in the rain, injuring dozens of people. The victims and their families filled the ER. I set aside my worries and concentrated on treating my patients.

I was just finishing up with the last of my roof-collapse victims several hours later when ambulances started rolling in with people injured in a three-car pileup on Sunset Boulevard that sent one vehicle hurling out of control into a crowded bus stop.

Nurse Alice Blevins quickly assessed the patients as they were wheeled in, deciding who was in the most urgent need of medical attention.

There were so many patients that doctors were called in from elsewhere in the hospital to assist. Dan Marlowe, Bart Spicer, Chet Arnold, and I hurried between exam rooms, treating patients and sending those needing more than emergency care on to specialists in orthopedics, cardiology, and neurology.

It was midafternoon by the time we cleared the emergency room of serious trauma patients and were left with only the typical walk-ins with minor injuries and simple ailments. Once the adrenaline wore off, I realized how hungry and tired I was. I told Alice she could find me in the doctors' lounge if any more emergencies came in.

I was starving, but too weary to go to the cafeteria, so I settled for a cold, soggy sandwich from a vending machine, then stretched out on the hard couch to take a nap.

This time sleep came easily.

I awoke three hours later, stiff and groggy and not the least bit recharged. I actually felt worse than I had before the nap. There was fresh coffee in the pot, so I got up, poured myself a cup, and sat down at one of the tables, waiting for the caffeine to kick in and revive me.

The lounge was our sanctuary, and the doctors were responsible for taking care of it. So, naturally, it was a mess. A week's worth of newspapers were scattered over the tables and chairs. Dirty cups and plates filled the sink.

The garbage can was overflowing. I figured it was my turn to clean up.

I started to gather up the newspapers and was about to throw them out when a tiny news item caught my eye. It was on the back page of the Metro section. The story didn't amount to more than three paragraphs. It was about a car accident on Mulholland Highway, which wasn't really a highway at all but rather a narrow road that wound around the northern edge of the Santa Monica Mountains. According to the article, Muriel Thayer, age nineteen, of Hollywood, died when she lost control of her car on the narrow, winding, rain-slick road.

I felt that tickle, the same mental shiver I'd gotten when I smelled the bath oil on Sally Pruitt's corpse.

I began organizing the newspapers on the couch by day, beginning with the morning the storms rolled in a week ago. Once I had the old newspapers laid out in chronological order, I began going through the news sections column by column, paying particular attention to reports about the storm and people injured by the downpour. I took careful notes as I went along.

When I was done, I had a list of two dozen names. I circled the victims who were alone when they were killed, and then I organized those names by sex and age. Among those half dozen names were two single women in their late teens. One died in a fall down a flight of stairs. Another was electrocuted.

There was nothing in the articles to indicate that either woman's death was anything but an accident. Neither article mentioned whether they were nursing students or not.

I wondered again about Muriel Thayer's death.

Was I jumping to conclusions?

All my fears were based on the similarities between Muriel and Sally and the fact that both of their deaths appeared to be accidents related to the storm.

I hadn't stopped to find out if there actually was

anything suspicious about Muriel's accident beyond my own feeling that something wasn't right.

There was one person I could ask—Dr. Jay Barbette, the county medical examiner. But how could I do it without revealing to him that I was investigating Sally Pruitt's murder?

Then again, it was Dr. Barbette who'd called me a born detective. Would he be any more surprised by what I was doing than Katherine was?

Probably not.

But that didn't mean he would approve of what I was doing. If I called him, he might tell Harry Trumble about it, and then I'd be in big trouble.

It was a risk I had to take, especially if there *was* a killer out there who'd already struck twice and might murder again.

I gave Dr. Barbette a call from the doctors' lounge, but he wasn't in. His assistant told me he was out at a crime scene. I said I'd call back later and didn't leave a message. I didn't want to take a chance that Harry Trumble would hear that I'd called.

I put my investigation aside and went back to work in the ER.

Alice Blevins assisted me as I put a plaster cast on a man's broken leg. The man had fallen off his roof while trying to plug a leak during a brief lull in the rain.

"Do you do any teaching in the nursing program?" I asked her casually as we worked.

"I'm not on the faculty, if that's what you mean," she said. "But I'm frequently asked to answer questions for the students or tell war stories about my tour of duty in Korea."

"The morale must be pretty low over there," I said.

"Why?" she asked.

"I heard a couple students died in accidents over the last week or so," I said.

"I only know of one. She drove off a cliff or something. Poor girl. I didn't realize there had been others."

I shrugged and told her I didn't know anything more, I was just repeating the scuttlebutt I'd heard around the hospital. What I didn't say was that I was disappointed that she couldn't give me any more details than I already had.

We finished up with the roofer and, as I was coming out of the exam room, I bumped into Bart Spicer. I thanked him again for letting us share a babysitter with him.

"Joanna is terrific, isn't she?" he asked.

I wondered if he knew, or suspected, what had happened between her and me. I wondered if it had happened to him, and if it had, if he'd pushed her away.

"How did you find her?" I asked.

"Word of mouth," Bart said. "Chet or Dan or Phil or one of the other doctors. Are you thinking about using her again?"

"We might," I said. "Have you ever hired any of the other nursing students to babysit? Joanna mentioned something about a list."

"There was one," he said. "I don't know what I did with my copy. Check the bulletin boards around the hospital."

I took his advice and set off down the halls, searching out bulletin boards in the coffee lounges, locker rooms, cafeterias, and anywhere else the hospital staff might congregate.

I couldn't find any copies of the list. And by the time I got to the bulletin board in the pathology lab, I was losing hope.

If I didn't find the list, there were a few other options. I could approach the other doctors and their wives to see if any of them still had a copy.

The easiest way, of course, would be to see Joanna Pate. She might know who the other nurses were. But the thought of seeing her again made me nervous. She was a very desirable young woman. I was afraid of what she might do and how I might react. I was thinking about that when one of the lab technicians tapped me on the shoulder, startling me. His skin and hair were almost as white as his lab coat.

"Weren't you here when the medical examiner picked up that lady who drowned?" he asked.

"Her name was Sally Pruitt," I said. "Yes, I was here. Why do you ask?"

"I'm glad I ran into you," he said, going to his desk. "The guys from Dr. Barbette's office left something behind the other day."

He brought me a plastic bag. Inside the bag was Sally Pruitt's rabbit-foot keychain and the single shiny key.

"Are you going to be seeing Dr. Barbette anytime soon?" the technician asked.

I would now that I had an excuse, I thought.

"Yes," I said, taking the bag and putting it in the pocket of my lab coat. "I'll be sure that he gets it."

I didn't know when I'd have an opportunity to go down to the county morgue, but I had a sinking feeling it would be sooner rather than later.

A strong wind beat the rain against the windows of the hospital, but despite the storm's fury the ER was surprisingly quiet. I spent the last hour of my shift catching up on all the paperwork generated by the chaos that had started my day thirty-six hours earlier.

I was on my way out to go home when I saw a woman in the waiting area, reading the evening edition of the newspaper. The headline was in big, bold type and immediately grabbed my full attention.

BABYSITTER MISSING, FOUL PLAY FEARED

It was the word "babysitter" that got me. Had The Storm Killer struck again?

There was another copy of the newspaper abandoned on an empty seat. I snatched it up and quickly read the article.

Tess Vigland, eighteen, disappeared from a home in Chatsworth last night while babysitting the two children of a single mother. When the mother, who'd been out on a date, returned a little after one a.m., she discovered the front door ajar, her children asleep in their beds, and the babysitter gone. The mother immediately called the police.

According to the article, a neighbor reported seeing Tess outside around eleven thirty p.m., talking to a man inside a large, dark sedan parked in front of the house. The witness didn't see the man's face and couldn't identify the make or model of his car.

Police told reporters that Tess left her shoes, purse, and wallet behind in the house, which indicated she wasn't planning on leaving and suggested foul play. Yet there were no signs of a struggle, leading police to believe she may have been abducted by someone she knew.

I tossed the paper aside. *The Storm Killer*. Good God, what was I thinking?

I'd worked myself up into believing there was some killer out there, stalking babysitters and using the storm to hide his crimes. I had absolutely no basis for leaping to that assumption.

Someone had murdered Sally Pruitt and made her death look like an accident, but that didn't mean every woman who died or disappeared in Los Angeles during the storm had been killed.

Muriel Thayer died in an accident on a rain-slick road. She was a nursing student and she babysat to earn extra money. That was all I really knew. It was hardly enough evidence to assume she was murdered.

I knew even less about Tess Vigland. She was a babysitter and she was gone. But her disappearance certainly couldn't be blamed on the weather, nor was she dead.

Yet.

That little voice in my head just wouldn't leave me alone, making my imagination run wild.

It was obvious what I needed to do: Go home, see my family, and get some rest. Everything would look different in the morning.

CHAPTER FOURTEEN

I didn't go home.

Instead, I called Katherine and told her I had to deliver Sally Pruitt's rabbit-foot key chain to Dr. Barbette right away.

"I hope you aren't thinking about cheating on me," she said, "because you're lousy at deception."

My heart dropped into my stomach, the blood drained from my face, and I nearly passed out. It was a good thing I was standing in the emergency room, because I was going to need one soon.

She knew about the kiss. She knew how it made me feel. She knew I'd kept it from her. How did she find out? Was it all over my face?

Maybe it was. Literally.

I felt a pang of panic. Had I walked back into our bedroom with another woman's lipstick on my face?

"I haven't lied to you about anything," I stammered.

"It's what you didn't say and you might as well have shouted it out," she replied. "The keychain is just an excuse to ask Dr. Barbette some more questions."

I took a deep breath and let it out slowly, relieved. This wasn't about Joanna. But it made me realize again just how guilty I felt about the kiss, for enjoying it, for wanting more. I would make it up to Katherine somehow, even though she didn't know she'd been slighted.

"You don't mind?" I asked.

"I'll wait up," she said. "I want to know everything."

"Really?" I said.

"This is better than an episode of *Perry Mason*," she said.

"I love you," I said.

"Of course you do," she replied, and I could hear the smile on her face. "I'm irresistible."

If Dr. Barbette was surprised to see me, he didn't show it. He was in middle of conducting an autopsy of a Hispanic man in his twenties with multiple stab wounds in his neck, chest, and stomach.

"What happened to him?" I asked as I came in.

"Horatio Ortega stabbed himself sixteen times with a steak knife," Barbette said. "Or so says the guy who was caught carrying Horatio's watch, wallet, and bloody steak knife."

The medical examiner peeled off his bloody gloves and shook my hand.

"What can I do for you, Dr. Sloan?"

I took the plastic bag out of my pocket and gave it to him. "You left this keychain behind the other day. It belonged to Sally Pruitt."

Dr. Barbette nodded and tossed the bag on an empty autopsy table. "You didn't make the trip all the way down here just to deliver that key."

"My wife said the same thing," I said.

"You want to ask me something about Sally Pruitt's murder," he said.

"My wife said that, too," I said.

"What else did she say? You could save me the trouble of having this conversation at all."

I told him what I'd learned so far about Sally Pruitt, how she was living with her parents and babysitting to earn money for tuition in Community General's nursing school.

"As fascinating as that is," Dr. Barbette said with a sigh, "I'd appreciate it if you got to the point, assuming there is one."

"Earlier this week, a woman died in a car accident on Mulholland," I said. "Her name was Muriel Thayer."

Dr. Barbette cocked an eyebrow. "What about her?"

"She was a nursing student at Community General," I said. "She was also babysitting to earn extra money."

"You think there's a connection," Barbette said.

"I was hoping you could tell me," I said. "Are you sure her death was an accident?"

"Yes," he said. "And no."

Goose bumps crawled up my back. He led me over to one of the morgue drawers as he spoke.

"She lost control of her car on one of those hairpin turns," he said. "The car went over the cliff and rolled over several times before reaching the bottom of the canyon."

"Were there any skid marks on the road?"

Dr. Barbette shrugged. "I just cut the bodies, but here's the interesting thing."

He opened the drawer in front of him, revealing a corpse I presumed to be Muriel Thayer. Beyond the Y-shaped autopsy incision, I noticed she was covered with deep bruises and numerous lacerations. She had a compound fracture of her right leg and a broken nose, and was missing several teeth.

"She was hurt pretty bad, as you can see," he said. "What you can't see is the collapsed lung, the cracked ribs, and the ruptured spleen."

"None of those wounds is fatal," I said.

"You must be a doctor," he said.

"So what killed her?" I asked.

"My best guess is a heart attack or heart arrhythmia," he said.

"Are you sure she wasn't dead before the car went off the cliff?" I asked.

He glared at me. "I may have been mistaken calling you a doctor. Think a minute."

I flushed, embarrassed that I'd asked such a stupid question. "If she was dead, she wouldn't have bled or bruised. Sorry, it's been a long day."

"You aren't used to thinking about death," he said. "You're more experienced in preventing it. If you're serious about investigating murder, you'll have to change the way you look at things."

I gestured toward the body. "Is she still here because you have some doubts about the circumstances of her death?"

"I don't have any doubts," he said. "Her parents are coming from Chicago to claim her body. The storm has delayed their arrival."

He may not have had any doubts, but I did, even though there was no evidence to suggest that she was murdered. Judging from the expression on Dr. Barbette's face, he knew exactly what I was thinking.

"Many factors can contribute to the sudden loss of life. Not every cause of death can be conclusively determined," he said. "That doesn't make them homicides."

I nodded, not really believing him.

"Do you think I'm incompetent, Dr. Sloan?"

"No, sir," I said, horrified that I might have offended him. "Of course not."

"I've been doing this a long time, young man. I've probably conducted hundreds of autopsies. If there was any evidence of murder, I would have found it."

"I'm sure you would," I said, trying desperately to make up for my mistake. "I didn't mean to imply, in any way, shape, or form, that you weren't doing your job. Of course you were. Exceptionally well."

"Then again," Barbette said, a contemplative look on his face, "the killer might not have left any evidence for me to find."

He gave me a tiny smile and, with it, a little encouragement. I smiled back appreciatively and with great relief.

"I'm sorry if I distracted you from your work, Dr. Barbette," I said. "I'd better be going."

"What's your hurry? As long as you're here, would you like to assist me on another autopsy? It's a dismemberment case. You don't get many of those."

"I wish I could," I said, "but I should get home to my wife."

"Very well," he said, sounding a bit disappointed. "Thank you for delivering Miss Pruitt's personal effects."

A thought occurred to me. "What happened to Muriel's things?"

"I have them," Barbette said. "They're in a box for her parents."

"Could I see them?"

"I don't see why not," Barbette said.

He led me to a storage room, drew a set of keys from his pocket, and unlocked the door. The tiny room was lined floor to ceiling with metal shelves. On each shelf were identical cardboard file boxes labeled with serial numbers and names. Dr. Barbette went to Muriel's box, pulled it off the shelf, and carried it back into the morgue, setting it down on the empty autopsy table.

"What are you looking for?" he asked.

"I don't know," I said, lifting the lid off the box. There wasn't much inside. Each item was in its own plastic bag. "I'm just curious."

Dr. Barbette smiled, amused. "That's how it starts."

"How what starts?"

"Every investigation," he said. "You think you're going to find Sally Pruitt's killer in that box?"

He didn't wait for an answer. He turned his back to me and returned to the corpse with the multiple stab wounds.

I sorted through Muriel's things. Her bloody, torn clothes had been neatly folded and placed in a bag, as if they might be worn again. Her raincoat, gloves, shoes, jewelry, and purse were each bagged separately, but the contents of her purse were collected together in one bag. I emptied the bag out on the table, the items spilling onto the metal with a loud clang.

I looked up apologetically at Dr. Barbette.

"Sorry," I said.

When I lowered my head again, my gaze fell on the bag containing Sally Pruitt's keychain. I didn't want it to be inadvertently included with Muriel's things, so I picked it up to set it aside. That's when I noticed Muriel Thayer's keyring on the table. I picked up the keyring and fanned out Muriel's keys, comparing them to the one on Sally's rabbit foot.

I found an exact match.

They both had the same key.

It wasn't evidence of murder—at least it wouldn't be to a court of law or any reasonable person.

But it was to me.

The back of my neck tingled. I could feel the killer's presence again, as if he was right there in the room with Dr. Barbette and me and the woman he'd killed.

I looked up and saw Dr. Barbette staring at me. "What have you found?"

"Sally Pruitt was murdered and tossed into the river. She didn't have her purse or her jewelry. All she had was this." I held up Sally's key with one hand. "Six days earlier, Muriel Thayer died from causes you can't conclusively determine. This was among her possessions."

I held up Muriel's key beside Sally's. Barbette walked over and examined them both. He frowned.

"You want to know my professional opinion, Dr. Sloan?"

"Absolutely," I said.

"It's creepy," he said. "But that doesn't make it murder. There could be a thousand innocent explanations. Even so, you should tell the homicide detectives what you've found."

I knew he was right, but I wasn't looking forward to

my inevitable encounter with Harry Trumble. There would be no talking my way out of the fact that I'd ignored his warning and investigated the murder anyway.

The phone rang. Dr. Barbette went to answer it. I studied the keys, as if staring at them hard enough would reveal what lock they fit into and where it was.

Dr. Barbette hung up and came back over to me. "Another day, another body."

"Anything interesting?"

"Nothing I don't see far too often," he said with a weary sigh. "Someone beat up a young woman and slit her throat. But it's going to get a lot of attention."

"Why's that?" I asked.

"Because it's that missing babysitter," he said. "Tess Vigland."

CHAPTER FIFTEEN

Dr. Barbette invited me to come along with him to the crime scene. I couldn't understand why, until he explained that Harry Trumble, the homicide detective working the Sally Pruitt case, was also assigned to the Vigland murder.

I followed the morgue wagon out to a vacant lot in Chatsworth, part of a large swath of land that had been cleared and graded for development.

It had stopped raining, but the relentless downpour of the last week had turned the unpaved streets into muddy riverbeds. A dozen dirt-splattered police cars were parked around a corner lot, which was illuminated by several huge lights powered by a loud portable generator on a trailer.

Dr. Barbette stopped his van beside the officer posted to keep people away from the scene. They exchanged a few words and the morgue wagon moved on, the officer waving me through behind it. I parked beside the morgue wagon and got out of the car, my feet immediately sinking into the thick muck. When I lifted my foot to take a step, my shoe almost came off with it.

Taking pity on me, Dr. Barbette offered me a pair of galoshes from the back of his van. I put the galoshes on and accompanied him through the crowd of officers, police photographers, and crime lab technicians towards the body, which was covered with a white sheet.

Harry Trumble was crouched beside a crime lab technician who was carefully pouring plaster into a set of tire tracks left in the mud. The technician was a heavyset man in a too-tight crime lab jumpsuit. I moved up quietly behind them.

"I couldn't get a set of tracks better than this if I put the plaster right on the tire itself," the technician said. "They're beauties."

"Yeah, they're a real work of art, Earl," Harry grumbled. "What can you tell me about them?"

"There are thousands of different tire tread designs, and each tire wears differently," Earl said. "They are almost like fingerprints for cars, though you can change a tire and you can't change your fingertip. That doesn't—"

"People don't ask you about your work much, do they, Earl?" Harry asked.

"I could talk about tires for hours."

"That's what I'm afraid of," Harry said. "How about you just tell me about this specific tire."

"It's a rayon custom super cushion tubeless tire, probably a B. F. Goodrich Silver Town, if I'm not mistaken," Earl said. "Judging by the deep, firm impressions left by the ribs and transverse grooves, I'd say they are relatively new. Only a few hundred miles on them, tops."

"What kind of car did they come from?"

"A large passenger sedan with a front and rear track of about sixty-two inches and a wheelbase of about a hundred twenty-nine inches. I'd guess we're looking at a Cadillac or a Chrysler or a Lincoln or—"

"I get the picture," Harry interrupted, rising to his feet. That was when he saw me. The look of shock on his face was almost comical and I couldn't help smiling.

"Hello, Harry," I said.

Every muscle in his face became rigid. It was a wonder he was still able to blink.

"What the hell are you doing here?" he asked.

Before I could answer, he yelled at the officers around

him, "I ordered this scene locked up tight. Who let this civilian through?"

"I did," Dr. Barbette said, peering under the sheet at the corpse. "He's found out some interesting things about Sally Pruitt's murder that I thought you'd want to hear."

Harry took a step towards me, getting in my face. I held my ground, mainly because my feet were sunk too deep into the muck for me to take a step back.

"I told you not to get involved," Harry said.

"I couldn't help it," I said.

"Seems to me I've heard that excuse before," Harry said.

He had. And the last time I said it, he decked me. I didn't think that was going to happen again, at least not at that moment.

Dr. Barbette stepped between us, forcing us apart. "I take it you two have some history together."

"We're old friends," I said.

"We used to be," Harry said. "Say whatever you came to say, Mark, and make it fast. I've got a homicide investigation to run here."

I quickly explained that Sally Pruitt and Muriel Thayer were both involved with the nursing school, Sally as an applicant to the program and Muriel as a student. They were both earning money babysitting. They were both killed during the storm. And they both had copies of the same key.

When I was done, Harry shook his head. "You came all the way out here to tell me that?"

"I thought it was significant," I said.

"That's why you're a doctor and I'm a homicide detective," Harry said. He turned to Dr. Barbette. "Was Muriel Thayer murdered?"

"No," Dr. Barbette said.

Harry looked back at me. "Kind of kills your point, doesn't it?"

"Dr. Barbette can also tell you her cause of death isn't

certain," I said. "That leaves the door open to other explanations."

"Like what?" Harry asked.

I glanced at Dr. Barbette. He looked back at me blankly.

"I don't know," I said. "But look at the connections. They were both babysitters." I gestured towards Tess Vigland's corpse. "And so was she."

"Do you know how many teenage girls in this city do some babysitting?" Harry said. "I'd guess just about all of them."

"How many of them are aspiring nurses? You should see if Tess Vigland either applied to nursing school at Community General or was already in the program."

"I *should?*" Harry said. "You're telling me how to do my job now?"

"I'm afraid there's a killer using the storm as a cover for murdering young women," I said. "Nursing students who do babysitting work."

Harry shook his head. "How many years have you been investigating homicides, Mark?"

"You don't need to be a detective to see the connections," I said.

"This morning, the waitress who served me breakfast at the Pantry sneezed," Harry said. "I saw two other people in the restaurant sneeze, too. Another one coughed. You want to know what I think? The cook is sick and is breathing germs all over the food. He's infecting us all. The health department should shut the place down before the plague spreads any further."

I saw what he was getting at. Just because all those people in the restaurant were sneezing, that didn't mean they'd caught a cold from the same person at the same place. It also didn't mean they all had colds. There were too many other factors at work to make that conclusion. Calling it a plague was a ridiculous leap, way out of proportion to the evidence he'd seen.

That was the point, of course.

He wanted me to say there was no connection between the people who were sneezing and the chef. That making the jump from a sneeze to a plague was outrageous. That if he was a doctor, he'd understand that.

It was a shrewd argument on his part. Especially since he was right. And I could tell from the smug look on his face that he knew it.

From his point of view, I was guilty of taking several unrelated bits of information about several different women, combining them with some superficial and irrelevant commonalities, and assuming that a mad killer was at work.

"This is different," I said.

That lame reply was the strongest defense I could muster without revealing how I knew for a fact that I was right.

I could feel it.

It was hardly a convincing argument. I'm not entirely sure I was convinced, but I was in too deep at that point. My pride was at stake. Maybe if it had been any other cop except Harry. Anyone except the man whose friendship I'd betrayed.

But it wasn't.

"Even if I thought that you were right, which I don't, this murder doesn't fit," Harry said, pointing at the corpse lying in the mud. "This isn't an accident. Tess Vigland was abducted by someone she knew, who beat her head in, slit her throat, and dumped her body in a vacant lot. There's a second killer."

"Check her keys, see if one of them matches these," I said, offering him the bags that contained the keys.

He snatched them from me and tossed them to the nearest uniformed officer.

"Stick to medicine, Mark," Harry said. "And if I find you interfering in this case again, I'll have you arrested."

Harry stomped away, splattering mud on his pants legs.

I remained where I was. I knew I'd keep investigating and I suspected that Harry knew it, too.

"You better get yourself a good criminal lawyer," Dr. Barbette said. "Or at least a dependable bail bondsman."

"Why?" I asked.

"So you're ready when Trumble catches you snooping around."

When I finally got home, it was nearly eleven p.m. Even so, it was earlier than usual for me. Katherine was sitting on the couch, feeding Steve his bottle, his chubby little legs kicking happily.

"Take off your galoshes," she said. "You're tracking mud all over the carpet."

I looked at my dirt-caked feet and realized I now had another excuse to drop by the morgue. I took off the galoshes, my shoes, and my wet socks and left them outside the front door to dry.

I padded barefoot back into the apartment. Katherine handed me Steve and a diaper to put over my shoulder.

"Burp him for me while I heat up your dinner," she said.

I held him, patted his back, and gently bounced. He nuzzled my neck and hiccupped.

"How was your day?" I asked.

She turned on the oven and took a tuna casserole out of the refrigerator. "Not nearly as interesting as yours," she said. "But there was one nice surprise."

Katherine picked up a letter from the kitchen table. It had the Chrysler logo on the envelope.

"Your Imperial Crown Southampton is waiting for you," she said. "They can deliver it to our door or you can pick it up. I think you should go get it or have them pick you up at the hospital. If they see where we live, they may change their mind about loaning it to us for a few days."

"I didn't know you liked cars so much," I said.

"I just think it'll be fun," she said. "We can make a night on the town out of it. A long night."

She winked. Katherine almost never winked. I would have winked back, but Steve reached out and gave my nose a hard squeeze, so instead I winced.

"Tell me all about your investigation," she said.

So I did, filling her in on everything I'd learned since discovering Sally Pruitt was murdered, right up through my encounter that night with Harry Trumble. The explanation carried me through dinner. When I was finished, Katherine put Steve to bed and came back to the table.

"There's one thing I don't get," she said, sitting on my lap. "How did you make the connection between Sally Pruitt and Muriel Thayer?"

I'd purposely danced around that part, but apparently not very well. I looked down at my plate, concentrating on the difficult task of rolling a pea.

"I asked Joanna, the Spicers' babysitter, if she knew Sally Pruitt," I said. "And then she mentioned how Muriel Thayer had also died."

This was my opportunity to tell Katherine about the kiss, to unburden myself of the guilt. But when I looked up at her face, I just couldn't do it.

Katherine slid an arm around my shoulder, a thoughtful expression on her face as she mulled over what I'd told her. I hoped she wasn't trying to decide if I was deceiving her or not.

"What about those other two women?" she asked.

"What other two women?"

"The two women you found in the newspaper who also died in accidents during the storm."

"I forgot all about them," I said. "Dr. Barbette got that call about Tess Vigland and before I knew it, we were racing out to the crime scene. In the rush of events, the names simply slipped my mind."

"Is the list in your pocket?" she asked. "You better take

it out now and put it in your wallet for safekeeping or it might accidentally get run through the wash."

"Good idea," I said. I pulled the list out of my pocket and glanced at the two names again. One was Ingrid Willis, nineteen, who slipped and fell down a flight of stairs outside her apartment, breaking her neck. The other was Clara Cohen, eighteen, who'd been buried alive in a mudslide in her backyard when a retaining wall on the hillside gave way.

"So Harry doesn't know about them," she said.

"I don't think so," I said. "I certainly didn't tell him."

"Then it's up to you, Mark."

"What's up to me?"

"To find out if Ingrid Willis and Clara Cohen were nursing students," she said. "And if they were working as babysitters, too."

"You want me to keep investigating, even after what Harry said to me?"

"Forget about Harry," she said. "He's not going to arrest you. Because if he does, he'll have to deal with me."

"I think he'd like that," I said.

"I doubt it. He blames you for stealing me from him, which doesn't say much about my own free will. He does it because it's a whole lot easier than accepting that he lost me all on his own."

"What does that have to do with whether or not he'll follow through on his threat?"

"Because if he tries to hurt you in any way, I'll remind him of all the reasons I left him for you and why you're a better man than he is," she said. "And that's the last thing he wants to hear."

"But that still doesn't explain why you want me to keep investigating."

"You mean besides the fact that you're going to do it anyway?"

I nodded.

"Because Harry is too stubborn to listen to you, and if

you're right and nobody does anything, more women are going to die."

I could feel Katherine's hand shaking ever so slightly on my shoulder. I put my arms around her and held her close to me. She was shaking all over. She was terrified.

"There's no reason to be afraid," I said.

"What's going to happen when he finds out what you're doing?"

"You just told me what's going to happen," I said. "If anybody should be afraid, it's Harry."

"I'm not talking about Harry," she said. "I'm talking about whoever is killing these women. What do you think he's going to do when he finds out you're pursuing him?"

"Maybe he won't know until the moment he's arrested," I said.

"Or maybe," she said, her voice quivering, "he knows already."

Despite my best efforts, I began to shake a little bit, too.

CHAPTER SIXTEEN

The next morning, shortly after I arrived to begin my shift, I gathered my courage and went to see Dr. Whittington. If anyone could tell me if Tess Vigland, Ingrid Willis, and Clara Cohen were nursing students or applicants, it was him. What I hadn't quite figured out yet was how to ask. On my way up the stairs to his office, I toyed with several possible ways to approach him.

I could say I'd been asked by each of them to write letters of recommendation but was so caught up in my work, I'd forgotten to get around to it. Was it too late to include my letter among their application materials? To which I was afraid he'd say, "Do you think I know the name of every young woman who applies to nursing school? And even if I did know these women, I'd refuse them admittance now purely on the basis of the astonishingly poor judgment they've shown by seeking you out for a recommendation. You're a disgrace to the entire practice of medicine. Go away before I pluck my eyeballs out with nails."

I could say I needed to contact the young women about babysitting and had misplaced their phone numbers. Would he mind putting me in touch with them? But I was certain he'd declare: "This is a hospital, not a babysitting service. Do you think I would violate the sanctity of the nursing school admittance process and the privacy of these vulnerable young women just so you could troll for the personal phone numbers of teenage girls? What kind of pervert are you? Get out of my sight, you miserable excuse for a doctor."

There was also the direct approach. I could say that I wanted to find out if there was a connection between their deaths and the murder of Sally Pruitt. But I knew what his response would be. "So you're a *detective* now? I applaud you for realizing that medicine is simply beyond your grasp. When you succeed in actually getting a badge, then you can ask me questions. For now, I'd appreciate it if you'd leave before my disgust for you makes me vomit my guts out."

So I arrived at his secretary's desk without the slightest idea what I was going to say. As it turned out, it didn't matter.

"If you're looking for Dr. Whittington, you can forget it," Imelda said, her face overwhelmed and literally overshadowed by her immense beehive hairdo. "He hasn't showed up or called in since yesterday."

"I know, that's why I'm here. He's sick at home," I said, surprisingly myself with my fluid improvisation. "He asked me to bring him the nursing school applications for"—I made a show of fishing around in my pockets for the list, which I then made an even bigger show of reading from—"Tess Vigland, Ingrid Willis, and Clara Cohen."

Imelda adjusted her batwing glasses, which were secured with an elaborate chain around her neck, as if she was afraid someone might try to snatch them from her beaklike nose.

"He could have called me," she said. "I am his personal executive secretary."

"I wish he had," I said. "He treats us residents like we're his servants."

She looked at me down her long, pointed nose. "You are, young man."

Imelda went to her file cabinet and thumbed through it for a moment, her back to me. My heart was pounding. I could feel trickles of sweat rolling down my back. I wasn't sure if I was nervous about my deception or about what I might find out.

She pulled several files from the drawer and handed them to me.

There was one for each of the three women.

I tried to thank her for the files, but I couldn't seem to speak. My throat was too constricted. All I managed to do was nod a few times and back away from the desk.

One nursing student. Four nursing school applicants. All from Community General. All dead.

Someone had murdered them all.

I told Nurse Blevins that Dr. Whittington had asked me to deliver some files to his house, and I drove out to Brentwood, leaving Chet Arnold and Bart Spicer to cover for me in the ER.

I knew I was going to get in deep trouble, but I didn't care. There was a killer stalking nursing students and applicants at our hospital. Dr. Whittington was the one man who knew all the victims. He could tell me who else had access to the enrollment and applications lists and what else, if anything, the victims might have had in common.

Of course, Dr. Whittington had no reason to answer my questions and wouldn't take kindly to an underling like me demanding answers.

I didn't care anymore. What was important now was finding and stopping the murderer before anyone else was killed.

The sky thundered and crackled with an anger that matched my own, reminding me of the storm's complicity in the deaths. Would the killings end when the storm left? Or would the murderer simply find a new cover for his crimes?

Then again, I wasn't certain there weren't more

killings yet to be discovered that had occurred *before* the storm.

I also couldn't figure out why the killer had been so careful to disguise the murders of Sally Pruitt, Muriel Thayer, Ingrid Willis, and Clara Cohen, and yet did nothing to hide what he'd done to Tess Vigland.

It didn't make sense, unless . . .

He'd stopped trying to use the storm to make the killings look like accidents because there was no longer any reason to. Because he knew his crimes had already been discovered.

Because he knew about me.

And there was only one way he'd know about me.

If I already knew the killer.

Before I could scare myself too much with that thought, I arrived at Dr. Whittington's house—and had new things to worry about.

It was drizzling, the sky dark with roiling clouds. Water dripped off the eaves of the house. The drapes on the large front windows were closed. I parked behind the big, black Imperial and got out with the files in my hand.

I decided I wasn't going to play any games. I'd come straight out and tell him why I was here. Five women were dead, maybe more.

I walked past the car towards the door when something made me stop. It was that tingle again. I turned back and crouched beside the Imperial, examining the tires. They were new, with no noticeable wear at all. And although I wasn't a tire expert, I was certain of one thing.

The tread pattern was the same as the one left in the mud beside Tess Vigland's corpse. Was Dr. Whittington the killer?

I thought about turning back, about finding the nearest pay phone and calling Harry Trumble.

But I didn't.

I couldn't assume that Dr. Whittington was the murderer simply because he knew all the victims and had the same tires as the killer. There were thousands of cars with the same tires.

As I got closer to his door, that little voice in my head wouldn't shut up.

But what if it was *his car?*

But what if he was *the killer?*

It would explain how the killer had managed to make the other deaths, particularly Muriel Thayer's, look like an accident. Dr. Whittington had the medical knowledge to concoct something that would fool even the best medical examiner.

Did he? And what would he do when he saw me at his door, holding the evidence that linked him to the victims?

By the time I asked myself that question, I was already at his door and the point was moot. Because there was a note thumbtacked to the door.

It was typewritten and wet. Some of the ink had run in the rain. But it was legible.

> *Do not enter. This is a crime scene. Call the police immediately.*

And it was signed,

> *Alistair Whittington.*

Of course I didn't do what the note instructed. I took a handkerchief from my pocket, reached out, and tried the doorknob. The door was unlocked. I eased it open slowly and peered inside.

"Dr. Whittington?" I called loudly. "It's Dr. Mark Sloan."

I didn't really expect a reply, given the note. The first thing I noticed was the smell. The unmistakable odor of decay and death. I'd never smelled it before, but the recognition comes hardwired in all of us. I covered my nose and mouth with the handkerchief and ventured inside the house. I was scared, but my curiosity was stronger than my fear.

The blinds were open to the backyard, filling the house with dim gray light. Everything in the room was neat and orderly. There were no signs of a break-in or violence. I moved slowly to the kitchen.

There was a coffee mug on the kitchen table and a tiny plate with leftover crumbs from a pastry. Yesterday's newspaper was neatly folded in the center of the table.

I turned back towards the living room and noticed that the double doors to the study were ajar. Flies buzzed in and out of the narrow opening and crawled on the doors. I knew what that meant and it made my stomach churn. My whole body was damp with sweat and I was filled with dread as I cautiously approached the study.

"Hello?" I said. "Dr. Whittington?"

I called out more for the comfort of hearing my own voice than to alert anyone to my presence. If there was anyone in the house, they already knew I was there.

I eased the door open. The stench hit me with almost physical force and I could hear the incessant, furious buzzing of flies.

The study was a stark contrast to the contemporary styling of the rest of the house. The room was decorated in dark leather furniture and rich wood, the walls hung with landscape paintings and lined with bookcases containing leather-bound volumes. One of the paintings was on the floor underneath the wall safe it had once covered. The safe was open and empty, all of its contents apparently stacked neatly on the coffee table. The papers included the deeds to two homes, the doctor's life insurance policy, his will, his passport, and a stack of Blue Chip stamp books tied with a ribbon and set atop the most recent catalog. There was also some women's jewelry and some cash in U.S. and British currency.

Dr. Whittington was sitting in his big red leather desk

chair, facing the door. He was sprawled facedown on his desk, a gun in his hand, blood and brain matter splattered on the curtains, the chair, and the typewriter behind him.

I turned away, gagging. The sight and the smell and the flies were too much. My whole body rebelled. I wanted to run outside. I wanted to vomit. But I wouldn't allow myself to do it. I fought against it with all my willpower. And once again, my curiosity overwhelmed my natural revulsion.

I had seen death before, many times, but nothing like this.

When I was sure I had myself under control, I made myself look back at him, to stare at Dr. Whittington until I could see him dispassionately, until I could forget that this was someone I knew and had worked with. Until he wasn't Dr. Whittington anymore.

He was a corpse. A cadaver. Just like the ones we worked on in med school.

He was wearing a white dress shirt and a cravat. I couldn't imagine what other man, besides Dr. Whittington, would wear a cravat even when relaxing alone at home.

I examined his head wound and took note of his degree of decomposition. From what I could tell, he'd been dead at least a day, perhaps longer. I didn't have any actual experience to draw on. I was basing my judgment entirely on my medical school training and what I'd learned growing up around cops.

I also determined that he'd killed himself. I was basing my judgment on the gun in his hand, the point-blank bullet wound to the head, and, most important, the suicide note under the paperweight at the edge of his desk.

The note was typewritten, with his signature in the bottom right-hand corner. Yesterday's date was in the upper right-hand corner. February 12, 1962.

I read the note.

Dear Sirs,

As you will have no doubt noticed by now, I am quite dead, my life taken by my own hand. But I'm saddened to say that my life was over long before I chose to put a gun to my temple and pull the trigger. My undoing has been slow and very painful.

I've made several large investments over the years, particularly in the bomb shelter development business, which haven't lived up to my expectations. In the last few months, I found myself facing the frightening prospect of complete financial ruin. In desperation, I turned to less honorable methods of acquiring funds.

I used my position at the nursing school to coerce the young applicants into trading sexual favors in exchange for admission to our prestigious program. I also intimidated them into selling their favors to others and paying me a percentage of the income from those endeavors.

But I underestimated their guile. They attempted to blackmail me, threatening to expose my infidelity and my criminality. Not only was I facing the loss of my possessions, but my family and career as well. This could not be tolerated. So I removed the threat. It was an act of self-defense.

Ultimately, however, it was futile. The bank will soon be coming to take the house, the car, and the appliances. The telephone and other utilities are about to be disconnected. My crimes will also soon be revealed.

So this, my final act, is a courtesy to myself and to my family, sparing them the pain and embarrassment of my inevitable ruination.

My dear wife has left me, returning to our home in London with our son. They can now make a new start, freed from the burden of my failures.

I've opened my safe and left all my pertinent pa-

pers on the coffee table for you. I've also left some li-
brary books for you to return. They are due Thursday.
 Sincerely yours,
 Dr. Alistair Whittington

I glanced back at Dr. Whittington. Everything in his
life was going wrong, yet even in his last few moments,
he was still trying to exercise some measure of control
over it anyway. The stuffy, intimidating, very British doctor was true to his character to the very end.

Using the handkerchief, I picked up the telephone re-
ceiver and dialed the police.

CHAPTER SEVENTEEN

The first thing Harry Trumble did upon arriving at Dr. Whittington's house was have me arrested. I was handcuffed by a police officer and driven downtown, where I was placed in a jail cell. I wasn't given the opportunity to make any phone calls—not that I would have anyway.

The confinement wasn't so bad, if you don't consider the stench of urine and sweat that permeated the walls. I'd smelled a lot worse that same morning. I was able to block it out of my mind. I spent the first two hours in custody going over all the details of the case again, this time fitting Dr. Whittington into the blanks.

Although Dr. Whittington had confessed to just about everything in his suicide note, he did it in a rather broad, vague way. I wished he'd taken the time to go into a bit more detail before shooting himself. I would have liked to know exactly how he staged the murders of Muriel Thayer, Ingrid Willis, and Clara Cohen without leaving any trace. I'm sure Dr. Barbette would also have liked an answer, especially since he would soon be facing the tiresome prospect of exhuming the corpses and conducting new autopsies.

At least there was no mystery about the mistakes Dr. Whittington made trying to disguise the murder of Sally Pruitt. The only reason I discovered that her death wasn't an accident was because of the sloppy way he dressed his victim after he drowned her. It was as if he'd been in a hurry, not paying attention to the crucial details.

With the other killings, however, he was careful and meticulous, leaving no sign at all that the deaths were anything but tragic accidents.

What had happened with Sally Pruitt that caused him to be so sloppy?

Tess Vigland's murder was even more puzzling to me. It was a vicious killing, his fury over his victim undisguised. Did he do it because he knew there was no point in going to such elaborate lengths to disguise his crimes anymore?

That didn't make a lot of sense to me. There was no downside to covering up a murder, unless he wanted people to know she'd been killed, perhaps so her gruesome demise could serve as a warning to others.

Who would those others be? Other nursing students involved in the blackmail scheme?

I thought of Joanna Pate and the kiss she gave me. Was she one of Dr. Whittington's call girls? Was she trying to seduce me that night into becoming one of her clients?

And if they were blackmailing Dr. Whittington, what was stopping them from extorting money from their other clients as well?

Despite Dr. Whittington's suicide and all that it explained, too much of what had happened was still a mystery to me for me to feel satisfied.

Perhaps I never would be.

As I pondered all the unanswered questions, I got sleepy, and so I spent the remainder of my four hours in jail enjoying a nice, restful nap on the hard, flat cot.

It was late afternoon when Harry Trumble finally came down to get me, kicking the cot to wake me up. Without saying a word, he led me into an interrogation room and slammed the door. I was thankful that at least he hadn't put me in handcuffs again. I would have liked a hot cup of coffee, but I wasn't about to ask for one. He was getting far too much pleasure already out of my discomfort. The less upset I appeared, the more it would irritate him.

I sat down at the table and watched him pace for a moment. He looked tired and angry. There was also a certain resignation in his posture, a palpable sense of defeat. I tried to appear unhurried, unperturbed, and uninterested.

"Did Dr. Whittington call you and ask you to pick up those files?" Harry asked finally.

"No," I said.

"So you lied to his secretary," he said.

"Yes," I said. "I did."

"How long have you known that Dr. Whittington killed these women?"

"I didn't know," I said. "I still don't."

Harry glared at me. "He confessed in his suicide note."

"He said he removed the threat," I said. "It's not quite the same as saying 'I killed four women, maybe more.'"

"More?" Harry said.

I shrugged. "We won't know until we check out the list of nursing school applicants."

"*We?*" Harry roared, slamming his fist on the table, startling me.

"It's just a figure of speech," I said.

"The hell it is," Harry said. "You've been running your own rogue investigation from the start."

"So what if I have?" I said. "If I hadn't, you'd still be stomping around in the mud looking for two killers instead of one. And nobody would ever have known that Muriel Thayer, Ingrid Willis, and Clara Cohen were murdered."

"We still don't know that," Harry said.

"They were all nursing applicants," I said. "They all knew Dr. Whittington, and they're all dead, just like Sally Pruitt and Tess Vigland."

"We can prove those two were murdered," he said. "We've got no evidence whatsoever on the others."

"Then find it," I said, my irritation coming through despite my best efforts. "I can't do everything for you."

Harry came around the table, grabbed me by the collar, and lifted me out of my seat. He looked as if he might strike me. I met his gaze, silently daring him to.

After a long moment, he released me, and I sat down again, straightening my shirt.

"I need you to make a statement," he said, standing over me, glowering. "Everything you know, and when you knew it, starting from the beginning."

"Not until you tell me a few things," I said.

"You want to go back to that cell?" Harry said, jabbing his finger in my face. "I can keep you in there as long as I want."

"And I can tell the officer who takes my statement just how little you had to do with the investigation of your first homicide," Mark said. "How's that going to look to your superiors?"

Harry's face reddened. I wondered how much was anger and how much was embarrassment.

"What do you want to know?" Harry asked.

"Have you found any keys belonging to Dr. Whittington that match the ones Sally Pruitt and Muriel Thayer had?"

"Not yet," Harry said.

"You should see if Tess Vigland, Ingrid Willis, or Clara Cohen had the same key."

"Have you got any other investigative pointers for me?" Harry sneered. "Because if you don't, I have advice to give you on your next surgical procedure."

I ignored the dig and the impulse to make a cutting rejoinder. There was no point making him any angrier than he already was, especially when I still needed more information from him.

"Did you match the tire treads on Dr. Whittington's car to the casts you made at the scene of Tess Vigland's murder?" I asked.

"Yeah," he said, practically spitting at me. "And the neighbor has identified the Imperial as the car she saw outside the house where Tess Vigland was babysitting. Not that it matters now."

"What happened to all of Whittington's money? How did he lose it?"

"You don't ruin yourself losing money you have," Harry said. "You ruin yourself by losing money that isn't yours. He borrowed against everything he had to invest a hundred thousand dollars in a bomb shelter development company."

"Safe Haven, Incorporated," I said.

"You knew about that, too?"

"He tried to sell me one."

"Shows you just how desperate he really was," Harry said.

"The bullet in his brain told me that," I replied.

Harry explained that Whittington was one of several investors, mostly professionals in other fields, who thought the bomb shelter business was going to boom. It didn't. The enterprise was going bankrupt and taking the investors down with it.

"Have you found any of Sally Pruitt's jewelry in Dr. Whittington's house?" I asked.

Harry shook his head. "He probably ditched it. Wouldn't you if you'd drowned some kid in your bathtub?"

"You think he killed her there?"

"Where else?" Harry said. "What the hell does it matter now anyway? They're dead, he's dead, it's done. Case closed. All that's left is for you to make a statement. You think you can do that now?"

I nodded. I started to rise from my seat, but he pushed me back down.

"I don't ever want to see you again," he said.

"I didn't do this to hurt you," I said.

"But you keep doing it anyway," Harry said. "Investigate *that*."

I lied in my statement.

I didn't change any of the facts, but as I told my story

to the officer, I made it seem as if I was consulting with Harry from the beginning, as if we were working hand in hand from the morning he visited my apartment.

It wouldn't be to my advantage to take credit for solving the murders. For one thing, I didn't feel as if I had. I never suspected Dr. Whittington until I was standing on his doorstep, bringing him the admissions files of those three dead women.

Besides, it wouldn't have done me any good. I was a doctor. I had no aspirations to be a homicide detective. And seeking recognition for what little I'd done would have deeply hurt the reputations and careers of Dr. Barbette and Harry Trumble. I cared too much about them both to do that.

And something Harry said to me had struck a nerve.

I'd taken the woman he loved. I wasn't going to take his career away from him, too.

I'd hurt him enough already.

This deserved to be Harry Trumble's victory. The problem was, Harry Trumble would always know that it wasn't.

CHAPTER EIGHTEEN

When I got home that rainy February evening, there was a message waiting for me from the hospital administrators. They'd told Katherine I was on paid leave until the controversy settled down. There was no need for me to come in to work until further notice. They were careful to say that this wasn't a disciplinary action, but rather something they felt was in my best interests, as well as the hospital's.

Needless to say, this message confused Katherine, who had no idea what they were talking about. So, as I ate my dinner, I went over everything once again, ending with my statement to the police.

When I was done, Katherine seemed dazed.

"He kissed my hand," she said. "Dr. Whittington killed all those women, and he kissed my hand."

I didn't know what to say to that. I took her hand and gave it a squeeze.

"At least it's all over," I said. "I can go back to being a doctor now. My days as a detective are finished."

"You can't go back to being a doctor just yet," she said. "You're on leave. Remember?"

I glanced at Steve in his playpen, gumming a plastic donut, his shirt drenched in drool.

"Then I'll put all my effort into being a dad," I said.

"What about putting some effort into being a husband?" she said.

"What did you have in mind?"

She gave me a smile. "I'm sure I can think of something."

The front page of the *Los Angeles Times* the next morning was dominated by the news of Dr. Whittington's suicide and his involvement in the murders of two young women. No mention was made of the other three possible victims. Something else wasn't mentioned—me. And I was glad for that.

The newspaper also reprinted most of Dr. Whittington's suicide note, omitting any mention of forcing would-be nursing students into selling their sexual favors and cutting him in on a percentage. I suspected those details had been withheld by the police to protect the reputations of the young women and their families.

I read the suicide note over many times, and each time I did, the tingle along my neck and between my shoulder blades got worse. Something wasn't right. Whatever it was, I was seeing it, and I *wasn't* seeing it, at the same time.

It was too frustrating. I gave up and read through the rest of the paper. A lot of column inches were given to storm coverage.

In one short but deadly downpour, half an inch of water fell on the city in a matter of minutes, causing flash floods throughout Los Angeles, turning canyon roads into impassable rivers. Cars were seen floating down Laurel Canyon Boulevard and onto Hollywood Boulevard. In Sierra Madre, hillsides scorched by summer wildfires disintegrated, burying five homes and trapping several people. In Pasadena, a car careened off the freeway and plunged into the Arroyo Seco storm drain, where it was carried two miles to the raging Los Angeles River. Somehow, the occupants of the car survived. LA mayor Sam Yorty declared a state of emergency in the city and ordered the Office of Civil Defense to coordinate operations.

Another article interviewed weather bureau forecasters, who predicted that a mass of unstable, moist air would pummel Los Angeles with "unusually heavy showers" and "extraordinarily high winds" for at least another day. Two water spouts, tornado-like spirals of wind-whipped sea, were reported off Malibu, prompting a warning to boaters and homeowners along the coastline. If the spouts touched land, they would become twisters and could cause enormous destruction.

Southern California wasn't the only place getting hammered by the weather. Rough seas in the Atlantic Ocean recovery area were forcing another delay in astronaut John Glenn's much-anticipated space flight.

And Hedda Hopper reported that actor Vince Edwards, who played Dr. Ben Casey on TV, visited St. Joseph's Hospital in Phoenix and managed to wake a girl from a coma just by saying "hello" to her.

It made me wonder if I should have taken acting classes instead of going to medical school. I would not only be able to cure the sick and help the injured, but I'd probably have my own situation comedy, too.

I was thinking about that when Katherine set Steve down in my lap and went looking for the stroller. She told me we were going to the Laundromat and that I was going to be in charge of the baby.

That sounded just fine to me. I was looking forward to a day of domestic tranquillity, far removed from the ugliness of murder and the chaos of the ER.

I felt like an intruder.

The Laundromat was filled with housewives, and they'd turned the place into a women's luncheon. They'd brought thermos bottles of coffee and milk and picnic baskets of sandwiches and cookies for themselves and their kids, who were playing in the playpen the mothers had set up. I was assigned to keep watch on the kids while the women, who included Mary Spicer, Gladys Arnold, and Irene Marlowe, gossiped and smoked and ate and folded their laundry.

I didn't mind. I stole a sandwich and some cookies and sat in a plastic chair beside the playpen, tickling the kids and eavesdropping on the conversation the women were having.

The big topic was, of course, Dr. Whittington's suicide and the revelation that he'd murdered two teenage girls.

"He's like Dr. Jekyll and Mr. Hyde," Irene Marlowe said. "They were both British, you know."

"Dr. Jekyll and Mr. Hyde?" Mary Spicer asked jokingly.

"Dr. Whittington and Dr. Jekyll," Irene said. "Though I don't think any secret potion drove Whittington to kill those girls."

"I feel sorry for his wife," Katherine said. "Think what she must be going through right now."

"She must have had an inkling something was wrong," Gladys Arnold said. "She left him, didn't she?"

"That was only because the money ran out," Irene said. "Not because he was a sex-crazed killer."

"Where does it say anything about him being sex crazed?" Mary asked.

"He wasn't playing backgammon with those girls," Katherine said.

"I ran into Constance Whittington at the supermarket once," Gladys said.

"You did?" Mary said. "You never told us that."

"She was lecturing the grocer on the proper care and presentation of vegetables in that very English accent of hers," Gladys said. "Her attitude seemed to be that everything was better in England than it is here and it was her job to educate all of us savages."

"They didn't make any effort at all to fit in," Mary said, nodding in agreement.

They kept talking, but I wasn't listening anymore. Mary's comment sparked a static burst in my mind. The letters and words that made up Dr. Whittington's suicide notes careened across my psyche.

I scurried around the Laundromat, looking for a copy of the morning paper. I finally found one, stuffed into a garbage can. I plucked it out and brought it back to my chair.

I borrowed a fat crayon from Gladys Arnold's three-year-old son and sat down in my seat, laying the news-paper open on my lap. I reread the suicide note and saw everything I'd missed before, marking up the newspaper in crayon as I went along. It was as if I'd read it the first time with blurred vision and now I was wearing glasses. Everything was clear.

Dr. Whittington didn't write the suicide note. It was written by whoever murdered him.

The same person who killed those five women was try-ing to trick us again by framing an innocent man.

There was a pay phone mounted on the wall not far from me. I hurried over to it, reached into my pocket for some spare change, and dialed Harry Trumble's number at the station house.

He answered on the first ring. "Trumble."

"Harry, it's Mark Sloan," I said. "Please don't hang up on me."

"Give me one good reason not to," he said.

"Dr. Whittington was murdered," I said. "The evidence is the suicide note."

"What are you talking about?"

"You didn't know him, but he was very British. You saw how he was dressed, didn't you? Who wears a cravat alone at home? He conducted himself as if it was his sole responsibility to uphold the British way of life among the savages," I said. "That's what's wrong with his suicide note. It's full of errors."

"I didn't see any typos or spelling errors," Harry said irritably.

"Because you're an American," I said. "That's why I

didn't see them at first either. But take a good look at the note, Harry. We spell some words differently than the British do."

I walked Harry through the suicide note, line by line, word by word. Dr. Whittington supposedly wrote "*In desperation, I turned to less honorable methods of acquiring funds.*" I pointed out that the writer used the American spelling of "honorable," not the British, which is "honourable." Likewise, he'd used the American spellings of "favours," "endeavours," "defence," and "programme." When I finished with my examples, Harry let out a frustrated sigh.

"That's it?" Harry said. "Did it ever occur to you that Whittington may have used the American spellings deliberately because he knew his note would be read by Americans?"

"He wouldn't have," I said. "But even if we assume for the sake of argument that he did, that doesn't explain the other errors.

"This isn't a goddamn spelling test, it's a suicide note," Harry said.

"He wouldn't say his books were 'due Thursday,' he'd say 'due back on Thursday.' And he signed the note 'Dr. Alistair Whittington.'"

"Now you're saying he wasn't a doctor?"

"What I'm saying is that he was an Oxford man, he wore a school tie, he was very class-conscious," I said. "These were supposedly his last words. He would have signed a genuine suicide note as 'Alistair Whittington FRCS,' indicating that he was a Fellow of the Royal College of Surgeons, and gone to his grave carrying his class distinction with him. By not doing so, Whittington was sending us a message, revealing in a subtle way that whatever he was signing was a fraud. And then there's the date. He would have started with the day first, not the month, and—"

"I'm hanging up now," Harry interrupted.

"You're making a mistake," I said, but it was too late. All I was hearing was a dial tone.

I hung up the phone and slumped back to my seat, tossing my marked-up newspaper onto the empty chair beside me in frustration.

The women were still talking and sorting laundry.

The kids were still playing and giggling.

Nobody noticed or cared what I was doing. Nobody saw my distress.

Well, that wasn't entirely true. One person did. I felt someone looking at me. I glanced at Steve. He was sitting in the middle of the playpen, oblivious to his friends, staring at me with big, moist eyes. He could tell something wasn't right with Daddy. Steve held up his chubby arms, signaling that he wanted me to pick him up.

I reached into the playpen, pulled him out, and set him down on my lap. He started to bounce, which was his way of telling me he wanted me to bounce him on my knees.

So I did.

I hummed the theme to *Bonanza* and, still holding him under his arms, bounced him to and fro to the beat of the song. He giggled with joy, his eyes wide, his mouth open in a big grin.

After a moment or two, he seemed satisfied that I was fine and reached his arms out towards the playpen. I got the hint and put him back down among his playmates.

I decided that it didn't matter whether Harry believed me or not. I knew I was right. The killer was still out there and had added another victim to his growing list.

I knew he existed. I knew what he had done. Somehow, I had to stop him.

But where to begin?

Obviously, the killer had forced Dr. Whittington to sign a blank piece of paper and then, after he shot the doctor, he typed the suicide note above the signature.

But why did he have Dr. Whittington open the safe

first? Was it to make it seem like the doctor was putting his affairs in order? Or was the killer looking for something? If so, what?

And more important, why did the killer pick Dr. Whittington to frame for his crimes? Was it simply because the doctor had a connection to each of the victims? Did Dr. Whittington know his killer, or were they strangers?

I didn't know any of the answers. I didn't even have any decent guesses.

I had nothing.

I gave up for the moment and began eavesdropping again on the conversation among the women.

"You won't believe what Bart got in the mail yesterday," Mary said. "A letter from Chrysler."

"So?" Irene said.

"They're offering us an Imperial Crown Southampton to drive for three days," Mary said. "Absolutely free."

"What's the catch?" Gladys asked.

"There isn't one," Katherine replied, folding socks. "They're sending those letters to thousands of doctors."

"They are?" Mary said, sounding disappointed.

"Mark?" Katherine held up the pair of socks she'd just folded, the top ankle portion of one pulled down over the other, the toe ends hanging out like floppy dog ears. "I don't recognize these socks. Where did they come from?"

"What makes you think I didn't buy myself some new socks?" I asked.

"Because you haven't bought a new pair of socks since we got married," she said. "You'd wear your socks until all your toes poked through, and your heel, too, if I didn't buy you new ones myself."

I gestured towards Gladys. "I borrowed them from Chet."

"Why would you borrow socks from Chet?" Katherine asked.

"It's a long story," I said. "And not very interesting."

Katherine handed the pair of socks to Gladys, who

promptly unfolded them. As I watched, she laid the two socks down on the table on top of each other, rolled them from up from the toes, then pulled the opening of one sock down over the whole roll. It took a few seconds and she did it while still talking about something.

I don't know what she was talking about because all I was hearing was the burst of static in my head. It was happening again. That physical tingle, coupled with a blur of images, facts, and thoughts in my mind, everything I'd seen and heard since Sally Pruitt was brought into the ER. And suddenly the bits and pieces all made sense.

I stood up, walked over beside Irene Marlowe and looked at her pile of socks. She stuffed one sock into the other, creating tiny balls.

I moved over to Mary Spicer and watched her as she placed one sock on the other, folded them in half, then turned them inside out, wrapping them around her hand like a glove. When she pulled her hand out, the folded sock resembled a sandwich.

"Haven't you ever seen someone fold socks before?" Mary asked me.

"Laundry is a mystery most men don't understand," Gladys said. "They just think their clothes magically show up washed, folded, and ironed in their drawers. Chet has never done a load of laundry in his life."

"I think that's why men get married," Irene quipped.

When I looked up again, I saw Katherine looking at me, bewildered. "Mark, are you okay?"

I nodded, forcing a smile to reassure her. It was amazing what you could learn at a Laundromat.

"I'm just fine, but I need to go," I said. "I need to take the car. Do you mind getting a ride home with one of these remarkable women?"

"Boy, do they lay it on thick when they want something," Irene said.

"Sure," Katherine said to me. "Where are you going?"

"There are some errands I need to run." I hurried out into the rain before she could see the lie on my face. I couldn't tell her the truth.

I couldn't tell her that I knew who the killer was and now I was going to prove it.

Chapter Nineteen

There was an enormous crystal chandelier hanging from the high ceiling of the Chrysler dealership on Santa Monica Boulevard. The showroom looked like an elegant living room that happened to be furnished with three Imperial Crown Southamptons instead of couches and chairs.

The salesman was dressed in a perfectly tailored suit and approached me as if I was a wet rat he'd just spotted running across his travertine floor.

I couldn't blame him. I was drenched, wearing an old raincoat, old slacks, old shirt, and old tennis shoes. I hadn't dressed to impress. I hadn't dressed for tracking a murderer either, but I didn't own a deerstalker hat, a cape, or a large magnifying glass.

"May I help you?" he asked, full of disdain.

I reached into my pocket and pulled out the rain-soaked invitation Chrysler had sent me. "I'm Dr. Mark Sloan, and I'm accepting your offer to try out a 1962 Imperial Crown Southampton."

He carefully unfolded the wet paper as if expecting to find a crude forgery. His entire demeanor changed when he saw the letterhead and my name neatly typed at the top of the page.

"Welcome!" he said heartily. "You should have let us deliver the car directly to you, especially in this storm."

"I couldn't wait," I said.

"You're that eager to experience the Imperial?" he stroked the hood of the car like it was a woman's thigh.

"If I said yes, I wouldn't have much of a bargaining position, would I?" I smiled and so did he, offering me his hand. I shook it.

"Thad Thorson," the salesman said, then swept his hand over the car, presenting it to me. "And this is undoubtedly America's finest fine car."

"Undoubtedly," I agreed.

"A steal at seventy-seven hundred," he said.

"Shamefully underpriced," I said.

I told him how much a friend of mine had enjoyed the Imperial, how he was the one who had urged me to hurry on down to take Chrysler up on the unbelievable invitation to drive the car for a few days.

When I gave Thad my friend's name, his face lit up. "Yes, I remember the gentleman well. In fact, you can drive the same car if you like. He returned it yesterday."

"It's black, isn't it?" I asked.

"With a sumptuous red leather interior and a chrome dash," he said.

"Perfect," I replied.

We went back to Thad's office and filled out all the necessary paperwork. He brought the car around to the covered carport, gave me a quick tutorial on the high-tech features, then handed me the keys.

I pressed DRIVE on the push-button transmission, gripped the rounded corners of the square steering wheel, and guided the land yacht out into the water. It was exactly the right car with which to brave the stormy sea that Santa Monica Boulevard had become.

The strangest thing about driving the car wasn't its immense size, its luxury, or a sticker price that was half the cost of a new house. No, the strangest thing was the knowledge that only a few short hours ago, the murderer had sat where I was sitting, his hands on that same square steering wheel, driving Tess Vigland to her death in a vacant lot.

I intended to deliver the car straight to the LAPD crime lab, but I had a few stops to make first, to gather the evidence I needed to convince Harry Trumble that I knew who the killer was.

My first stop was Joanna Pate's apartment. I'd avoided her ever since the kiss, but now I saw things in an entirely different light. Dr. Whittington's suicide note was a fraud, but perhaps much of what the killer wrote was based on truth—only it applied to him, not Dr. Whittington.

Joanna Pate lived only a few blocks from the Chrysler dealership. I parked in front of her apartment and ran through the wind-driven rain to her door. I leaned on the bell until I heard her voice.

"Who is it?" she asked.

"Dr. Mark Sloan." I had to yell to be heard over the roar of the storm.

She opened the door and I hurried in, dripping water on her linoleum entry. It was a simple two-bedroom apartment, with a small living room furnished with matching couch and easy chairs that were cheap, basic, and probably rented. The only personal touches were some vases of fresh flowers, a few throw pillows, and an old rug on the pile carpet.

Joanna was barefoot, wearing Capri pants and a sleeveless white blouse. Her entire face lit up when she saw me.

"Is your roommate here?" I asked.

"No, she's waiting tables at Norm's." She smiled coyly. "We're all alone. May I take your coat?"

"I'm not going to be here that long."

"You were just in the neighborhood and you thought of me." Joanna wiped some water from my cheek. "I think that's very sweet."

She kept her hand on my face and rose up on her tiptoes to kiss me, but before our lips could meet, I spoke.

"How much do you charge?"

"Fifty cents an hour for one child," she said. "Fifteen cents more for each additional one."

"Not for babysitting," I said. "For sex."

She dropped her hand from my face. Her eyes turned cold. "Get out."

"Dr. Whittington was murdered by the same man who killed your friends Sally and Muriel," I said. "Maybe you know him. Maybe he's one of your regular customers."

"If you don't go now, I'll call the police," she said, backing away from me.

"Please do," I said, advancing on her. "Ask for Homicide Detective Harry Trumble and tell him everything you know. Tell him how you slept with Dr. Whittington and the men you babysat for. Tell him how you were blackmailing all of them. It might just save your life."

"I wasn't blackmailing anybody," she said. "None of us were."

I noticed she hadn't denied the rest of my charges. I didn't really know if she was blackmailing anybody or not. I was just taking wild shots in the dark, hoping something would stick. But if she was telling the truth, and none of the girls were involved in blackmail, then Dr. Whittington's murder made a lot more sense. And so did the opening of his safe.

"Where did you take the men you slept with, Joanna? I'm sure it wasn't here. A motel? An apartment?"

"Why should I tell you anything?"

"Because it could help me stop the killer before he murders someone else," I said. "Someone like you. It wouldn't surprise me if your name was the next one on his kill list."

The color drained from her face. "Dr. Whittington had this house in Northridge," Joanna said. "In one of those new subdivisions."

I thought back to Dr. Whittington's party and the bomb shelter brochure that encouraged us to make an appointment to visit their model home in the valley "before the inevitable day the A-bomb is dropped." I also remembered the deeds to two properties that were among the papers removed from his safe.

"Did all of you take your men there?" I asked.

She nodded. "Dr. Whittington insisted."

I had a pretty good idea why, and it wasn't because it was a distant, discreet location unlikely to be accidentally stumbled upon by the men's wives or anybody who knew the babysitters.

I asked her for the address of the house and the key. She gave me the address, fished the key out of a big bowl on her kitchen counter, and tossed it to me. I caught the key and pocketed it. I didn't have to look at it to know it matched the keys found on the dead women.

"I'm going to Northridge. Make that call to the police now," I said. "Tell Harry Trumble everything you told me."

"And end up in a reformatory for girls?" she said. "No, I don't think so."

"Would you prefer to end up in a coffin?"

She stared at me. "There must be another choice."

"Why did you kiss me that night in the car?" I asked. "Was it really a misunderstanding? Or were you trying to seduce me into being another one of your clients?"

She looked me in the eye. "What would you like it to be?"

"Call him," I said, and I walked out.

The contemporary ranch-style homes in the Walnut Acres subdivision were set back from the street on perfectly square, flat lots with wide lawns bisected by a ribbon of concrete leading to big front doors trimmed with decorative rectangles. The dominant feature of each house on Langelinie Street was a bold two-car garage that reached out to the street. Although the houses all had the same floor plan, they were distinguished by superficial architectural flourishes. A steepled roof and an Asian symbol on the garage made it a Pagoda Ranch. A simulated-thatch roof and half-timbered walls made it a Danish Ranch. A red-tile roof and fake-adobe walls made it a Spanish Ranch. A flat, white-gravel roof and large front windows made it a Moderne Ranch. And so it went throughout the neighborhood.

Most of the homes on Langelinie, in keeping with the street name, were Danish Ranch. The trees on the street were recently planted, spindly and naked, barely held in place with wires and wooden stakes against the driving wind and rain. The front yards were soaked. Entire flower beds floated free, tossed by the whitecaps on the surface of the submerged lawns.

The Danish Ranch home where Dr. Whittington's aspiring nurses brought their men was indistinguishable from any of the others on the street. And there was nothing about the place that indicated it was the display home for a bomb shelter. Several cars were parked on the street, but none of them directly in front of Whittington's house. The blinds were closed and no lights were on inside.

I parked the Imperial in the driveway, got out, and slogged through the water on the front walk to the door. I used Joanna's key to unlock the door and entered the house without knocking or announcing myself.

The home was as sterile as any uninhabited model home I'd seen on my drives with Katherine and Steve. It was decorated with brightly colored, high-heeled furniture. There was a stone fireplace and a large sliding glass door that opened to the back patio. The kitchen was separated from the living room by a broad counter. A picture-framed sign that said THE FAMILY ROOM OF TO-MORROW was mounted beside a set of double doors off the kitchen. I figured that had to be the entrance to the bomb shelter.

There wasn't a single personal knickknack or photo in evidence. No newspapers, no magazines, no grocery lists taped to the refrigerator. This wasn't a home people lived in. It was one they walked through. Or, in the case of the nursing students and their clientele, it was a place to exchange money for sex.

I walked down the hallway to the master bedroom and found definite signs of life.

The wallpaper was ripped away, the air vents removed, light fixtures pulled down from the ceiling. Huge holes had been smashed into the walls with a pickax, which had been discarded on the floor. A tiny cubbyhole had been revealed in the wall across from the bed. An 8 mm Honeywell camera was mounted inside. I pushed my hand against the back of the cubbyhole. It was a hatch that opened into a closet in the hallway.

The women weren't blackmailing Dr. Whittington. *He* was the blackmailer. He was using *them* to extort money from the men they were sleeping with. Whether the women knew it or not didn't matter.

One of the men was making them all pay.

Now I knew why the safe was open in Dr. Whittington's study. It wasn't enough to kill the women involved. The killer wanted the film. He ransacked the office and forced Whittington to open the safe. The killer cleaned up after himself, laying out everything he removed on the coffee table to hide the fact that the room had been painstakingly searched.

Judging by the mess in the bedroom, the killer hadn't found what he was looking for. He still hadn't found the film.

I went into the master bathroom. There were two sinks, a shower, and a large bathtub. I crouched beside the rim of the tub and examined it, the tiles, and the linoleum floor. I figured Sally must have put up a fight, kicking and splashing water everywhere. Judging by the haste with which the killer had dressed her, I didn't think he'd done a thorough job of cleaning up.

I was right. There were traces of red dye on the tile

caulking and where the edge of the linoleum met the bathtub.

This was where Sally Pruitt was murdered.

I rose to my feet and became aware of a slight draft. I shivered, but not from the cold. I went back into the bedroom and noticed the shades billowing gently. The sliding glass door in the bedroom wasn't entirely closed and the carpet was wet.

Was it that way when I came in?

I left the bedroom and was heading back down the hall when I noticed something else.

The double doors that led to the Family Room of Tomorrow were open, revealing the second set of steel doors that they hid.

The steel doors were ajar.

And then I sensed a shift in the air, a presence displacing space. It was a presence I'd felt before, in the morgue, at that instant when I matched Sally Pruitt's key to the one that belonged to Muriel Thayer.

"Hello, Chet," I said and turned around slowly to face the man behind me.

Dr. Chet Arnold stood in the doorway of the open linen closet. He was wet. He was angry. And he was holding a gun.

"You don't seem surprised to see me, Mark."

I'd never had a gun pointed at me before. I couldn't take my eyes off the barrel.

"Believe me, I am," I stammered.

"But you knew I killed those girls." He stepped towards me and I backed up into the living room, raising my hands even though he hadn't asked me to. "And Whittington, too."

"Yes," I said.

"What was my mistake?"

There was a calm, casual attitude about his voice that I found thoroughly unnerving, nearly as much as the gun aimed at my chest.

"The socks," I said, almost apologetically. I didn't want him to shoot me, but of course I knew he would. And if he didn't, he'd find some other way to kill me. He had to.

"The socks?" he said. "What socks?"

"The ones you loaned me," I said.

"What did they have to do with anything?"

"It was the way they were folded," I said. "It's not how your wife folds them, but it's the way Sally Pruitt's mother does. And probably it's the same way Sally did, too. She washed your clothes when you had your trysts, didn't she, Chet?"

"I couldn't take the risk that Gladys would smell another woman on me," he said, shaking his head in disbelief. "So that was it? The socks?"

I nodded. "You also made some mistakes with the suicide note you wrote for Dr. Whittington, but it wasn't until the salesman at the Chrysler dealership told me you'd returned a black Imperial yesterday that I knew for sure you were the killer."

"But lucky for me, you still had to come here looking for more evidence," Chet said.

I shifted my gaze from the gun to Chet's face for the first time. In doing so, I saw two things.

I saw from the expression on his face that he hadn't known I was chasing him until I walked into the house.

And I saw Harry Trumble creeping out of the master bedroom.

"You didn't know that I was investigating the murders, did you?" I wanted to keep him talking and distracted, to give Harry time to get a clear shot from the hallway if he needed to.

"I knew you'd figured out Sally was murdered," Chet said. "I saw you leave the hospital with the medical examiner. But I didn't know you were playing detective until you walked in here and went straight to the bathroom to check the tub."

"Why did she dye her hair?"

"Because I asked her to," he said. "I like redheads. I wish I'd married one."

A floorboard creaked behind Chet. He whirled around, firing his gun at the same time Harry fired his. A vase exploded beside me and I hit the floor, the shots ringing in my ears. When I looked up, I saw Harry on the floor, twitching in an expanding pool of blood.

Chet kicked the gun away from Harry. It skittered down the hall into the bedroom.

"Who the hell is he?" Chet yelled.

I scrambled over to Harry, not caring whether Chet would allow me to or not.

Harry was shot in the throat. Blood was oozing out of his wound. He made a gurgling, sucking sound as he tried to breathe through his perforated and blood-choked trachea. If I didn't do something fast, he would die.

"He's a homicide detective," I said, getting to my feet and marching into the kitchen, my back to Chet.

"You already called the police?" Chet railed in fury. "Goddamn you, Mark!"

I wasn't listening. I yanked open cupboards and cabinets until I found a spray bottle of window cleaner under the sink and a steak knife in one of the drawers. I turned back towards the hallway and the barrel of Chet's gun.

Chet yelled at me. "Put that knife down."

"He's dying, Chet," I yelled back. "He needs an emergency tracheotomy."

"I don't care," Chet cried out furiously. "He's a dead man and so are you."

That's when I realized we were both yelling to be heard and not because of the ringing in our ears. The house was filled with an increasingly loud roar, like a squadron of helicopters was hovering over us.

I looked out the sliding glass door behind Chet and couldn't believe what I was seeing. An enormous funnel cloud loomed over the street, its swirling point cutting through the neighborhood, kicking up trees, blasting through fences, and ripping houses apart into splinters of wood and glass. Chet turned and saw it, too.

I stood in slack-jawed amazement, staring at the tornado, power lines and patio furniture spinning within its furious whirling clouds of debris.

The air in the room was electric and alive. There was a tremendous boom, and every window in the house exploded, spraying glass, the shards slashing me all over.

The surprise and the pain snapped me out of my shock. I went to Harry, crouching down beside him, and that saved my life. It put the kitchen counter and a piece of the hallway between me and the living room when the twister peeled the roof off the house.

"Help me with Harry," I yelled.

Chet shook his head and ran for the door. He was going to leave us behind to die, letting the twister do his dirty work for him.

But he never reached the door. He was sucked off his feet into the maw of the furious cloud, disappearing in the maelstrom of wind-driven shingles, glass, rocks, and wood.

My ears popping, I dragged Harry to the entrance to the bomb shelter, dodging an uprooted tree and a cartwheeling couch as they flew overhead. I opened the doors and pulled Harry into the cement stairwell that led down to the bunker. I slammed the steel doors of the bomb shelter shut behind us, just as the twister hurled the Imperial into the kitchen like a child's toy. The car covered the stairwell, trapping us below.

I dragged Harry down the concrete stairs, opened the doors to the bunker, and wrenched him inside, shoving the doors shut.

As the twister tore at the earth above us and wailed against the concrete walls, I fumbled in the pitch-blackness, feeling my way with my fingertips from the wound in Harry's throat to a spot just below it. I stabbed the steak knife into Harry's trachea and jammed the plastic tubing from the spray bottle into the crude incision, creating an airway so he could breathe.

I took off my shirt, wadded it up into a ball, and pressed it against the gaping bullet wound, hoping to stop the bleeding.

I closed my eyes and prayed that Harry would survive and that the walls would hold.

CHAPTER TWENTY

Today

It was ten minutes past midnight when Mark Sloan finished telling his story to Steve, Amanda, and Jesse in the living room of his beach house.

There were a few slices of cold pizza left in a takeout box on the coffee table. Embers glowed in the back of the fireplace. Outside, the rain still fell. It felt like it had been falling since 1962.

Nobody asked what had happened to Harry Trumble. They all knew firsthand how his story ended.

Harry survived, with a scar on his neck and a ragged voice that sounded like every word had to claw its way out of his throat. He remained a homicide detective. But one case would end up becoming his obsession and defining his career: the Clown Killer, a serial murderer who painted the faces of his female victims with clown makeup.

The killer eluded capture, and over time the task force was slowly whittled down until it consisted of only Harry. For more than a decade, Harry single-handedly and single-mindedly pursued potential leads from his cubbyhole of an office, long after the public and the police force stopped looking for or caring about the Clown Killer.

On the eve of Harry's retirement, with the Clown Killer all but forgotten and still at large, the detective faked a letter to himself from his nemesis. The act flushed out the killer, but at a terrible price. Furious about the faked letter, the killer came out of hiding to murder two more women. Harry managed to catch him at last, with Mark's help.

However, that wasn't enough for Harry. The detective gunned down the Clown Killer in cold blood. Harry wanted to be assured of justice before dying himself of a long illness that he'd kept hidden from everyone.

"I never knew there were tornados in Los Angeles," Jesse said finally.

"Until then, neither did I," Mark said. "I remember the twister destroyed some homes, a gas station, and a grocery store, but miraculously, there was only one fatality, and that was Chet Arnold. They found him impaled on a picket fence a block away."

"How long were you and Harry stuck in that bomb shelter?" Jesse asked.

"A few hours," Mark said. He glanced at his son, who was staring into the dying embers of the fire. "You're awfully quiet."

"It's a lot to absorb," Steve said, his voice flat and even.

"You can dig up the old case files," Mark said. "I'm sure the facts are all there."

"I'm not talking about the murders," Steve snapped back. "I learned a lot about you, about our family history, that I didn't know until tonight."

"You sound angry," Mark said.

"I don't understand why it took a murder for you to tell me that you've known Harry Trumble most of your life and that he was in love with Mom."

Jesse shifted uneasily on the couch and stole a glance at Amanda, who seemed lost in thoughts of her own.

"I didn't see what purpose it would have served," Mark

said. "You worked in the same building for years. Harry could have told you himself and never did."

"In a way he did," Steve said. "A couple of days before he died."

Mark raised his eyebrows in surprise. "What did he say?"

"We were in a car together on a stakeout. He said he was sorry we didn't get to know each other better, that he saw a lot of Mom in me. I told him I didn't know he knew Mom. He just smiled and said he introduced you to each other, and he left it at that."

Mark and Harry never spoke of what happened in Northridge, or the storm killings, after that terrible day, although they worked together briefly on the Clown Killer task force. But they also made their peace, shortly before Harry's death.

Harry confessed that he never really hated Mark for stealing Katherine from him. The truth was, he hated himself for not being the man Katherine wanted him to be. Every time he looked at Mark, he saw that man and the domestic life he was afraid to have.

It was easier to hate Mark than himself and, in doing so, he pushed away the closest friend he ever had.

Even so, Mark never let go of the guilt. Harry had been his best friend, and he couldn't help thinking that by taking Harry's first and only love, he was responsible for the man's loneliness and lifelong bachelorhood.

"How come I've never heard about the Storm Killer case?" Amanda asked, speaking up finally. "A serial killer would have made big news in 1962."

"Which is exactly why LAPD buried it, to avoid the scandal over their mistakes," Steve said and looked at his dad. "Am I right?"

"Yes, but it was more than just that," Mark said.

"Some things never change," Steve said.

Jesse stared at Mark. "I can't believe you went along with the cover-up. That's not the Mark Sloan I know."

"I was a different man then," Mark said quietly.

"Obviously," Steve said, the bitter edge of his voice not lost on Mark.

"Constance Whittington was told the truth," Mark said defensively. "I made sure of that myself. But it didn't matter to her. Even though her husband didn't actually kill anyone, she felt his actions were ultimately responsible for what happened. He was still a blackmailer and a panderer. The family was disgraced regardless."

"So Chet Arnold's family was told that he was a murderer?" Amanda asked.

Mark shook his head. "We couldn't prove it anyway. All the evidence was destroyed with the house. All the police had were my doubts about Whittington's suicide note and my word about a pair of socks."

"And the bullet in Harry's throat," Jesse said.

"The gun was never found," Mark said.

"But you and Harry were there," Amanda said. "And so was Chet."

"No, we weren't—at least not in any record you'll ever find," Mark said. "As far as the news reports on the tornado go, Harry and I were never there. Two unidentified people, one with a throat injury, were rescued from a home bomb shelter by neighbors. Our names were never mentioned."

"Did Mom know?" Steve asked.

"Yes," Mark said. "She knew everything."

"*Everything?*" Steve pressed, looking his father in the eye.

"So how did the police explain what Dr. Arnold was doing in a Northridge neighborhood he didn't live in?" Amanda asked, sparing Mark, at least momentarily, from having to answer his son's question.

"They didn't," Mark said, grateful for the reprieve. "It remains a mystery, at least to the public."

"But what about the families of those other women?" Jess asked. "Muriel Thayer, Ingrid Willis, and Clara

Cohen? Didn't they deserve to know the truth about what happened to them?"

"We couldn't prove that those women were murdered," Mark said. "We didn't exhume Ingrid Willis or Clara Cohen, but Dr. Barbette and I thoroughly examined Muriel Thayer's body before releasing it to her parents. There was no evidence of foul play. We didn't know how Chet could have killed them and made it look accidental."

"We do now," Amanda said.

"We do?" Jesse said.

"Succinylcholine," Amanda said. "They were killed the same way as the woman who washed up in front of this beach house."

Muriel Thayer drove off a cliff. Ingrid Willis fell down a flight of stairs. Clara Cohen was buried in a mudslide when the retaining wall in her backyard gave way. But now Mark knew what had really happened. Each woman was injected with the paralytic drug, rendering her helpless to save herself from the horrific fate her killer staged for her. Chet put Muriel behind the wheel of a car and pushed it over a cliff. He threw Ingrid down a flight of stairs. And he buried Clara Cohen alive under a hillside of mud. The last minutes of their lives must have been filled with unimaginable terror.

"Why couldn't you and Dr. Barbette find the drug in Muriel Thayer's body?" Steve asked his father.

"Succinylcholine was undetectable at the time because it breaks down so quickly in the body," Mark said. "It wasn't until 1966, and the Coppolini murder case, that toxicologists finally discovered a way to detect the presence of the drug in a corpse."

"It's a textbook case in forensics," Amanda said, and went on to explain that Dr. Carl Coppolino, an anesthesiologist in Florida, had murdered his wife, Carmela, and, allegedly, Colonel William Farber, the husband of his mistress, Marjorie, by injecting them with the paralytic drug, which was commonly used in his work. Initially, the cause of death for both victims appeared to be coronary thrombosis.

The crime might never have been discovered but for the bitter end of the relationship between Coppolino and his mistress. Marjorie went to the police and told her story, leaving authorities with the difficult task of proving it.

"It took months," Amanda said, "But toxicologists isolated metabolites of succinylcholine in the brain tissues of Coppolino's wife. Coppolino was convicted of second-degree murder for his wife's killing, but his lawyer, F. Lee Bailey, managed to win him an acquittal on Farber's death. Now we routinely test for those metabolites, among others, in every autopsy."

"But we still wouldn't have known how Chet Arnold killed those three women if not for the dead body that washed up in front of this house," Steve said. "Whoever killed her knew exactly how those women were murdered and wanted you to know it."

"Only one person could have known that," Jesse said. "Their killer. And he's been dead for over forty years."

"That's what scares me the most," Mark said.

"I don't believe in ghosts," Amanda said.

"Neither do I," Mark said. "Especially ones who have digital cameras and can transfer a JPEG of an old *LA Times* front page to a memory card."

"Maybe it's a very tech-savvy ghost," Jesse said.

Steve got up and stretched. "Which brings us to the present and our Jane Doe in the mermaid suit. Her murder was a riddle we were supposed to solve. I figure the red hair relates to Sally Pruitt, and the slit throat evokes Tess Vigland, and the succinyl-whatever refers to the other three victims. But what's the point of the mermaid suit?"

"The killer is saying he knew about the house in Northridge," Mark said. "It was on Langelinie Street. There's a world-famous statue of Hans Christian Andersen's *The Little Mermaid* on a rock in Langelinie Quay in Copenhagen. Whoever the killer is, this is a game to him."

"So who are we dealing with here?" Jesse asked.

"One very sick and scary individual," Amanda said. "Who doesn't like women very much."

"Or it's someone who blames Mark for what happened to Chet Arnold," Jesse said. "Someone who wants revenge."

"If so, why wait over forty years to get it?" Mark asked. "And why not kill me instead of an innocent woman?"

"Maybe he wants to toy with you first," Jesse said, "and was waiting until another storm hit on the same days in February to do it."

"I don't think this is the first time since 1962 that there's been rain in mid-February," Steve said. "But I suppose it's worth checking out."

"We also need to track down Chet Arnold's wife and children as well as Constance and Roland Whittington," Mark said, "and anybody else who was even tangentially involved in what happened in 1962."

"What can they tell you?" Amanda asked.

"I don't know," Mark said. "Maybe they'll say something that will help me figure out what the motive for this latest killing could be. Once we know that, we'll be a lot closer to discovering who the murderer is."

"Unless he decides to make you his next victim first," Steve said.

CHAPTER TWENTY-ONE

Mark slept deeply that night, but he relived the past once again in vivid, detailed dreams. When he awoke the next morning, it was as if he'd lived his life twice.

He awoke with several questions from the past nagging at him. If he could find the answers, they just might be the keys to solving the new murder.

Why did Chet slit Tess Vigland's throat and make no attempt to disguise her murder as an accident?

What happened to the blackmail film? And why didn't Alistair Whittington try to save himself by giving the film to Chet?

He got out of bed and trudged to the kitchen to discuss the questions with Steve, but it was well past nine a.m. and his son had already left for work. Mark couldn't blame him for wanting to get an early start. Steve had a homicide investigation to lead, and he wouldn't get far until he identified the victim.

The fog was thick over Santa Monica Bay, the ocean breeze blowing the light drizzle and the sea spray against the windows. He liked these gray days almost as much as the sunny ones. There was something comforting and beautiful about a deserted, windswept, foggy beach.

Mark made himself a bowl of cereal with strawberries, washed it down with a few cups of strong coffee, then showered, dressed, and braved the traffic to Community

General Hospital. The morning drizzle had become a heavy shower. The traffic barely moved.

He turned on the radio to listen to the news, but his thoughts immediately drifted back to the murder and to the past. Old memories kept coming back, making it difficult to think about anything else.

Maybe that was the whole idea.

It occurred to him that the past might just be a clever distraction. The new killing could have nothing at all to do with what had happened in 1962.

The killer could be an old adversary playing an elaborate mind game, showing just how much he knew about Mark and how easily he could manipulate him.

There was only one man Mark knew who was capable of that.

Carter Sweeney.

The man's homicidal tendencies were hereditary. His father, Regan Sweeney, was a mad bomber who had terrorized Los Angeles and killed dozens of people. Mark captured Regan and sent him to the gas chamber, where he was put to death. Regan's son, Carter, became obsessed with revenge. He and his sister, Caitlin, tried to destroy everything Mark held dear—his reputation, his career, his family, and his friends. And when that failed, the Sweeneys blew up Community General Hospital, trapping Mark, Steve, Amanda, and Jesse in the flaming rubble.

Mark survived that encounter, only to be kidnapped by the Sweeneys and forced to engineer a daring hundred-million-dollar robbery. He managed to foil the Sweeneys again, leading to their capture. They were sentenced to multiple life terms in prison for their homicidal rampage.

Carter Sweeney was a brilliant and resourceful man. Could he have reached out from his prison cell and enlisted someone to terrorize Mark again?

Mark doubted anybody was devoted enough to the Sweeneys to murder for them, but it wasn't a possibility he could entirely dismiss. If his investigation didn't turn up some compelling leads soon, he would make the journey to Pelican Bay Penitentiary and confront his cunning adversary face-to-face once again.

Steve's first stop when he got to headquarters was the Scientific Investigation Unit, which was analyzing the stuff the beachcomber had found at Point Dume, the place where the unidentified victim was most likely dumped into the sea.

The items included a Hot Wheels car, a charm bracelet, an earring, a watch, a fingernail clipper, a class ring, a fishing lure, a coat button, a nipple ring, and a cell phone. Most of the stuff was mass-produced and virtually untraceable.

The easiest item to trace was the cell phone, which belonged to Tia Davidoff, twenty-seven, of West Covina. Officers were sent to her home and found her alive and well. She'd lost the cell phone on the beach a week before the murder, so she wasn't even a potential witness.

The watch was identified as a Fossil, and from the serial number on the back the techs were able to trace it to a gift shop at Universal City Walk, a shopping center adjacent to the movie studio. It was a discontinued style, purchased three years earlier. The manufacturer was being contacted to see if whoever bought the watch had sent in a warranty card. Otherwise, there wasn't much hope of identifying the owner of the timepiece.

The coat button, with a distinctive hawk etched on the surface, came from a Stanton-brand men's raincoat, a line carried exclusively by Nordstrom department stores. Tens of thousands of Stanton raincoats had been sold over the years.

The techs had better luck with the class ring. It was manufactured in China under license by the Rossiter Jewelry Company of Clayton, Nebraska. The ring was the company's popular "Continental" style, individualized for the graduating class of Northgate High School in Santa Clarita, north of Los Angeles, two years ago. A police officer had been sent out to the school to get a copy of the class yearbook.

Steve left them to their work and went to see the file clerk in the basement. They spent two hours trying to dig up the files on the Sally Pruitt and Tess Vigland homicides. They finally found them in a water-stained, dust-covered box deep in the bowels of the storage room. Steve blew the dust and cobwebs off the box and brought it upstairs to his desk.

The files were undamaged and surprisingly complete. He found crime scene photos of Sally Pruitt and Tess Vigland, as well as their autopsy reports. He also found black-and-white studio portraits, most likely school photos, of Muriel Thayer, Ingrid Willis, and Clara Cohen. There were also crime scene photos of Alistair Whittington and his home, inside and out.

Steve found Harry Trumble's typed reports, pecked out on a manual typewriter with a crooked "T," and his personal notebooks, filled with his almost illegible handwritten scrawl. From what Steve could tell, Trumble's investigation concentrated on the family members and boyfriends of the two known victims, Sally Pruitt and Tess Vigland. Harry also interviewed known sex offenders in the area, all to no avail.

He read the statement his father had given to the police after his arrest at Whittington's house. Harry's own report did nothing to contradict Mark's version of events, which made it seem as if he'd been working hand in hand with the police from the outset.

There was a detailed background file on Mark Sloan, calling him a "member of the police family" by virtue of his father, Detective James Sloan, and suggesting that LAPD should consider using the doctor as a consultant in the future.

They had come to regret that, Steve thought wryly.

There was no mention in any report of Dr. Chet Arnold, or Harry Trumble's gunshot wounds, or the house in Northridge, or anything that exonerated Alistair Whittington of the murders.

Enough of the past, he decided. There was a killer on the loose today and he wouldn't be found in a musty file. Steve made a list of all the players from the 1962 drama and began working the phones, and his computer, to track them down. He'd nearly completed his task when, as if on cue, an officer showed up at his desk with a Northgate High School yearbook.

Steve started with the senior class, scrutinizing each page, until he found the photo he was looking for. Brooke Haslett was smiling brightly, full of hope and eagerness, ready to fulfill her destiny, never imagining that it was a knife's edge across her throat and the eternal embrace of a cold emerald sea.

Mark was shocked to find Dr. Dan Marlowe emerging from the operating room in sweat-soaked scrubs, a smile of satisfaction on his face. The big man went to the waiting room, where a frail woman in her fifties, flanked by her two adult sons, rose from their hard plastic seats to hear his news. Her sons steadied their mother on her feet. Judging by her wan appearance and loose skin, and the telltale impression under her shirt of an IV port on her chest, Mark guessed that the woman was chronically ill and undergoing chemotherapy treatment.

Whatever news Dan told the family must have been good, because the woman practically flew into his arms, giving him a strong, grateful hug that nearly knocked the brown wig from her head. When they parted, she was crying tears of relief and joy. Her sons each shook Dan's hand in turn, and then the doctor made his way to Mark, who stood at a respectful distance from the family.

"What are you doing, Dan?" Mark asked angrily.

"What I was born to do," Dan said. "And it feels damn good."

"What were you thinking? How could you possibly have operated on someone?"

"Because he was in desperate need of angioplasty," Dan said.

"Surely you could have referred him to another cardiologist," Mark said.

"Rufus King has been my patient for thirty years," Dan said. "He trusts me, his family trusts me. And they've endured so much tragedy lately, I had to do this. I couldn't let those boys face losing both their parents."

"You could just as easily have killed him," Mark said. "You're in no condition to be performing surgery."

"I told you I intend to keep practicing as long as I can."

"I thought you'd use your good sense and stay out of the OR. You've got cancer, Dan. You're heavily medicated on painkillers. If your patient knew that, do you think he'd really want you passing a catheter into his heart? One slip—"

"Damn it, Mark. I feel fine," Dan interrupted. "The minute I think I'm a danger to my patients, I'll stop."

"Really? Based on what you've done, I don't think you're capable of making that judgment." Mark yanked up Dan's left sleeve, revealing a Fentanyl patch on his inner arm. The patch released a powerful pain medication that was absorbed into the skin and could cause dizziness, slurred speech, and slowed reflexes. "You got someone else to write you a prescription for this patch, because you knew if I discovered you were in that much pain, I would never have let you into the operating room. If someone dies under your scalpel, I'll be equally responsible because I helped you hide your condition."

Dan took a deep breath and let it out slowly. "I'm sorry, Mark. The last thing I want to do is put your career at risk."

"It's not my career I'm worried about," Mark said.

Dan studied his friend's face. "But you're definitely very worried about something, and it wasn't this. You didn't come down here to talk to me about performing an angioplasty. You didn't know about that until you saw me."

Mark nodded solemnly. "Let me buy you a cup of coffee. I need to tell you a story."

CHAPTER TWENTY-TWO

It would have taken most of the day for Mark to tell Dan Marlowe everything, so he gave him only the key points. He revealed that Dr. Whittington didn't commit suicide, he was murdered by their friend Chet Arnold, who also killed five women. Now someone had murdered another woman in a manner that mimicked those earlier killings. To solve the crime, Mark was revisiting the past for clues and needed Dan's help.

They sat in the same booth where, only a few days ago, Mark had told Dan Marlowe he was going to die.

"How could you have kept the truth about what happened secret all these years?" Dan asked.

"I did it for the good of the families involved," Mark said.

"I don't know if Constance Whittington would agree with you."

"She knew the truth, but I didn't see how it would help Gladys Arnold and her kids to know Chet was a serial killer."

"But they're going to know now, aren't they?" Dan said. "Do you think it's going to feel any better forty years later than it would have then?"

"No, of course not," Mark said. "They will feel betrayed not only by Chet but by me and the entire police department. I was hoping they'd never have to know. But the killer has made that impossible. Maybe that was the point."

"I don't see what I can do for you," Dan said.

Mark wasn't sure either. His entire investigation, at least as far as the past was concerned, was a matter of stumbling around in the dark, hoping to trip over something significant.

"Did Chet ever confide in you?" Mark asked.

"He never told me he was a murderer, if that's what you're getting at," Dan said. "I know he wasn't happy in his marriage."

"What was his problem?"

"Being married," Dan said. "He talked more to Alice than he did to me."

"I didn't know they were close," Mark said.

"They weren't," Dan said. "He just enjoyed listening to her war stories and had to contribute something personal to the conversation to get her to talk."

"I lost track of Alice. She left Community General not long after Dr. Whittington's death," Mark said. "Do you have any idea where she might have ended up?"

"Yeah, as a matter of fact I do," Dan said. "She gave up nursing. She's a veterinarian out in Agoura now."

Mark looked surprised. "You two have kept in touch?"

"Not at all. I lost track of her the same time you did. My daughter, Emily, and her family live out there. Their dog got a burr in his paw, so she took him to the vet, who turned out to be Alice. That was three, maybe four months ago."

Mark looked past Dan to see Steve entering the cafeteria and heading their way. Dan twisted around in his seat to follow Mark's gaze.

"Hey, Steve," Dan said, shaking the detective's hand. "You look pretty grim."

"Murder is grim business," Steve said with a shrug.

"On that happy note, I better go clean up," Dan said. "Thanks for the coffee, Mark. I'll keep our discussion to myself."

"I appreciate it," Mark said.

"Just returning the favor," Dan said, walking away.

Steve looked after him, then turned to his dad, speaking up once the cardiologist was out of earshot.

"What favor?" Steve asked.

"One I can't do for him any longer," Mark said with a sigh. He knew he couldn't keep Dan's condition a secret from the hospital administration, not after this. Dan's privileges would surely be suspended immediately.

"But that's nothing for you to worry about," Mark said. "What's up?"

"A few things. I checked out Jesse's weather theory. Since 1962, there have been many rainstorms over these same days in February, though none quite as destructive as that one was."

"So we're still left with no clue why the killer waited until now to resurrect the past."

"I've also managed to track down everyone you worked with back then," Steve said. "I'd like you to be with me when I talk to them."

"I wouldn't miss it," Mark said, "though it feels strange to actually be invited."

"You're the key to this case," Steve said. "You're the only one who can break it. But there's one visit I have to make that you might want to sit out."

"What's that?"

"We've identified the murder victim," Steve said. "Now I have to tell Brooke Haslett's parents that their daughter is dead."

Mark filed his report on Dan Marlowe with the hospital chief of staff, then accompanied Steve out to Valencia, where Brooke Haslett's parents lived. It was a thirty-minute drive they made in silence, both lost in their thoughts.

Mark was thinking about what he'd just done to Dan and how his old friend would take the news, once it came down. There was no doubt in Mark's mind what the hospital would decide to do. Dan would be stripped of his hospital privileges immediately. And it would be entirely Mark's fault. First, he'd told Dan he was going to die. And tomorrow, he'd probably have to tell Dan he was taking away his right to practice medicine. Mark was going to prevent Dan from doing what he loved most, perhaps the one thing that gave him the strength to fight the cancer that was ravaging his body and would soon claim his life.

Steve was thinking about what he was going to have to tell the Hasletts. He wasn't just telling them their daughter was dead. She was murdered. Without knowing a single detail, they would be tortured by that fact alone. They wouldn't be able to stop themselves from imagining the terror and pain their daughter must have experienced. But the real nightmare would come when they inevitably found out the atrocities that she had suffered.

There was no soft or easy way for Steve to do this, and he'd yet to develop a thick enough skin not to be emotionally affected himself.

Steve Sloan would never admit it, but he was grateful to have his father with him. Mark was experienced at delivering devastating news to family members on an almost daily basis. His bedside manner was impeccable. He was a natural, calming presence. Many families had found comfort and strength in his warmth, good humor, and integrity. Steve hoped his dad would apply those same skills in this unpleasant situation.

The Hasletts lived in a sprawling, brand-new neighborhood of tract homes, duplexes, and condominiums crowded around a shallow man-made lake that was, essentially, a massive duck pond. The nicest homes were "lakefront" properties with tiny docks for their pedal boats, some of which were tricked out to look like aircraft carriers, ocean liners, Rolls-Royces, and even the Starship *Enterprise*.

The sun had broken through the gray clouds for a moment, and people were out on the wet sidewalks and bike paths, taking full advantage of the intermission in the storm.

Ginny Haslett was outside her colonial-style lakefront duplex, washing duck droppings off her unadorned pedal boat with her garden hose, when Mark and Steve approached her. She was tall and sun-bronzed, wearing a wide-brimmed straw hat, baggy shorts, and leather flip-flops in a show of bright optimism in the face of certain showers.

"Excuse me," Steve said. "Mrs. Haslett?"

She turned and, startled, nearly lost her balance. Mark rushed forward and took her by the arm to steady her from falling.

"Are you all right?" Mark asked. "We didn't mean to frighten you."

Mrs. Haslett laughed. "You didn't scare me, Doctor. I'm just surprised to see you again."

Now it was Mark's turn to be startled. "You know me?"

"I'll never forget you, but I certainly don't expect you to recognize me," she said. "I've changed a lot in forty years."

Mark suddenly felt as off balance as Mrs. Haslett had only a moment ago. If he hadn't still been holding on to her arm, he might have tipped into the lake himself. He exchanged a look with Steve, whose blank expression revealed none of the anxiety his father knew he must be feeling.

"Please forgive me, Doctor, but there is one thing I've forgotten," she said. "And that's your name."

"Mark Sloan," he said. "And this is my son, Steve."

"The last time you saw me, I was twelve years old and came close to drowning in the LA River," Mrs. Haslett said. "I had a dislocated shoulder. I'm sure it wasn't nearly as big an event in your life as it was in mine."

Mark stared at her. It was during the rescue of her and

her little brother that firefighters had found the corpse of Sally Pruitt.

"I remember," Mark said, his voice barely above a whisper, feeling the full impact of the killer's careful planning, the cruel significance of Brooke Haslett's murder, and the true scope of the evil that was unfolding.

Whatever horror had started on that rainy February day in 1962 had come full circle. The killer was saying that there was no escaping the past. Not for Mark Sloan. Not for Ginny Haslett. And not for their children. The only way out was death.

Mark knew now that Brooke's class ring was intentionally dropped on the beach. The killer wanted the police to discover who his victim was, but he also wanted them to have to work at it a bit first.

More manipulation.

More games.

Ginny Haslett must have read something on Mark's face, or suddenly realized he was here for a reason and, judging by his expression, it wasn't a pleasant one. Her surprise quickly faded, uneasiness and dread washing over her.

"Where's your husband, Mrs. Haslett?" Steve asked gently.

"At the grocery store. He'll be right back." She turned to Mark, and when she spoke, her voice trembled. "Why are you here, Dr. Sloan?"

There was so much Mark wanted to say, so many apologies he wanted to make, but he couldn't find the words or the voice to speak them.

Steve pulled out his badge and held it up for her to see. "I'm a homicide detective, Mrs. Haslett. Perhaps we should go inside and wait for your husband to get back."

"Oh my God," she said, crumpling into Mark's arms and breaking into deep, guttural sobs.

Mark held her tight and thought he felt some of her tears on his cheek before he realized they were his own.

CHAPTER TWENTY-THREE

Mark and Steve left the Hasletts' home and the grieving parents, who were sobbing quietly in each other's arms over the loss of their only child.

Steve maintained his professionally stolid composure throughout the agonizing, and ultimately fruitless, interview, but he could feel the stomach cramps wrought by his suppressed emotions. As soon as he got home, he intended to jog the cramps and the pain away on the beach, no matter how hard it was pouring outside. In fact, the more soaked he got the better, to wash away the stink of his ugly job.

Mark wasn't as successful at hiding his sorrow, his pain, or his fury. The emotions clashed within him, a battle visible on his face and in his eyes. He felt personally responsible for the horror and misery inflicted on the Hasletts. They were suffering so that he would, too. And this, of course, brought the anger. Whoever was doing this to Mark, and to the Hasletts, had to be stopped.

No, it was more than that.

Whoever was doing it had to be punished.

As soon as Mark got into the car, Steve started the motor and glanced at his father.

"I'm no doctor, but you don't look well to me," Steve said. "I can drop you off at home if you aren't up to this."

"You said it yourself, Steve. I'm the key to this murder.

I fit into the motive somehow. I need to be at these interviews," Mark said. "But you're right, I'm not well. I've never felt so emotionally sick or encountered such a cold, calculating evil in my entire life."

"You've seen worse," Steve said. "We both have. The difference this time is that it's personal. The killer is making this about you."

"I wish I knew why," Mark said.

"Let's try revenge for starters." Steve opened his notebook. "Alistair Whittington was never publicly or officially cleared of the killings. And his son, Roland, just happens to be in Los Angeles for the first time in thirty years."

"What's he doing here?" Mark asked.

"He's an attorney for a British pharmaceutical company, working on a merger with an American competitor," Steve said. "And maybe he's also taking care of some unfinished family business."

Roland Whittington's lavish suite at the Century Plaza Hotel had a breathtaking view of West Los Angeles, clear to Santa Monica Bay. From where he stood, his back to the Sloans, he could see Community General Hospital and the Brentwood neighborhood where he had once lived.

The attorney bore an uncanny resemblance to his father in looks and bearing. He certainly had his father's taste in clothes, wearing an impeccably tailored four-button charcoal-gray, single-breasted Brioni suit, a Turnball and Asser shirt, and a crisply knotted Oxford tie.

"I assure you, it's a coincidence," Roland said, turning to face the Sloans, who were sitting on the couch in the suite's small living room. "Though I will admit I had reservations about coming back to Los Angeles. But I felt it was time to confront the past."

"It's how you've chosen to confront it that concerns me," Steve said.

"Are you accusing me of murder, Lieutenant Sloan?" Roland asked.

"No," Steve said. "I just have a hard time accepting coincidences."

"The confrontation I speak of is being waged entirely within myself," Roland said. "I have no resentment towards anybody except my father, which is unfortunate, since he long ago escaped being held accountable to me for any of his myriad sins."

"Then you won't mind if we look into your activities while you've been here," Steve said.

"Not at all," Roland replied. "You should talk with my executive secretary, Miss Lawson. She controls my calendar and has kept a detailed record of all my billable hours."

"And what about when you've been off the clock?"

Roland glanced, perhaps inadvertently, at the neatly made king-sized bed. "You can check with her about that, too."

"What do you know about what happened in 1962?" Mark asked.

"My mother told me everything—that my father lost all that we had," Roland said. "Our home, our money, and our good name. Although he didn't kill himself, he was surely to blame for his own murder."

"You're pretty clinical about it," Steve said. "It almost sounds like you're talking about a stranger."

"In some ways I am," Roland said, taking a seat in a chair across from them. "I was nine years old when my mother left him."

"Why did she leave?" Mark asked. "Was it just about the money?"

"If it was only the money, she would have stayed. You can always make money again. Other losses, like trust and love, are harder to restore," Roland said. "She caught him late one night watching a home movie. Only it wasn't a film of my birthday, our Hawaii vacation, or one of our Disneyland trips. He was watching himself in bed with one of his nurses."

"Do you know which one?" Mark knew it was unlikely that Roland would, but he had to ask anyway.

"Alice Blevins," Roland said, surprising Mark and seeming to take some pleasure in it. "You didn't expect me to know, did you?"

"Honestly, no."

"If it had been anybody else, it wouldn't have hurt my mother quite as much. Alice and my father met in Korea, during the war," Roland said. "She was a frequent visitor to our home when I was growing up. My mother didn't realize that Alice was also a frequent visitor to my father's bed. Not the marital bed, of course, but some hideaway my father had expressly for his assignations."

"The house in Northridge," Mark said.

"Presumably," Roland said. "My mother had suspected an affair between them for some time. The film only confirmed it."

At least now Mark knew why Whittington, with a gun at his head, had refused to turn over the film to Chet Arnold. Whittington was afraid of being blackmailed himself.

"Was your father sleeping with any of the other nurses?" Steve asked.

"Not that I know of," Roland said. "But he liked to watch himself in action, or so my mother told me. It excited him."

"How did she catch him watching the movie?" Mark said. "I doubt he was screening it in his office where she could just walk in on him."

"I don't know," Roland said.

"Does she know where your father hid the films?"

"If she did," Roland said, "she never told me."

"I'd like to ask her myself," Mark said. "Can you tell me how to reach her?"

"She can't be reached, I'm afraid," Roland said. "She's

in a nursing home being treated for Alzheimer's disease. Mum doesn't even know who I am."

Mark sighed with disappointment. If only he'd talked to her years ago. Then again, it had never occurred to him to call her again after telling her what really happened to her husband. The investigation was over and seemed best left undisturbed, for the sake of everyone involved. There seemed to be no purpose, and no good to be accomplished, by finding the film and embarrassing the people involved with their past indiscretions.

"What was life like for you and your mother after your father's death?" Steve asked.

"Murder," Roland corrected him. "I was too young to appreciate the shame and disgrace my mother endured. People assumed she'd known what kind of man my father was and turned a blind eye to it. Or, worse, that she was so bereft of decent character and judgment, she wasn't able to detect his inherent monstrosity. She was never able to remarry. No man of any stature wanted to be associated, even remotely, with the scandal. Never mind that she was as much a victim as any of those dead women."

"What about you?" Mark said, gesturing to Roland. "How did you cope with the disgrace?"

"Beyond watching what it did to my mother, and feeling utterly powerless to help her, I was untouched," Roland said. "By the time I was ready to pursue my own life, my father and the scandal he created were entirely forgotten."

"Clearing him of murder might have created more sympathy for your mother," Steve said. "It might have made her life a lot easier."

"It wouldn't have erased the financial, sexual, and criminal improprieties he committed. There's no disputing he was an adulterer, blackmailer, and pimp. The disgrace was complete and irrevocable, whether he was a murderer or not." Roland met Steve's gaze. "You're wondering whether I would gain any measure of comfort by murdering a young woman in the same fashion as my father's killer did as a way of punishing Dr. Sloan for burying the truth."

"Yeah," Steve said, "I am."

"The answer is no," Roland said, shifting his gaze to Mark. "That would make me more of a monster than my father ever was."

"Do you buy it?" Steve asked his father as they emerged from the crowded elevator and walked across the hotel lobby, which was crowded with people seeking refuge from the storm outside. There wasn't even standing room in the bar.

"He's persuasive," Mark said. "But I don't believe he's forgiven me for failing to exonerate his father and for participating in the cover-up. I'm not sure I forgive myself."

There were a dozen yellow CAUTION: SLIPPERY SURFACE cones, featuring a drawing of a stick figure losing its footing, positioned every few feet throughout the marble lobby like markers for a slalom course.

For a moment, Mark longed for his roller skates so he could give it a try. Thinking about that reminded him of the horrified look on Dr. Whittington's face the first time he saw Mark skate past him down the hospital corridor.

"It sounds to me like you did the right thing at the time," Steve said.

Mark shook his head in disagreement. "I was young, inexperienced, and lacked the confidence I have today. Now I would never let the police pressure me into hiding the truth, no matter how ugly and embarrassing it might be. It's better to let the truth out and deal with whatever trouble is going to come. The cover-up only makes things far worse, as we are discovering today."

"You had no way of knowing something like this would happen."

"I knew Constance Whittington and her son would have to live with the consequences," Mark said. "Who knows how the disgrace affected them, and what it has driven Roland to do."

"You think he murdered Brooke Haslett?"

"I don't know yet," Mark said, "but I'm troubled by the coincidence that he's here at all right now and that he works for a pharmaceutical company."

"Which you figure would give him access to succinyl-whatever."

"Motive, means, and opportunity," Mark said. "He has them all."

"I know somebody else who as all those same charming qualities," Steve said.

"Who?"

"Drake Arnold," Steve said. "Chet's son."

CHAPTER TWENTY-FOUR

The Pacific View Motel on Sunset Boulevard didn't have a view of the Pacific. Its fourteen rooms overlooked a Chevron gas station, an alley, and the motel's cracked asphalt parking lot. The only incentives the motel had to offer its guests were free twenty-four-hour satellite TV porn, a coupon for two dollars off a pizza delivery from Domino's, and a bar of soap in the bathroom.

Drake Arnold seemed perfectly relaxed in his surroundings, sprawled out on the bed, his back against the headboard, a bag of Cheetos in his lap and a six-pack of beer on the nightstand beside him. He wore two days' worth of stubble, a loud Wal-Mart Hawaiian shirt, and a wrinkled pair of ten-dollar cargo pants. His eyes were on an X-rated movie that played silently on the TV, which was mounted on the wall behind Mark and Steve. The storm disturbed the satellite reception, creating streaks of digitization across the picture.

"You're looking at a genuine playboy, Dad," Steve said. "This man is irresistible to women."

Mark glanced at Drake, who was grinning stupidly at Steve's description of him, his eyes never leaving the TV screen.

"I find that hard to believe," Mark said.

"Believe it, Doc. The babes can't get enough of me,"

Drake said, shoving a handful of Cheetos into his mouth. "All they want is a slice of the big pie."

"That's the crux of his defense against the three women who accused him of spiking their drinks with roofies, dragging them to a motel room, and raping them," Steve said. "Drake is out on bail pending trial."

"I don't need to drug women to sleep with me, Detective," Drake said. "I exude masculinity."

"I can smell it from here," Mark said.

Drake chuckled. "Women are drawn to me like moths to the flame."

"Which usually kills the moths," Steve said.

Drake shrugged. "Maybe I picked the wrong metaphor. Fact is, when it comes to me, women can't help themselves."

"That much I believe," Mark said. "Rohypnol impairs judgment, enhances euphoria, and causes short-term memory loss."

"You want to turn up the sound on the TV?" Drake gestured to Mark. "The remote is broken and this is the best part."

"I'd rather hear about your father," Mark said.

For the first time since they entered the room, Mark got Drake's undivided attention.

"What the hell for?" Drake said.

"There's been a murder," Steve said. "We think it may have something to do with activities your father was involved with before his death."

Drake snorted. "You mean like screwing nurses?"

"You knew he was having affairs?" Mark asked.

"My mom told me, said she figured it out after the twister. A tornado in LA, who'd a thunk it?" He snorted again and finished his beer, crumpling the can in his hand and tossing the empty across the room. The can bounced off the rim of the garbage pail and clattered to the floor among the other crumpled empties. "She read in the papers how they found his body not far from a couple of people trapped in a home bomb shelter. It rang this big old bell in her head. She found out the house belonged to my dad's boss, a doc who was getting nurses to whore for him. The doc had a great idea, if you ask me. Nothing sexier than a woman in a nurse's uniform."

"So your mom assumed you dad was in the valley having sex with one of Dr. Whittington's nurses," Mark said. "Did you believe her?"

"Have you ever met my mother?"

"Yes," Mark said, "I have."

"Then you know why my dad would pay to have sex with someone else." Drake reached for another beer. "Mom says God smote him for it with a tornado. She found Jesus after that."

"Makes me wonder what God might do to you," Steve said.

"Look around," Drake said. "This is it."

"Like father, like son?" Steve asked.

They were in the car, driving back home to Malibu, stuck in the darkness and the downpour. Traffic was crawling on Sunset Boulevard, the intersections flooded with water, the stoplights out of order. It was going to be a long, slow drive.

"Chet Arnold was drugging women and killing them," Mark said. "Now his son is drugging and raping them. You think it's in the genes?"

"You tell me," Steve said. "Your father was a cop. You're a consultant to the police. I'm wearing a badge."

"It's the old nature versus nurture debate," Mark said. "Is it in the genes or is it how you were raised? I grew up around police officers. You grew up seeing me actively involved with homicide investigations. But Chet was killed while his son was still in diapers."

"You have to admit the parallels are creepy," Steve said.

"They certainly are," Mark said. "Forty-odd years ago

I was a young doctor investigating a homicide, one that never would have come to light if not for Ginny Haslett being rescued from the LA River. Now Ginny's daughter is dead and my son is investigating the murder. Maybe that's exactly the picture the killer wants us to see."

"You can look at the big picture. I'll look at Chet," Steve said. "I see a guy who gets off drugging women and doing whatever he wants to them while they are powerless. He gets off on the control. Maybe he found that controlling whether they lived or died was the ultimate kick."

"It's possible," Mark said. "But what's he got against me?"

"You nailed his father for murder," Steve said.

"Until I told you last night, nobody knew that except me, Harry Trumble, his commanding officer, and the chief of police. No one is still alive but me. So how did Drake Arnold find out?"

"Stranger things have happened," Steve said. "But after what you just said, I may know why whoever killed Brooke Haslett is tormenting you."

"Why's that?"

"Because you're the only one left."

It took Mark and Steve two hours to make what ordinarily would have been a thirty-minute drive back home. While Mark prepared dinner, Steve brought in the dry-erase board from the garage and began making a chart of the investigation in the living room.

He taped crime scene photos and pictures from the 1962 investigation onto the board, drawing lines with different-colored markers to delineate the connections between each person and each place. When he was done, he put up photos from the current investigation, adding a line from Brooke Haslett to Mark Sloan, from Mark Sloan to Ginny Haslett, from Ginny Haslett to Sally Pruitt. Along the edge of the board, he attached photos of the various items collected on the beach at Point Dume. And finally, he posted the police mug shot of Drake Arnold and a company photo of Roland Whittington and drew a line from each man to the picture of his dead father.

By putting everything he had up on the board, Steve hoped to get a clear overall view of the case and glean a better idea of where he stood. What he saw instead was a drawing of a multicolored ball of twine with some photographs taped to it.

Mark put a bowl of spaghetti and meatballs down on the kitchen table and came out to look at Steve's board. He saw the past staring back at him in the faces of the dead—Alistair Whittington, Chet Arnold, Harry Trumble, and all those young women.

In the upper right-hand corner of the board Steve had written CLUES, underlined the word, and left space below it to fill in. So far, that space was empty.

"Does anything pop out at you?" Steve asked as he heaped spaghetti onto his plate.

"You've got nothing written in the clues column."

"That's because we don't have any yet," Steve said.

"What about all those things you found on the beach at Point Dume?"

"You mean besides the ring that helped us identify Brooke Haslett?" Steve asked.

"That doesn't count," Mark said. "We both know the killer left that for us."

"It could have slipped off her finger or out of his pocket," Steve said. "If he wanted us to ID her, why not leave the ring on her hand?"

"He didn't want to make it too easy," Mark said. "Just hard enough so we had to work at it a little bit, so we were committed to the search."

Steve sighed. "I wish he'd left more for us intentionally, because the rest of the stuff isn't leading anywhere."

"What about the memory card we found in her stomach?"

"The lab guys tell me there isn't anything unique about it that would allow them to track it back to any single individual. There are millions of those memory cards manufactured and sold around the world."

"Can you get anything off the picture of the *LA Times* front page?" Mark said, his frustration obvious in his voice.

"It could have been downloaded from dozens of different Web sites using a computer at any Internet café or public library."

Mark sighed wearily. "So we're nowhere."

"I'm there so much," Steve said, "I'm thinking of buying some property and settling down."

Mark examined the board as he ate his dinner. He followed each line Steve had drawn. Unlike other cases and other boards he'd studied, each of these lines represented part of his life, times he'd experienced, people he'd known. He wondered if his personal connection was clouding his ability to see the facts clearly. Maybe he was wrong about his approach to solving the crime.

Maybe he wasn't the key to understanding why Brooke Haslett was murdered.

Maybe he was a handy distraction to throw the police, and himself, off the real motivation for the crime.

"How much do you know about Brooke Haslett?" Mark asked his son.

"Nothing beyond what her parents told us," Steve said. "She was studying political science at Cal State Northridge, was well liked, and had no enemies that they knew of."

"Everything on that board is about me and the past," Mark said. "If someone was trying to totally distract us from looking too closely at her, they've succeeded."

"I'll start digging into Brooke Haslett's life first thing in the morning, though I still think we're on the right course."

"While you're at it, you might see if Carter Sweeney has had any visitors up at Pelican Bay lately."

"I wasn't going to say anything, but that occurred to me, too. I'll look into it," Steve said. "What about the other people on our list from your deep dark past?"

Steve reached into his pocket, pulled out a piece of paper, and handed it to his father. Two names and addresses were written on the paper: Alice Blevins and Dr. Bart Spicer.

"I think you're missing a name," Mark said.

"Joanna Pate," Steve said. "I haven't been able to track her down, but I haven't tried very hard yet. She may have moved away, changed her name, or got married. Do you still want to talk to Blevins and Spicer, or should I?"

"I'll talk to them tomorrow," Mark said without any enthusiasm. He felt like a windup doll, simply going down the path the killer had set him on.

CHAPTER TWENTY-FIVE

For a woman in her seventies, Alice Blevins looked like she could wrestle a bear, so the St. Bernard was no match for her at all. She hefted the huge animal up onto the exam table and expertly inserted a thermometer into his rectum.

"The great thing about animals is they don't complain," she said to Mark.

"He doesn't look too happy to me," Mark said.

"They're also loyal, obedient, and uncomplicated," she said. "Sadly, the same thing can't be said for most human beings."

Beyond her gray hair and some wrinkles on her face, Alice hardly showed her age. He saw it in her eyes. She had a gaze like an ugly scar, hinting at battles fought and wounds sustained.

"Is that why you gave up nursing?" Mark asked.

"One of them," Alice pulled out the thermometer, examined the reading, then tossed it in a biohazard bucket. "Hold Hubert for me."

Mark put his arms around the big slobbering dog while Alice examined the animal's ears.

"You left Community General after Dr. Whittington's suicide," Mark said. "Was his death one of the reasons?"

"Between the patients and the doctors, there was just too much heartbreak to deal with every day," she said. "I should have left nursing after Korea."

"What about Dr. Whittington?" Mark asked. "Should you have left him after Korea, too?"

Alice frowned, tore a piece of cotton off a large roll, then picked up a bottle and squirted some liquid into the dog's ear. Before the dog could shake his head, she shoved the cotton into his ear and worked it around inside, cleaning it. Hubert cocked his head towards her and panted happily.

"Everybody who went to Korea died there, even the ones who came back. We just resembled the people who left," Alice said. "Nobody came back. We were either the walking dead or the reborn."

Alice took the dirty cotton from the dog's ear. The cotton was black. She tossed it in the trash, tore off fresh cotton from the roll, squirted some liquid in the dog's other ear, and started cleaning again.

"You can't imagine the misery of serving in a M.A.S.H. unit," she said. "There's a never-ending stream of young boys, butchered and bloody, screaming in agony and despair. There is no happiness, no victory, just constant dread and fear. There is so little humanity or pleasure that when you can find some you take it, regardless of the consequences. Alistair and I saved each other. It wasn't an affair. It was survival."

"And when you came back?" Mark said. "What was it then?"

"We forged a bond separate and distinct from his marriage. There were no lies or illusions between us. I knew he was married. He never stopped loving his wife and I didn't expect him to," Alice said. "But the man Constance married was not the man who came back to her. It was thanks to me that she had a husband left to love at all. We had a shared experience that nobody but us could ever understand. We kept each other's soul alive when the darkness threatened to become too much."

"So when you learned about his suicide, you left the hospital and nursing because you blamed yourself for his death."

"No, I blamed you." She threw the dirty cotton into the trash and looked for a syringe. "Alistair didn't kill himself and he didn't kill those girls. It was all a lie to discredit him."

"Why did you blame me for it?"

"Because I know you went to his house to deliver those papers the day he died. You found his body and yet your name wasn't mentioned once in the papers," Alice said. "That told me volumes."

"You think I staged what happened to him?" Mark asked.

She filled the syringe with an antibiotic and gave the dog a shot. If the dog felt it, he didn't show it. "I don't know what you did, Mark. Or why you did it. I just knew Alistair."

"Not as well as you think. You didn't know he was using nurses as prostitutes or filming their sexual encounters."

She shook her head and dumped the used syringe into the biohazard bucket. "No. Alistair would never have done that. It's a lie."

"He even filmed the two of you together," Mark said. "He had a camera hidden in that house in Northridge."

"More lies," she said.

"Constance saw him watching it and that's why she left the country with her son," Mark said. "Roland told me himself yesterday."

She opened Hubert's mouth and examined his teeth and gums. "What difference does any of it make now?"

"Someone killed a young woman the same way those nursing students were murdered forty years ago," Mark said. "Whoever did it made sure I found her body."

"You think I did that, a woman who has spent her life easing the pain of others, man and beast."

"You were having an affair with Dr. Whittington and you blame me for covering up the murder of the man you loved."

Alice looked up at him. "You admit that it was murder?"

"Dr. Whittington was a panderer and a blackmailer, and he secretly filmed everything that went on in the bedroom of that house in Northridge, but he didn't kill himself or anybody else."

"Do you know who killed him?" she asked.

"Chet Arnold," Mark said.

"You knew that and you didn't bother clearing Alistair's good name."

"What I knew and what I could prove were two different things," Mark said.

"And that makes it all right?" Alice said, shaking her head in disgust. "He's a better man dead than you are right now."

"Is that what you were trying to prove by killing Brooke Haslett?"

She lifted the dog and set him on the floor. "If I did, you think I'd tell you?"

"So tell me you didn't," Mark said.

"Would that give you some peace, Mark?" she asked, attaching a leash to the dog's collar. "The way I see it, that's the last thing you deserve."

She led the dog past Mark and out the door.

Dr. Bart Spicer was the one person besides Dan Marlowe whom Mark had kept track of over the years. It was easy because Bart was always in the news, at least among people who were kept informed by the *Globe*, the *Star*, the *National Enquirer*, and *People* magazine. Mark wasn't a regular reader of those publications, but issues were often left behind in the hospital waiting rooms and it was hard not to read them, the same way he found it impossible to ignore a bowl of potato chips.

Bart got the most media attention just before the major awards shows, like the Oscars and the Emmys, when Hollywood's royalty inevitably rushed into his Beverly Hills clinic for appearance tune-ups, earning him the nicknames Dr. Frankenstar and Doc Botox. He didn't mind the nicknames. He even had business cards made up with the nicknames in italics under his own. Every talent booker on every talk show on television or radio had one of those cards in the Rolodex.

The plastic surgeon was also a frequent guest on makeover reality shows, where he helped transform earthy, sour-faced Midwesterners into smiling, synthetic West Coasters.

But now Bart was getting some very unwelcome publicity, thanks to a massive malpractice lawsuit filed by an aging action star whose plastic surgery obsession made his famous face resemble something carved out of Styrofoam.

The star's attorneys accused Bart of encouraging their client's unhealthy obsession with plastic surgery, advising him to have multiple unnecessary and potentially hazardous procedures. To bolster their claims of the plastic surgeon's unethical behavior, the lawyers leaked documents showing that Bart received six-figure payoffs and lavish tropical vacations from the manufacturers of his Botox and collagen injections to "talk up at every opportunity" the benefits of the controversial procedures to his patients, his colleagues, and the media.

Although Mark was familiar with Bart's activities, the two men hadn't actually seen each other face-to-face in ten years, and even then it was only briefly, in a chance meeting at a trendy Malibu restaurant.

So Bart Spicer was suitably stunned when he walked into one of his exam rooms to find Mark Sloan waiting for him. He gave Mark a hug. Mark was smiling and he assumed that Bart was trying to smile as well, but the plastic surgeon's face was as stiff as plastic and about as lifelike. He looked like a man wearing a mask of Bart Spicer's face.

"It's been way, way, too long, old friend," Bart said, "though I can see why you're here."

"You can?" Mark asked.

"You can't outrun Mother Nature or Father Time, but you can certainly fool the senile old coots," Bart said. "Just look at me!"

Bart opened his arms wide, pointing his outstretched thumbs at his shiny, stiff face, his capped teeth, his colored contacts, and his full head of implanted hair.

"You look incredibly well preserved," Mark said, though he thought "pickled" or "embalmed" might have described Bart Spicer's appearance more accurately.

"Don't worry, my friend, we'll lift those sagging cheeks, smooth out those wrinkles, and remove those bags from under your eyes," Bart said. "Have you thought about coloring your hair?"

"No," Mark said, stealing a glance at himself in the mirror. He'd had no idea he looked that bad.

"Think about it," Bart said. "You might also consider shaving a little off that nose of yours. I'll throw it in at no charge as a favor to a friend."

Mark didn't think his cheeks were sagging, or that he had bags under his eyes. He knew there were a few wrinkles, but he thought they gave him character.

"Actually, I didn't come here for plastic surgery," Mark said.

"Botox isn't plastic surgery, Mark. It's an injection of youth."

"It's a deadly neurotoxin derived from the same bacterium that causes botulism."

"That, too." Bart said. "Isn't it poetic that something so potentially deadly can also create such beauty and happiness?"

"I need to talk to you about what happened during this same week in 1962."

"Dr. Whittington blew his brains out," Bart said. "And half the doctors at the hospital cheered."

"Probably because they were the ones he was blackmailing," Mark said. "Whittington was running a prostitution ring made up of nursing school students and applicants. Many of the girls offered their babysitting services as a way to meet the doctors they later enticed with sex. Whittington filmed their trysts with a hidden camera and blackmailed the men involved."

"Yeah, I know," Bart said. "I was one of those guys."

The admission took Mark completely by surprise. Of course, Mark had gone there intending to ask Bart if he was involved with any of the nursing students, but he'd figured it would take some finesse to get a truthful answer. The last thing he'd expected was an unprompted confession. It was so unexpected, Mark wondered if perhaps he'd misunderstood Bart's comment.

"I know you hired nursing students as babysitters," Mark said. "Are you saying you also paid them for sex?"

"Absolutely! They'd babysit your kids *and* have sex with you. Who could ask for more?" Bart said. "The girls were smart, beautiful, and conscientious about their health. The whole thing was convenient, safe, and inexpensive, too."

"Until they blackmailed you," Mark said.

Bart waved the notion away. "It didn't bother me any."

"You didn't mind paying extortion?" Mark asked in disbelief.

"I didn't pay anything," Bart said. "I told them to show my wife the film. She'd enjoy it."

"Mary *knew* you were sleeping with call girls?"

"We had an open marriage," Bart said. "We still do. We even did threesomes, though we're a little old for that activity now. I thought you knew all about that."

"Why would I?"

"Because Mary invited Katherine to join us once, but she politely declined," Bart said. "Didn't your wife ever tell you?"

Mark shook his head. "I would remember something like that."

"I thought you two told each other everything. Mary and I certainly do. Complete honesty. That's been one of the secrets to the success of our marriage. That and Viagra, of course."

Bart winked and gave Mark a nudge.

"Did you ever see one of the films?" Mark asked.

"I wanted to. All they ever showed me was a tiny filmstrip that I held up to the light," Bart said. "It was definitely me on the film. I remember thinking that I looked pretty good."

"Who asked you for the money? Was it Whittington?"

"Hell no, it came from one of the girls," Bart said. "I didn't know Whittington was even involved until I saw that bomb shelter brochure at his party. I recognized the house out in the valley. I'm sure a lot of guys in that room did. Whittington must have been in pretty desperate trouble to let that happen. I'm not surprised he holed up in his bunker and ate his gun."

Mark was about to correct him, to remind him that Whittington had died in his office, when he had a revelation.

If Alistair Whittington really believed a nuclear attack was imminent, and that everybody needed a home bomb shelter, wouldn't he have had one himself?

And Whittington wouldn't have told anybody about it, either, hiding its existence so neighbors and friends wouldn't try to take refuge with him in a nuclear attack.

But he wouldn't have left his bomb shelter, the "Family Room of tomorrow," sitting empty and unused until the atomic apocalypse. No, he would have found a way to enjoy the extra square footage.

A bomb shelter would have been the perfect place for Whittington to watch his movies . . . and hide them from others.

His pulse quickened with excitement. He knew he was onto something good, and without Bart's offhand remark it might never have occurred to him.

Why didn't he think of it forty years ago?

Mark would call Steve later and ask him to pull the original blueprints for Whittington's home from county records and copies of any permits for additional construction. But he doubted Whittington had followed the rules. If he'd built a shelter, he wouldn't have wanted anyone to know it, including the clerks downtown.

If the bomb shelter still existed, and if they found the film, and if the footage hadn't deteriorated after all these years, there was no guarantee it would lead them to the motivation behind the murder of Brooke Haslett.

So far, all they'd managed to do was reinforce information that Mark already knew. Somehow they needed to break new ground in the investigation.

"You still there, Mark?" Bart asked. "You look lost."

"In a way I am. Do you remember which one of the nursing students made the blackmail demand?"

"I don't remember. It could have been any of them—not that it mattered to me," Bart said. "I didn't hold a grudge."

"You mean you continued to pay them for sex? Even after they tried to blackmail you?"

"Sure, why not? It was a sweet deal for me and my wife. We both got a nice night out away from the kids and I got some action, too. The babysitting service, and the sex, stopped the day Whittington killed himself. It took us months to find another good babysitter."

"Were you sleeping with Joanna Pate?"

"Of course," Bart said. "Weren't you?"

"She made a pass at me," Mark said, "but I declined the offer."

"Your loss," Bart said with sigh. "She was a gymnast in the sack."

"Do you know what happened to her?"

"Why? Are you interested in making up for your mistake? I've got a few spare Viagra pills I can give you if you need them."

Mark wasn't amused. "There was a murder this week that mimicked the killings of those young nursing students. That's why I'm here. I'm talking to everybody I knew then, hoping someone can lead me to the killer."

"I've read about you over the years," Bart said. "I never understood why you enjoy going after murderers so much."

"I don't enjoy it," Mark said.

"C'mon, Mark. Can you look me in the eye and tell me you don't get any pleasure out of it at all? Not even the chase?"

Mark avoided his gaze. "What do you know about Joanna Pate?"

Bart smiled to himself and wagged a scolding finger at Mark, but he answered the question anyway.

"Last I heard—and we're talking forty-three years ago—she got knocked up by one of the doctors she was sleeping with."

"Do you remember which one?"

"No, but I sure remember her," Bart said. "She was a hell of a babysitter."

Chapter Twenty-six

Lieutenant Steve Sloan spent most of his day discovering that Brooke Haslett was a woman without an enemy in the world, with the exception of the person who murdered her.

All her ex-lovers remained friends with her. Her professors at Cal State Northridge described her as intelligent, enthusiastic, and popular. And she was well liked at the Nordstrom store where she worked.

It wasn't until he was in the middle of a phone call interviewing a fourth coworker of Brooke's that he noticed the possible connection between her job and her killing.

His pen ran out of ink and he was reaching for a fresh ballpoint when he knocked over the Haslett file and the pictures of the items gathered at Point Dume spilled out on the floor.

And he saw the photo of the button from a Stanton-brand raincoat, a line sold exclusively at Nordstrom.

Brooke worked in the men's department.

Steve immediately asked Nordstrom for a list of customers who'd bought Stanton raincoats in the last twelve months. Even if the killer had bought a coat from her, his name wouldn't show up on the list unless he'd used a credit card for the purchase.

Steve doubted the killer would be so careless, but he had to check anyway.

In the meantime, he looked at Brooke's boyfriends, coworkers, and teachers to see if any of them had a history of sexual assault or violent crimes.

He came up empty.

So he checked to see if her killing matched the characteristics of any other unsolved murders in California or nationwide, on the off chance that she was the latest victim of a serial killer from outside Los Angeles.

He found no matches.

The more Steve looked into her life, the more he came to believe she wasn't killed by someone who knew her. She was killed for what she symbolized: a link to the past.

Steve called Pelican Bay Penitentiary and requested a list of Carter Sweeney's visitors over the last year. Sweeney had had only one visitor—his lawyer.

The prison was screening Sweeney's mail, so Steve asked the warden if they'd seen any mention of Mark Sloan or any of the people he was involved with in 1962.

The warden said Mark's name had appeared, but only in legal documents and trial transcripts that Sweeney's defense attorney had sent his client in preparation for their latest appeal.

Steve was satisfied, at least for the moment, that Carter Sweeney wasn't behind Brooke Haslett's murder and that the killer wasn't anyone else in her life.

That meant he was back where he'd started.

Back to his father and a string of murders that occurred while Steve was a baby.

Back to the list of names from Mark Sloan's past.

Mark was talking to Alice Blevins and Bart Spicer, so that left only one person for Steve to interview.

Joanna Pate, the former nursing student, babysitter, and teen call girl.

Steve had made only a cursory effort to find her before. Now he would have to roll up his sleeves and get his hands dirty. He unearthed files from Community

General's nursing school to locate her parents, but they'd both died years ago. A little more digging revealed that Joanna was an only child, so he couldn't locate her through her siblings either. She must have lied when she told Mark she was the oldest of three children and therefore an experienced babysitter.

On the assumption that she probably got married, Steve used LAPD's computers to access wedding license databases throughout California from 1962 to 1972, the odds being that she was most likely to have wed while still in her twenties.

When he found no mention of her in the California databases, he widened his search to marriage licenses granted in other states, starting with Nevada, and he immediately scored a hit.

Joanna Pate had married Nelson Lenhoff on June 17, 1963, at a drive-through chapel on the Las Vegas strip.

On a hunch, Steve checked the roster of doctors on the Community General staff in 1962 and found a Dr. Nelson Lenhoff in the pediatrics department.

Some more pounding on the computer keys revealed that Dr. Lenhoff had a private practice in Pasadena until 1981, when he divorced his wife and moved to Florida.

By the time Steve came up with Joanna Lenhoff's home address, which was somewhere on the San Fernando Valley side of Coldwater Canyon, his neck and shoulders were sore and his eyes were stinging from the hours spent hunched over the computer. But he felt a sense of satisfaction that was stronger than his discomfort. He liked the methodical process of basic detective work, especially when it paid off.

Steve got up, stretched, took out the tiny bottle of Advil in his desk drawer and dry-swallowed a couple of tablets. He grabbed his car keys and decided to drive out to see Joanna Lenhoff without calling her first. In his experience, it was always better to catch people off guard and unprepared, especially when he expected them to lie.

*   *   *

Joanna Lenhoff lived in a small, unassuming Craftsman nestled in the curve of a narrow side street that wound from Coldwater Canyon to a dead end at the base of the Hollywood Hills. Sandbag dams, three or four bags long and two bags high, were laid at angles from the curb, creating steps that were intended to slow the flow of runoff down the street.

But the mud and water still clogged the gutters, one of which was right in front of Lenhoff's house, creating a deep mud puddle in the curve that submerged the sidewalks on both sides of the street.

Joanna's home wasn't in any danger of flooding. It was hunched up against the steep, craggy hillside and was surrounded by overgrown trees. A steep asphalt driveway led up to a detached garage, which was covered with dead leaves and bordered one end of her sliver of a backyard.

Steve parked in the driveway to avoid the mud and had to kick his driver's-side door open to keep it from immediately closing back on him as he got out of the car. Rain blew inside the car, drenching the seats and dashboard, but there was no way to avoid it. He climbed out, letting gravity slam the door behind him, and walked up railroad-tie steps that led to her front porch.

He was hunched over against the rain, so he didn't notice the note thumbtacked to the front door until he reached the porch. The white paper was so bright against the dark door it appeared to be illuminated. The words on the printer paper were printed in bold black twenty-point type.

**DO NOT ENTER. THIS IS A CRIME SCENE.
CALL THE POLICE IMMEDIATELY.**

The note wasn't signed. It wasn't necessary. Steve knew who'd written it.

He called for backup and drew his gun, more out of protocol than necessity. Whoever left the note did it on his way out, not his way in. Even so, there was no harm in protecting himself.

Steve braced his back against the wall and eased the door open with his free hand. The smell of rotting flesh hit him immediately. He holstered his gun, certain now that he wouldn't need it. He dabbed some Vicks VapoRub under his nose to combat the stench, put on a pair of disposable gloves from the ever-present stash in his jacket pocket, and went inside.

The air was still and heavy. He could almost feel it seeping past him, freed by the open front door. The chill from outside made him realize how warm it was inside the house. The heater had been cranked up. He could hear the patter of rain and the scratching of windblown tree branches against the house, and his own heartbeat pounding in his ears, but otherwise the house was silent.

It was more than that. It was lifeless.

The shades were drawn and it was dark, a gloominess that was deepened by the black leather furniture, paneled walls, and hardwood floors. Framed family photos of all sizes were propped on every flat surface and covered the walls. Joanna was in nearly every one of them. She was shown alone, with her two children, with an older couple he assumed were her parents. There were no pictures of her ex-husband. When Joanna walked through the house, gazing at those pictures, it must have been like walking past a hundred mirrors, each reflecting her image back at her from a different time.

He walked into the kitchen and jerked back, startled, the breath catching in his throat.

Joanna Lenhoff was lying on her back on the center island, her head lolling over the edge of the counter, facing the doorway, her wide, dead eyes staring right at him.

By the time Mark Sloan arrived at the crime scene, it was nightfall and the tiny street was completely clogged with official vehicles, their flashing, twirling, multi-colored bubble lights casting an eerie strobe over the neighborhood.

Because of the flooding in front of Joanna's house, most of the police vehicles were parked where the side street met busy Coldwater Canyon Boulevard, creating a bottleneck for local residents trying to get past the roadblock to their homes. The steady downpour turned what would have been an irritating inconvenience for drivers into a commuter's nightmare, causing a massive traffic jam on the boulevard in both directions, north into Studio City and south into Beverly Hills.

Mark left his car in a church parking lot and walked to the house, his long overcoat getting soaked by the rain and splashed with mud by every car that passed on Coldwater Canyon Boulevard.

The officer manning the roadblock waved him through and he wove through the parked cars to Joanna Lenhoff's house. Someone had constructed a crude bridge made of plywood and sandbags over the torrent of water to the front steps.

When Mark reached the covered porch, he took off his wet overcoat and muddy shoes so he wouldn't leave tracks all over the crime scene.

He found Steve in the living room, conferring with someone from the crime lab. They'd already spoken on the cell phone, but the connection was bad, so Mark didn't know entirely what to expect. All he knew was that Joanna was dead.

Mark's attention was immediately drawn to the photos of Joanna on the walls. He could see the young woman he knew in all of them, despite her age, the lines on her face, the family and friends around her. Nobody looking at those pictures could ever have imagined that the refined, conservatively dressed woman at the center of each one had ever been a prostitute. She'd aged very well, a sixty-year-old who easily looked ten years younger.

Steve held a sealed, transparent evidence bag out to his father. The note was inside. Mark didn't read the words on the paper as much he felt them, clutching his throat like cold fingers, the past reaching out from the grave to strangle him.

"This was on the door when I arrived," Steve said. "It was written on her home computer. The message is still on the screen. Was the note on Whittington's door ever made public?"

Mark nodded. "It was in all the press reports."

"She's in there." Steve cocked his head towards the kitchen. "I'll be right with you."

Mark entered the kitchen, where Dr. Amanda Bentley was standing with her back to him, inadvertently blocking his view of the body. But the large amount of dried blood splattered on the tile floor indicated he should brace himself for the worst.

"How bad is it, Amanda?" Mark asked softly.

"Terrifying," Amanda said, stepping aside so Mark could see for himself. "Whoever did this knows how to use a knife."

Joanna Lenhoff was on her back on top of the center island.

On the cutting board, Mark thought.

She was naked from the waist up, her shirt and bra had been cut away, frayed halves of the clothing open like bloodstained wings on either side of her.

The killer had made a crude, Y-shaped incision with a kitchen knife, extending from each of her shoulders to her sternum and then down along the middle of her body to her waistline.

"He started my autopsy for me," Amanda said. "While she was still alive."

"Was she injected with succinylcholine?" Mark said, his voice hoarse.

"Probably." Amanda pointed out a tiny pinprick on

Joanna's throat. "I'll let you know when I get the lab results."

There was a question Mark needed to ask, but he found it difficult, the words coming out slowly, barely audible. "Have you found anything inside of her?"

"Like another memory card?" Amanda asked. "Not yet, but that doesn't mean there isn't some nasty surprise waiting for me when I get her on my autopsy table."

"How long has she been dead?"

"A day," Amanda said. "Give or take a few hours."

Steve came in behind Mark. "She was posed for us. The killer wanted us to see her face when we came through the door."

"Brooke Haslett's murder was carefully staged for maximum dramatic effect, too," Amanda said. "The mermaid suit, the red hair, the location where the body was found."

"This killing is very different," Mark said, stepping out of the kitchen so he could think more clearly, undistracted by the horror of Joanna's body. Steve and Amanda followed him.

"Everything about Brooke's death was carefully planned long in advance," Mark said. "First, he had to find her, which couldn't have been easy. She was selected because of who she was and what she symbolized. He probably watched her for a long time, waiting for the perfect time and place to abduct her or lure her to him. He had the mermaid outfit and the memory card ready and waiting for when that right moment came. The victim, every detail of her death, the disposition of her corpse, and the discovery of her identity were all chosen to convey a specific message."

"I'm sure Joanna Lenhoff was chosen for the same reason," Amanda said. "She knew the victims in 1962, and she knew you."

"Ginny Haslett knew me, but whoever is behind this didn't kill her. He murdered her daughter instead," Mark said. "Brooke was the same age as the other victims. Why not kill Joanna's daughter instead?"

"How do we know he hasn't?" Amanda asked nervously.

"Her two children are safe," Steve said. "There are officers at her daughter's home in San Diego and campus police have located her son at Boston University. We'll be protecting them both until the killer is caught."

"With the exception of the syringe full of succinylcholine that the killer brought with him, it appears he used whatever was at hand to commit the murder," Mark said. "It suggests this murder wasn't as well thought out. It's missing the details that would give it symbolic significance beyond the murder itself."

"What about the note on the door?" Steve said. "It's a direct reminder of Whittington's staged suicide."

"The note was written here, on the home computer, almost as an afterthought. Why didn't he have her sign it first, to really evoke the past?" Mark said. "I don't think the killer decided to kill Joanna until shortly before he did it. At the moment, it suggests to me that Joanna was murdered for a different reason than Brooke Haslett was."

"You don't think she was killed to tell you something?" Steve said.

"I think she was killed so she *wouldn't*," Mark said.

"So what was the point of cutting her open like this?" Amanda said.

"Pleasure," Mark said. "I think he enjoys it."

"Just like whoever killed those nurses in 1962," Steve said. "He got off on their terror, knowing they were paralyzed, powerless to save themselves from certain death."

"We know who killed those nurses," Mark said.

"Do we?" Steve took a deep breath and considered his words carefully. "Are you sure Chet Arnold was the right man?"

"He told me he killed the girls," Mark said.

"Yes," Steve said, "but which ones?"

Mark stared at his son, the full significance of what he was saying sinking in.

"What if Harry Trumble was right?" Steve said. "What if there were two different killers? One who killed Sally Pruitt and Tess Vigland, and one who killed the others?"

"Someone who was never caught." Mark took a seat, his legs feeling weak.

"That would certainly explain why the murders of Sally Pruitt and Tess Vigland were so different from the others," Amanda said. "And how Brooke Haslett's murderer knew enough about the details behind the 'accidental' deaths of those other nursing students to suggest they were killed with succinylcholine."

"He knew it because he killed them, too," Steve said, looking now at his father.

It all made such perfect sense. In his youth and arrogance, Mark had missed the obvious clues.

He didn't solve all the murders in 1962. He solved two of them.

And by participating in the police cover-up, he saw to it that Whittington was blamed for all the killings, the case was closed, and nobody ever looked at the "accidental" deaths of those nurses again. Mark made it possible for a murderer to go free without any fear of ever being pursued or punished for his crimes.

Mark knew with heart-wrenching clarity that Steve's theory was correct. There were two killers. One was Chet Arnold and the other got away.

"It all makes sense, except for one thing," Mark said. "Why wait forty-three years to kill again?"

"Maybe he hasn't," Amanda said. "Maybe he just waited until now to tell you about it."

CHAPTER TWENTY-SEVEN

When Steve came home at nine p.m., he found his father in front of the dry-erase board, studying the pictures, the clues, and relationships between them all.

"Come to any fresh conclusions?" Steve asked.

"Just that you're right," Mark said. "There were two killers. And if he's been killing all these years, we may never be able to prove it. We can't go back and double-check every accidental death of a young woman for the last four decades."

Mark thought back to Harry Trumble's last case, the capture of the Clown Killer. One reason he'd eluded capture for so long was because he'd gone overseas, exporting his gruesome brand of murder. What if this killer had done the same thing?

"He might even have been away for most of that time," Mark said.

"Or put away," Steve said. "He could have been in prison, serving a sentence for another crime. I'm checking recently paroled or released violent offenders who were originally incarcerated at least twenty or thirty years ago."

"It's a long shot," Mark said.

"Right now, I'm willing to explore any possibilities," Steve said.

Mark heated up some leftover spaghetti for Steve, who briefed his father on what he'd learned over the last few hours. Officers canvassed the neighborhood, but nobody reported seeing anything suspicious at Lenhoff's house during the last twenty-four hours—not that they would have noticed anyway. Most of the neighbors who drove past her house said their attention was on their driving, concentrating on not having an accident as they made the turn through the flooded curve in the street. There were no signs of forced entry in the house, leading Steve to believe the killer simply knocked on the front door and either was invited inside or pushed his way in. No fingerprints, tire tracks, shoe impressions, or other useful forensic evidence had been uncovered yet, and Steve was still waiting on Amanda's autopsy report.

Mark reciprocated by telling Steve everything he'd gleaned from his interviews with Alice Blevins and Bart Spicer. He also shared his theory that Whittington must have had a home bomb shelter of his own and that it might have been where the blackmail films were hidden.

"If that footage still exists," Steve said, "it could be the break we've been looking for."

"What makes you think the killer is on the film? And even if he is, how would we know? There are probably dozens of men on the film, many of whom it might be impossible to identify now."

"I'll worry about that once I've seen the film." Steve got up from the table and made two calls. The first was to a junior detective in homicide, asking him to wake up someone in the building department and find the original blueprints of Whittington's home and any improvements that might have been made to the property. His next call was to a judge to get the process moving on a search warrant so they could check out the house first thing in the morning.

When Steve hung up, he found Mark in front of the board again, looking at it as if it was the first time he'd seen it, tracing the lines between people, events, and objects with his finger.

Alistair Whittington was in deep financial trouble. To get himself out of it, and perhaps to satisfy his own prurient interests, he coerced nursing school students and applicants to work for him as hookers. The women met the men they would later seduce by first offering their services as babysitters.

Later, the women would bring the men to Whittington's house in the valley, where he secretly filmed their encounters as leverage for blackmail.

Chet Arnold was one of those men, and rather than pay blackmail, he killed the women he slept with, framed Whittington for the crime, and then murdered Whittington, making it look like suicide.

Mark saw through it and the rest was history.

Until now.

Brooke Haslett was murdered in the same way as Chet's victims. She was also the daughter of a woman Mark had treated forty-three years ago.

Joanna Lenhoff was one of Whittington's nursing students and call girls. Now she was dead, too.

There were three people on the board with personal ties to those past events who Mark thought might be involved in some way in the murders of Brooke and Joanna.

Bart Spicer readily admitted to paying for sex and being blackmailed by Whittington. But was he really as easygoing about it as he seemed? He was a doctor then and was still one now, which meant he had access to succinylcholine and knew how to administer it. If Bart did kill the two women, what was his motive? And what did he have against Mark?

Roland Whittington had the clearest motive for wanting to see Mark suffer: vengeance for making Roland and his mother endure the disgrace of Alistair Whittington's financial misdeeds, sexual improprieties, and violent murders. Mark could have eased some of their burden by revealing publicly that Dr. Whittington wasn't a killer. Instead, Mark had helped cover up the truth.

Now Roland was back in Los Angeles during the same week his father was killed forty-three years ago.

It was a disturbing coincidence.

And as a lawyer for a drug company, Roland could probably get his hands on succinylcholine without any trouble. Was Roland back in town to mark the anniversary of his family's shame by murdering two women with ties to his past?

Roland wasn't the only son with reasons to hate Mark Sloan.

Drake Arnold was a lot like his father, Dr. Chet Arnold. He enjoyed drugging women and taking advantage of them while they were helpless. Was it a genetic predisposition? Was it a disturbing coincidence? Or was it something more?

It couldn't be, Mark thought. Drake hadn't been old enough at the time of his father's death to know anything about Chet's psychological quirks or the murders he committed.

Drake would certainly loathe Mark if he knew the truth about his father, Chet, and the circumstances of his bizarre death on that stormy February day.

But he didn't. He couldn't.

Except for Mark Sloan, all the people who knew the secrets about Chet Arnold were dead.

What if Drake did know? What if his father had kept some sort of diary or left behind some other evidence of his crimes that Drake had found? What if Drake was intentionally following in his father's footsteps?

"You have any theories on the identity of the killer," Steve asked, "and why he's decided to come out of hiding now?"

"I wish I did," Mark said.

"Want to hear my theory?"

Mark turned to his son. "You have one?"

"I'm just looking at where all the clues point, and it's right here." Steve tapped the picture of Alice Blevins.

"Alice?" Mark frowned. "What possible reason would she have had to murder all those young women?"

"We know she was in love with Whittington and that he was running that call girl ring. Maybe Alice resented the women for trying to entice him away. Or maybe he was sleeping with them and she hated them for that. Or maybe she was sleeping with them and being blackmailed."

Mark gave Steve a disbelieving look. Steve threw up his hands.

"I don't know her motive yet, Dad. But look at the facts. She knew all the victims. She knew all the men. She knew Ginny Haslett, she was there with you when you set her dislocated shoulder. And Alice had access to succinylcholine then and she has access now."

"Based on that logic," Mark said, "you might as well consider me a suspect, too."

"If you weren't my father, maybe I would," Steve said. "But I've got to say, if you are the killer, it's a twist I didn't see coming."

"It would also be the end of your career as a homicide detective," Mark said.

"I've always known you'd destroy it eventually," Steve said. "That's why I bought Barbeque Bob's restaurant with Jesse."

Mark stared at Alice's picture, mentally drawing lines from her to all the suspects and all the relevant clues. He didn't see it before, but he did now. Steve was right—the facts fit.

"Assuming it's her," Mark said, "why is she killing now?"

"I don't know," Steve said. "But she's definitely got a good reason for hating you."

"So why doesn't she kill me instead of Brooke Haslett and Joanna Lenhoff?"

There was a knock at the door. Steve got up to answer it. He peered through the peephole and opened the door to welcome Amanda, who strode in, a file under her arm.

"My autopsy report won't be ready until tomorrow, but I figured you'd like to hear my preliminary findings right away," Amanda said. "So I thought I might as well stop by on my way home."

"You live in the opposite direction," Mark said.

"I bought a new car," Amanda said. "I'm looking for excuses to drive."

"You bought that Chrysler 300 six months ago," Steve said.

"Do you want to hear what I found or do you want to interrogate me some more?" Amanda asked. "I'm doing you a favor, remember?"

"Sorry," Mark and Steve said in unison.

"I found succinic acid in Joanna Lenhoff's system, confirming our suspicion that she was immobilized with succinylcholine," Amanda said. "It's a toss-up at the moment whether she died of asphyxiation from being unable to breathe due to the paralysis or bled to death from her wounds."

"Did you find anything unusual?" Steve said.

"There were strands of hair in her wounds." Amanda removed several photos from the file in her hand. They were magnified images of the hairs. "I also found the hairs on her clothing, so I think they might have come from physical contact with her killer."

"What kind of hair are we looking at?" Steve asked, studying the photos, which meant nothing to him.

"Cat hair and processed human hair," Amanda said.

"What is processed hair?" Mark asked.

"It's straight, black, coarse hair donated by Indians, Indonesians, and Chinese for use in human-hair wigs," Amanda said. "The hair is bleached, and stripped of its outside cuticle layer and dyed a new color. A wig will eventually begin to shed through repeated combing and brushing. This particular wig was dyed light brown."

"Did Joanna have a cat or own any wigs?" Mark asked Steve.

"She didn't have a cat and I didn't find any wigs in the house," Steve said. "But I imagine a veterinarian spends a lot of time around cats and might even own a few wigs. I'm putting Alice Blevins under surveillance."

Steve got up and went to the phone, leaving Amanda alone with Mark and the case board.

"Alice Blevins? The head nurse?" Amanda asked. Mark nodded. "You don't look convinced."

"She's a strong suspect based on all the connections between her and the victims, but there's no actual evidence and way too many unanswered questions."

"Answer them and you'll find the evidence," Amanda said. "A wise man once told me that."

"You make it sound so easy."

"For you, it usually is," she said. "You're the wise man who gave me that advice."

"I thought I had all the answers and the evidence forty-three years ago," Mark said, gesturing to the board. "Look where that has got us now."

CHAPTER TWENTY-EIGHT

Driving up the driveway to Whittington's house was like moving back through time for Dr. Mark Sloan. The house was exactly as he remembered it, only without the suicide note taped to the front door. There was even a blazing red 1962 Cadillac convertible parked out front, its enormous fins and chrome grill gleaming in the early morning sunshine. The dark clouds had fled during the night, leaving the sky a clear, brilliant blue.

The drapes on the home's distinctive picture windows were wide open to take in the light, revealing the brightly colored vintage furnishings inside. While the decor wasn't identical to what the Whittingtons had owned, it was eerily similar.

Steve emerged from their car first and motioned to the driver of the crime lab van behind them to stay put for the moment. Mark joined his son and they strode side by side to the front door just as it was opened by a bald man in a tank top and shorts. He was in his early thirties, his nose, lips, chin, eyebrows, and ears pierced with jewelry, his bare arms covered in elaborate tattoos of skeletons, naked women, and religious iconography.

"Eldon Wurzel?" Steve asked, flashing his badge.

"Phlegm," the man said.

"Excuse me?" Steve said.

"I'm Phlegm," he said. "Lead singer of Spew. Don't you recognize me?"

"Afraid not," Steve said. "I'm Lieutenant Steve Sloan, LAPD, and this is Dr. Mark Sloan, a consultant to the department. Are you Eldon Wurzel, owner of this house?"

"Nobody's called me Eldon since grade school," Phlegm said. "But yeah, I own this house. I've been trying to get it declared a historical landmark ever since I bought it."

"Because Phlegm lives here?" Mark said.

"Because it's one of the few residential homes designed by architect Randolph Felich that hasn't been demolished for a subdivision or denigrated by 'remodeling,'" Phlegm said. "I've stripped all the 'improvements' and restored it to pristine condition. It's the same now as the day it was built."

"Does that include the bomb shelter?" Steve asked, handing Phlegm the search warrant.

"What bomb shelter?" Phlegm said, reading the warrant.

"That answers one question." Steve waved to the driver of the crime lab van to come over, then turned his attention back to Phlegm. "I don't know if you're aware of this, but your home was the scene of an investigation in 1962."

"Yeah, I know. Some doctor guy. It's one of the reasons this house hasn't been ruined. Nobody stays in it for very long. They get creeped out, scare themselves into thinking it's haunted. Realtors always have a hard time unloading it. I stole this house." Phlegm smiled at Steve. "That's a figure of speech, of course."

"Thanks for clearing that up," Steve said, glancing back at the van, where the crime lab technician was taking out a machine that looked like the offspring of a romance between a metal detector and a lawn mower. "The thing is, Mr. Phlegm, we think there might be evidence in the house that's relevant to two murders committed this week."

"You think I killed somebody?" Phlegm said, his voice rising in pitch.

"No," Steve said. "We don't think you or anybody currently living in this house had anything to do with those crimes. But we believe crucial evidence was left here over forty years ago, and that warrant gives us the authority to look for it."

"The floors have been redone, the walls painted, and the cupboards and counters have been cleaned a couple times since then," Phlegm said, with more than a hint of sarcasm in his tone. "Where do you think this evidence is?"

"That's what he's going to tell us." Steve cocked his head towards the crime lab technician, a portly man in a loose-fitting jumpsuit who was approaching them now, lugging his equipment. "We're going to survey your home and property with ground-penetrating radar."

The technician slowly pushed the two-wheeled GPR unit over the floor as if he were mowing the carpet, watching the readout on what looked like a laptop computer mounted on the long arm of the device.

As the technician explained to Mark, the GPR units were typically used by surveyors, archaeologists, and engineers to detect pipelines, electric lines, structural components, storage tanks, tunnels, and buried artifacts, among other things.

The crime lab used it to find graves.

After two hours, the technician found a "sizeable void" under the carpeted floor of the walk-in closet in Phlegm's recording studio, a soundproof room filled with elaborate audio and computer equipment that he used for cutting demos. The closet stored hundreds of CDs, diskettes, and tapes of all shapes and sizes, neatly arranged on shelves designed especially for that purpose.

Steve glanced at Phlegm and motioned to the floor. "We're going to have to pull this carpet up."

"Be my guest," Phlegm said.

The technician set aside the GPR device, crouched on the closet floor, and pulled at the edge of the carpet in one of the corners. Then he stepped back, lifting the carpet and the padding as he went, exposing the concrete underneath.

There was a section of concrete that was a different shade and texture than the rest. It was square-shaped and had clearly been added after the rest of the cement was poured.

Steve and Mark shared a look and the same thought. Constance Whittington must have had the entrance to the bomb shelter sealed and concreted over before she put the house on the market.

"Get the jackhammer," Steve said to the technician.

After an hour of arguing over the phone with Phlegm's irate lawyer, and repeated assurances from Steve that the city would pay for all damages, Phlegm reluctantly cleared his recordings from the closet and the technician brought in his jackhammer.

It took only a few minutes to break apart the thin layer of concrete that had been spread over the steel door, then another half hour to clear away the rubble and pry the exposed steel door open with a crowbar.

"Cool," Phlegm said, his fury forgotten in his excitement over the new discovery. "I always wanted a secret room. Whatever you find down there, besides dead bodies and your evidence, is mine, right?"

"It's your house," Steve said.

He took out a flashlight and aimed it into the opening, revealing a steep concrete stairwell that descended into blackness. The air was dank, the walls damp. Spiders and other insects scurried away from the light.

"Dad, come with me," Steve said. "You two stay up here in case we run into trouble down there."

Steve descended carefully into the bunker, pointing his flashlight at another heavy door at the bottom of the steps. When he reached the door, he pulled it open, the hinges grinding with a loud metallic squeal that echoed off the thick concrete walls.

He swept his light over the pitch-dark room, glanced up at his dad behind him, and stepped inside. Mark followed Steve in, noticing that the door could be locked and bolted from the inside, a grim reminder of the paranoia and fear of the time.

The interior of the bomb shelter itself was about the size of the living room of the apartment Mark had shared with Katherine and Steve.

Katherine was right, he thought. We could have lived in one of these and parked our Imperial out front.

The shelter was separated into three distinct living spaces—a kitchen, a living room, and sleeping quarters. There was a Geiger counter, shovels, picks, an emergency medical kit, and a fire extinguisher on the wall beside the door.

The kitchen was dominated by a generator, a hundred-gallon water tank, a makeshift sink, and shelves stacked with dishes, cooking utensils, canned goods and bags of rice, sugar, and flour. Other shelves held a radio, flashlights, and batteries.

The bedroom area consisted of four bunk beds bolted to the wall and separated by curtains, and several storage trunks, presumably for clothes and bedding. There was also a curtained area in the corner that concealed the toilet, waste buckets, and personal-hygiene supplies.

The living room was the largest section of the shelter. It was furnished with an area rug, a couch, several card tables, and a recliner. A small bookcase was stocked with a twelve-volume encyclopedia, books, and board games. But the most interesting item was set up within arm's reach of the recliner—an 8 mm movie projector, aimed at a blank space on the wall.

"Homey, isn't it?" Steve said.

"Whittington was ahead of his time," Mark said. "This wasn't a bomb shelter, it was his personal home theater."

"That's what it's gonna be when I'm done with it," Phlegm said, entering the bunker behind them and holding another flashlight. "My secret hideaway, a place to watch all my porn I don't want my wife to know about."

"Oddly enough, that's exactly what this room was used for," Steve said, starting to open the storage trunks in the sleeping quarters. "We're looking for the late owner's collection."

Mark scanned the room for other possible hiding places and could find only one. He opened the cast-iron stove. It smelled of vinegar and was stuffed with small, round film canisters.

"Heat up the popcorn," Mark said. "It's movie night."

Phlegm was so excited about the discovery of a hidden bomb shelter in his home that he told Steve not to worry about LAPD reimbursing him for the damages. Before they left, a grateful Phlegm thrust autographed copies of Spew's latest CD into their hands.

Steve dropped Mark off at Community General and took the film back to the crime lab to see what could be salvaged and viewed.

There wasn't anything Mark could do for the time being on the investigation, so he concentrated on the hospital administrative work he'd neglected. He returned calls and sorted through his paperwork, which is how he came across a memo from Community General's chief of staff.

The memo informed Mark that Dr. Dan Marlowe's medical privileges at the hospital were being suspended immediately, pending review by the Physician Well-Being Committee and the Medical Staff Executive Committee the following week. In consideration of Mark's long relationship with Dr. Marlowe, they were giving him the option of informing the doctor of their decision himself.

Mark called the chief of staff, thanked him for his

thoughtfulness, and said he would tell Dr. Marlowe today about the hospital's decision.

He wasn't looking forward to the meeting with Dan, but it certainly was no worse, and no more difficult to deliver, than the other news he'd had to give his old friend in recent weeks.

On his way to Dan's office, Mark ran into Dr. Jesse Travis in the elevator. Jesse grilled Mark, who apologized for not having the time or the energy to answer his questions.

"I'm feeling entirely left out of this investigation," Jesse said.

"That's because you have been," Mark replied.

"See?" Jesse said. "I'm a natural detective. I'm acutely aware of what's going on around me."

"Someone has to keep the hospital running while I'm ignoring my professional responsibilities."

"Since you put it that way," Jesse said, "I feel honored."

Mark stepped out of the elevator, leaving Jesse behind, and went to Dan's office, where he was told by his nurse that the cardiologist had called in sick and was staying at home today. He thought about calling Dan, but decided that what he had to say was best communicated face-to-face.

The only problem was that Mark had no way to get to Dan's house. Since Steve had dropped him off at Community General, Mark didn't have a car of his own, so he headed down to the pathology lab to see if Amanda would let him borrow hers.

"Perfect timing," she said as Mark entered. "I just finished my autopsy report on Joanna Lenhoff."

"Discover anything new?"

"Do you really expect me to tell you before I tell the detective in charge of the investigation?"

"I'm here first," Mark said with a grin.

"All my preliminary findings were confirmed," Amanda said. "She was injected with succinylcholine, which should have prevented her from breathing and killed her within a few minutes. But she didn't die right away."

Nearly all the people who are given the drug, Mark knew, don't die immediately. They are injected with the neuromuscular paralytic as part of general anesthesia. They don't die because they have some help breathing.

So did Joanna.

"The killer kept her alive while he cut her," Mark said, "For how long?"

"Five or ten minutes," Amanda said.

"My God," Mark muttered. The killings were clearly more about the perverse pleasure the murderer derived from his victims' suffering than about tormenting Mark Sloan. That was simply an added benefit.

"He's going to kill again," Amanda said. "He likes it too much to stop."

Mark agreed. It made him wonder once again why the killer was stepping so boldly out of the shadows now after forty-three years in hiding.

"You better let Steve know right away," Mark said, turning to leave when he suddenly remembered his reason for coming down to see Amanda in the first place. "Speaking of Steve, he dropped me off here, leaving me stranded."

"And you want to borrow my car," Amanda said.

"Do you mind?" Mark said. "Dan called in sick and I need to tell him the chief of staff's decision."

"He's no fool, Mark. He's probably figured it out for himself by now," Amanda said. "It may be why he stayed home."

"Even so, it's something I should tell him myself," Mark said. "I owe him that much."

"I don't envy you." Amanda opened her desk drawer, took out her keys, and tossed them to Mark.

Chapter Twenty-nine

Crime lab technician Moses Depp approached the cardboard box of 8 mm film canisters as if they were infected with the Ebola virus. The barrel-chested African American man wore safety goggles, a respirator with organic vapor cartridges, and protective gloves as he examined the film recovered from the bomb shelter.

As Depp opened the canisters, he gave a play-by-play in his booming baritone over the intercom to Steve, who was watching through the window in the next room. It sounded to Steve like he was listening to Darth Vader.

"The rusted or bulging metal cans indicate deterioration of the film inside. Eight millimeter film is on triacetate," Depp explained, sorting through the box and separating the plastic canisters from the metal ones and placing them on different trays. "Over time, as moisture interacts with the acetate base in the film, it creates acetic acid, giving it that vinegar smell as it deteriorates. It can also be covered with mold. Even if it hasn't deteriorated to that degree, the film might have shrunk, warped, or turned brittle."

"How much of the film is salvageable?" Steve asked.

"Probably most of it," Depp said, carefully opening each canister and inspecting the stock inside. "But it's a laborious and costly process. What you should be asking me is how much of it is viewable now."

"Okay, I'm asking," Steve said.

"Looks to me like the majority of it is in pretty good shape, considering the fluctuating heat and humidity and the proximity to the other deteriorating stock," Depp said. "It's the plastic canisters that saved most of it."

Depp carried the tray of plastic canisters out to Steve as if they were a selection of party hors d'oeuvres.

"You can start with these," Depp said. "I'll set you up on a viewer."

Dan Marlowe had lived in the same house in Sherman Oaks for forty years. His children were born there. His wife had died there. And more than likely, Dan would die there, too.

The house didn't belong in the San Fernando Valley. It was a quaint seaside cottage that should have been on Nantucket. Or in Maine someplace. Not sandwiched between a Sante Fe ranch on one side and a Spanish Revival bungalow on the other.

Mark had visited Dan's home many times over the years. For dinner parties and birthdays, to watch football games and play poker. Those visits became less and less frequent as their kids grew up, their wives died, and they themselves pursued other interests.

It wasn't as though they never saw each other. They worked in the same hospital together every day. Hardly a day went by when they didn't say hello to each other, perhaps discuss the latest gossip, a recent movie they'd seen, the progress of a shared patient, or whatever happened to be in the news.

Now Mark tried to remember the last time he'd come to Dan's house. It was for a poker game, he knew that much, with some of the other doctors from the hospital. He'd lost. He always did. Their long years of friendship gave Dan an unfair advantage against him at the card table. Dan could see right through his bluffs.

That was one reason Mark hadn't even tried to soften

the news when he told Dan about his cancer. And it was why he wouldn't soften the news now.

Mark knocked on Dan's door. He heard the TV shut off and the heavy footsteps approaching the door. Dan opened the door wearing a pair of surgical scrubs. The last time Mark had seen Dan he'd been dressed the same way. He wondered if Dan was feeling so ill that he'd gone home yesterday and fallen into bed without even bothering to change.

"Mark. I didn't know you made house calls," Dan said, opening the door wide.

"Only for special patients." Mark stepped inside. Although it may have been months since he'd last been in the house, he felt immediately at home. Everything was familiar. The antique coat-tree chair by the front door, the family pictures on the walls, the his-and-hers matching recliners in TV room.

"How are you feeling?" Mark asked, hanging his jacket on the coat-tree chair.

"Like I've got cancer," Dan said. "I know the body is made up of two hundred and six bones. Today is the first time I've felt each and every one of them."

"You're experiencing bone pain?"

"Isn't that what I just said?" Dan said, walking into the TV room. "I knew Martha would overreact when I called in sick."

"It wasn't your nurse's fault," Mark said. "I didn't come here to check up on you."

"Then why are you here?" Dan sat down in his recliner. His wife's recliner was as she'd left it, her hand-sewn afghan draped over the back. She'd died sitting there, of heart arrhythmia, a decade ago.

"The hospital has suspended your medical privileges pending review by the Physician Well-Being Committee and the Medical Staff Executive Committee next week."

"Why?" Dan asked evenly.

"Because you were performing surgery while heavily

medicated," Mark said. "What did you expect would happen?"

"I suppose you told them that," Dan said.

"You didn't give me much choice," Mark said.

"You always have a choice, Mark. But you always choose the option that will make you feel good about yourself. And nothing makes you feel better than judging others."

"This isn't about me," Mark said. "It's about what's in the best interests of you and your patients."

"Ask Rufus King how he's feeling today," Dan said. "He's glad to be alive."

"You're missing the point."

Mark remembered his shock when he saw Dan emerge from the operating room.

And then he remembered some other things.

The anxious family, waiting for Dan to tell them how the operation went . . .

The woman whose wig nearly fell off when she flew into the doctor's arms to give him a grateful hug . . .

"It doesn't matter anyway," Dan said. "I'm in no shape to go back to the hospital."

"Speaking of which, I'd better get back." Mark rose from his seat, suddenly eager to leave and trying hard not to show it. "I have a lot of patients to see."

"I appreciate that you came out to see me, Mark. A lesser man would have called or left the task to someone else."

Dan started to get up, but Mark waved him away, glancing again at Irene's empty chair beside him. For an instant, he could see her ghostly image sitting there, knitting.

It was Dan who found her.

"Don't trouble yourself. I can find my way to the door. Call me if you need anything."

"I will," Dan said.

Mark went to the entry hall. His heart was pounding as

he reached for his jacket and examined the other garments on the coat-tree.

There was a raincoat hanging from one of the hooks. It was a Stanton.

And one of the buttons was missing.

Suddenly all the clues snapped into place.

When the woman in the waiting room hugged Dan, she transferred processed hair from her wig and cat dander from her pet to his scrubs. And Dan transferred them to Joanna Lenhoff . . .

. . . when he killed her.

Dan murdered those nurses in 1962. And Mark knew why he'd waited until now to kill again.

Because Dan had just discovered he was dying.

Mark had started towards the door when he felt a sharp sting in his back. Instantly his breath caught and his entire body froze.

Dan caught him as he fell, grabbing Mark under his armpits.

"I knew you'd figured out it was me when you looked at Irene's chair," Dan said. "We've played poker together too many times. You never could bluff me. I could always read your cards on your face."

Mark couldn't swallow. He couldn't breathe. He couldn't even blink. All he could feel anymore was terror. It was as if he was entombed in concrete.

He knew he'd been paralyzed by an injection of succinylcholine. Within a minute or two he would die. And there was nothing he could do to stop it.

"It's a good thing you came today. I don't know if I would have had the strength to do this tomorrow," Dan said, dragging Mark into the kitchen and hefting him up onto the counter.

His lungs screamed for oxygen. His soul screamed for life. They were screams only Mark heard as the final darkness began to spread across his consciousness, Dan's voice fading into a haunting whisper.

"I hope you aren't squeamish about having a man's mouth on yours, but we're old friends, right? And you do want to live for a few more minutes. Well, maybe you won't once you know what those minutes are going to be like."

Dan gave Mark mouth-to-mouth for a few breaths, then stopped, walking back into the entry hall for his medical bag, letting the seconds tick by as Mark slipped into hypoxia and to the edge of death once again.

"You've witnessed autopsies, even performed a few, but this will be a chance to experience one yourself from the other side of the knife. Quite an educational experience—not one Joanna could appreciate, I'm afraid. I did, though."

Dan gave Mark mouth-to-mouth again, then took a scalpel from his bag and slit Mark's shirt open. The ripping sound, and the point of the knife so close to his flesh, sent waves of fear through him.

It took a full second to expand the lungs and two to three seconds for them to deflate with each breath. Three or four breaths would take about fifteen seconds for Dan to give. Mark knew that gave Dan a full thirty to forty seconds to do something else, something horrible, before having to repeat the mouth-to-mouth.

Depending on what *else* Dan was doing to him, the ordeal could go on for some time. For Mark, it could be an eternity of excruciating pain. Dan smiled, as if reading Mark's thoughts.

"That look in your eye right now, that's what makes this experience so incredible for me," Dan said. "That's what I missed all those years when I wasn't able to kill."

CHAPTER THIRTY

Steve spent hours in the tiny cubicle, hunched over the hand-cranked tabletop viewer. As he turned the cranks on the spools, the tiny film strips were run over a lens that projected the grainy images onto a small rear-projection screen.

The colors had faded to red or magenta and sometimes were blurred due to buckled film, but Steve could make out what was going on and, for the most part, could clearly see the faces.

He recognized the women who'd been killed and even a few of their companions. Bart Spicer was a frequent customer and so was Steve's pediatrician, who'd only recently retired to Palm Springs. Most of the men, however, meant nothing to Steve and would have to be identified by his father later.

Watching the faded footage of the perfunctory, hurried couplings of men and women was depressing, dull, and soulless. It was like studying crudely produced scientific film on the random mating habits of a particular species of ape. Steve couldn't imagine what pleasure Whittington derived from watching the films, beyond academic interest. The picture was poor. There was no sound. There were no close-ups, angles, or editing. Except when people entered the room, the camera rarely captured their faces once the sex began.

Still, Steve was able to begin compiling an index of sorts. It was clear to him already that Bart Spicer was familiar with each of the victims. He had yet to see Whittington in any of the films, though there were plenty more rolls to watch.

His eyes were beginning to blur. All the bodies and couplings were beginning to look the same. He was getting ready to quit, to put off further viewing until later with his father, when an image grabbed his complete attention.

There were two women in the room. Muriel Thayer and Joanna Pate. And Steve couldn't believe who was with them. He grabbed his cell phone to call his father.

Dan gave Mark mouth-to-mouth. Mark hated how much he craved the air, how much his whole body silently pleaded with Dan to give him just one more breath.

"You're the reason I haven't been able to really indulge myself doing what I love most. I was always afraid you'd catch me, and that fear, and my frustration, only grew over the years as I watched you catch one murderer after another. But now I have nothing to lose, do I?"

Dan opened his medical bag and carefully selected a variety of surgical tools, making sure to show them to Mark before he laid them on a towel on the counter.

"I'm going to give you satisfaction, Mark, before I take my own. I'm going to answer all the questions you have. It would be cruel to let you die without knowing the truth. And I'm not cruel. Well, at least not in that way. I didn't kill those nursing students because they were prostitutes or in retaliation for blackmail. I only slept with Muriel and Joanna once, together. I'm a man of big appetites. Neither one of them blackmailed me. Nobody did."

Although Mark couldn't close his eyelids, darkness was closing over his vision anyway. He knew it was hypoxia, the lack of oxygen in his blood, and so did Dan.

The killer leaned over Mark and resuscitated him with more mouth-to-mouth before continuing. Each time Mark started to fade as Dan spoke, Dan revived him.

"I killed Muriel because I wanted to and because I knew I could get away with it. I wanted to see what it was like to look into a healthy person's eyes, someone untouched by illness or old age, at the instant they realized they were going to die and were powerless to stop it. It's unbelievably exciting. Better than sex. Better than anything.

"I didn't know someone else was killing nursing students until the same time you did, and once Whittington was blamed for all the deaths, I realized how lucky I was to escape detection. But I never stopped yearning to do it again. I'm sure you're wondering why I waited so long to kill Joanna. She was never a danger to me as long as she thought the killer was caught. But if you talked to her, and told her otherwise, she might remember the one customer she and Muriel had in common. I couldn't risk that. I had to rush over there and make sure she couldn't talk to you again."

Mark felt his consciousness drifting, a coldness seeping into his bones. Death was only a few seconds away. It was almost like sleep. It was almost welcome.

Dan glanced down at Mark's eyes, studying his face for a moment before reviving him again with more air.

"I think this kill is going to be the best ever because you understand what's happening to you in a way nobody else ever did." He picked up a scalpel and made a show of appreciating the blade. "Not the nursing students. Not my wife. Not your cat. Not anyone. The perfect end for us both, wouldn't you say?"

At that instant Dan stabbed the knife into Mark's upper right shoulder, drawing the blade slowly down towards the center of his chest. The pain was intense and yet, at the same time, distant. For the moment, the inability to breathe was a blessing to Mark. The light-headedness caused by the oxygen deprivation dulled the pain, made it feel apart from him, from his consciousness. He was aware of the ripping flesh, of the blood on his skin, but the agony was separate. It wasn't sinking in.

"No, no, no. You want to be awake, old friend. You want to appreciate this."

Dan set down the bloody blade and gave Mark some more air. With the oxygen came the pain. Deep, sharp, and intense.

"That's more like it." Dan smiled as he straightened up, Mark's blood on his scrubs. "And we're only getting started. You may even live long enough for me to show you your own heart."

He picked up his blade and Mark braced himself as best he could for the torture to come. As the point of the scalpel pierced his flesh again, there was a deafening explosion and Dan dropped from view.

For a second, all Mark heard was the ringing in his ears, all he saw was the recessed light on the kitchen ceiling. And then the darkness washed over his senses again. His limbs went cold. He felt buried alive, his body a coffin he could never escape.

A blinding light blasted away the darkness. The hot intensity of pain obliterated the cold. As his dry, stinging eyes focused, he saw the recessed light again before it was blocked out by Steve's worried face.

"Hold on, Dad. I won't let you die."

Steve gave his father mouth-to-mouth, straightened up, and pressed a towel to Mark's wounds to stop the bleeding.

"It's over," Steve said. "You're safe. You're going to survive. I promise you."

He leaned forward, gently closed his father's eyes, and gave him more air.

Mark was on a bed in the ER, propped up in a sitting position, as Dr. Jesse Travis checked the bandages on his shoulder and chest.

"I had a plastic surgeon do the suturing," Jesse said to Mark. "It was a clean cut. The scarring will be barely noticeable."

"Where's Steve?" Mark asked hoarsely, his throat ragged from the intubation.

He'd learned that Steve had kept him alive with mouth-to-mouth for fifteen minutes until the paramedics arrived and took over with an ambu bag. In the ER, Jesse immediately intubated Mark and put him on a ventilator until the effects of the succinylcholine wore off. He was also put on an IV of painkillers and he drifted off into sleep.

This was the first opportunity Mark had had to speak since Dan had thrust the needle into his back.

"He's on his way in," Jesse said. "He had to stick around at Dan's house until the officer-involved shooting team arrived to take his statement. You know how it goes. Amanda is out there, too, doing her ME thing."

Mark nodded. He was still in a state of shock, physically and mentally, and he knew it.

He was stunned that he'd survived. He'd never been so close to death. He'd never experienced such fear.

Despite what he'd been through, Mark still found it difficult to accept that the man who did this to him was the same man he'd considered a close friend for more than forty years. The man who had raised a family, who was a loving grandfather, and who was beloved as the hospital's Santa Claus in the children's ward at Christmas.

How could Dan have been such a monster? How could he have hidden it so well from everybody?

And with the knowledge of Dan's true nature came a deep sense of betrayal. Dan Marlowe betrayed everything in his life. He betrayed his wife, his children, his grandchildren, his profession, and in his last act, Mark Sloan.

All those years, Dan blamed Mark for stopping him from indulging his passion for murder. He used his own fatal illness as one last opportunity to kill again and to make Mark suffer for depriving him of his gruesome pleasure for so long.

Mark couldn't help believing that although he'd survived, ultimately Dan had won.

Dan had escaped punishment for his crimes. The punished were the loved ones of his victims and his own family, who would always be haunted by the atrocities he'd committed.

And so would Mark.

"Dad?"

Mark looked up to see his son standing in the doorway, his shirt stained with his father's blood.

Jesse slipped out quietly, giving Mark and Steve some privacy. Steve approached his father's bedside.

"How are you feeling?" Steve asked.

"Alive," Mark said, his voice unsteady. "Thanks to you. I owe you my life."

"Now we're even," Steve said with a smile. "Besides, I couldn't let you die, at least not until you give me the recipe for Chocolate Decadence a la Sloan."

Mark smiled and gave his son's hand a squeeze. "I've never been so relieved to see anybody in my life. What were you doing at Dan's house?"

"I saw him with Muriel and Joanna in one of Whittington's 'home movies.' I realized why the killings had started again and why Joanna was murdered. When I tried to reach you, Amanda told me you'd gone to see Dan. I knew you were in danger."

"I wish I'd known that I was," Mark said. "I didn't realize it until it was too late, until he gave me the injection."

"At least it's over now," Steve said.

It was and it wasn't.

As Mark lay there on that kitchen counter, his son giving him mouth-to-mouth, he realized the full implication of something Dan had said, something that would torture him more than anything Dan had planned to do to him.

"I think this kill is going to be the best ever because you understand what's happening to you in a way nobody else ever did. Not the nursing students. Not my wife. Not your cat. Not anyone . . ."

It raised a deeply troubling question, the answer to which Dan took to his grave.

Did Dan Marlowe murder his own wife?

If so, it had terrifying implications for Mark Sloan.

Because Mark had never owned a cat.

But he was married to a wonderful woman who died too young.

Katherine Sloan died of a heart attack.

Some people called her "Kat."

Mother Nature was schizophrenic. After drenching Los Angeles with rain, she baked the city with temperatures in the eighties. The storm washed the smog from the sky, leaving the city looking crisper, cleaner, and brighter than Mark could remember seeing it in years.

He felt renewed and refreshed as well. Somehow coming so close to death had made him appreciate every detail of each day since then. Like the feel of sand between his toes, the taste of a good cup of coffee, the smile on his son's face, the company of good friends—all of which he was enjoying today.

Mark stood on his deck cooking shish kebabs on the grill, while on the beach below Amanda and her son made sand castles, Steve and Jesse tossed a football back and forth, and Jesse's fiancée, Susan Hilliard, sunned herself on a chaise lounge.

Whatever malaise Mark had been feeling over the last few weeks was gone, surgically removed when Dan Marlowe cut him open. He was healed, physically and emotionally.

Life was good.

Of course he'd made mistakes and he had regrets, just like any man. But he knew he was so incredibly lucky, in so many ways, that he had no excuse for being depressed or worried about the future.

Mark was a rich man by every measure, but what he treasured most was his close relationship with his son, which would endure no matter where Steve lived. The relationship might change, but the deep connection they shared would never weaken.

He realized now that getting old wasn't something to be feared. It was to be embraced and enjoyed. He might be losing his youthful vitality, but age and experience only deepened and enriched his appreciation of life.

Mark had lost people very dear to him. Loved ones and old friends. He would lose more. Steve could get married and move somewhere else. Amanda and Jesse could leave someday, too, to pursue new relationships and opportunities.

It would be painful and yet, at the same time, those changes could invigorate his life in unforeseen and challenging ways. And that was what would keep him forever young—that was what would keep life exciting.

Yes, things were changing, he thought. And he couldn't wait to see what was going to happen next.

Read on for a preview of
Mark Sloan's adventures in the
next Diagnosis Murder novel

THE DEAD LETTER

Coming from Signet in February 2006

On Monday morning, Bert Yankton showed up promptly at 7 a.m. at his Wilshire Boulevard offices looking fit and rested. He smiled at the receptionist, picked up his mail, and sauntered into his bright corner office.

He emerged a few moments later to get a cup of coffee and a donut from the snack room and went back to his desk to check the stock market, catch up on his email, read the newspaper, and go over his calendar for the day. This was all part of his morning routine.

Ordinarily, Yankton would spend the next two hours preparing for his first meeting of the day, which would either be with a client or members of his staff.

But that morning he had a meeting that wasn't on the books.

The man who strode uninvited into Yankton's office looked like he would be much more comfortable wearing a tank top, shorts, and sandals than an off-the-rack suit and scuffed-up Florsheims. He had the even tan and sun-bleached hair of a surfer, but there was nothing laid-back about his attitude. The man radiated authority and probably would have even without the badge and the gun clipped to his belt.

"Bert Yankton?" The man asked.

"Yes." Yankton rose from his chair. "How can I help you, officer?"

"It's detective. I'm Steve Sloan. LAPD Homicide."

"Who died?" Yankton asked.

"People who die aren't my problem, Bert. Just the ones who are murdered."

"All right," Yankton said. "Who has been killed and what does that have to do with me?"

"Where have you been since you left the office Friday night?"

"I went home for a few hours and then I drove down to La Quinta," Yankton said. "I have a place there."

"Is there anybody who can confirm your whereabouts?"

"I was by myself. But I stopped for gas in Montclair on my way down, got some groceries at Jensen's market on Saturday night, and filled up the tank again on the way back this morning, at a Chevron in Redlands. I used my credit card for all those transactions, if that matters."

"It will."

"Are you going to tell me what this is about?"

"Where's your partner?"

Yankton's face tightened and he glanced at his watch. "Jimmy doesn't come in until ten."

"When did you last see Jimmy Cale?"

"Not since Friday," Yankton said. "We met with a client for lunch at Le Guerre in Studio City. Jimmy had other meetings in the Valley and I had an appointment back here at the office."

"Who did you meet with?"

"I'm not answering any more questions until you tell me what is going on."

"You met with a private investigator who calls himself Nick Stryker," Steve said.

"What should he be calling himself?"

"Zanley Rosencrantz, that's his real name, but that doesn't sound half as cool as Nick Stryker, does it? Think about it for a second, Bert. Would you have hired a guy with a name like that to follow your wife?"

Tiny beads of perspiration were beginning to make Yankton's brow shine. "If you already knew who I met with and why, what was the point of asking me?"

"To catch you in a lie, of course." Steve said. "It's a big part of what I do."

"Has Stryker been murdered?"

Steve shook his head. "No such luck."

Yankton shifted his weight in frustration, clearly trying to keep his voice steady and his demeanor professionally aloof. "Then who has?"

"That's a tricky question," Steve said. "We aren't entirely sure yet."

"We?"

"Me, your wife, and the La Quinta Police," Steve said. "I'll tell you more about it on the way down to the parking garage."

"What's in the garage?"

"Your car," Steve said. "Which reminds me, you better bring your keys."

The two men didn't speak to each other again until they were alone in the elevator. Yankton hit the button for the parking garage and turned to Steve.

"You mentioned my wife and the La Quinta Police," Yankton said.

"I don't know what your weekend has been like, but let me tell you about mine," Steve said. "After you trashed your house with a sledgehammer, your wife, Vivian called her lover, your partner Jimmy Cale, who set her up in an apartment in Marina Del Rey. He was supposed to join her there again Saturday night. When he didn't show, she got worried and went over to his place. His car was parked in the driveway, but his front door was wide open. She went inside and found everything smashed, blood on the floor, and no sign of Cale. That's where I come in."

Yankton cleared his throat. "Is Jimmy dead?"

"You tell me," Steve said. "But if you're going to confess, wait until I read you your rights."

"I didn't kill Jimmy," Yankton said.

"Did you trash his house?"

"No," Yankton said.

"It must have been another angry husband with a sledgehammer," Steve said. "Right, Bert?"

Yankton didn't answer. He reached into his jacket for his cell phone to call his lawyer, but thought better of it after remembering two things: There was no reception in the parking garage and his lawyer didn't know the first thing about criminal law.

They reached the garage with a disconcerting jolt. The elevator doors slid open like the curtains on a stage at the opening of a play. Yankton gasped involuntarily at the drama that was already unfolding.

His parking space was cordoned off with yellow police tape. The trunk and all four doors of his BMW were wide open. Several uniformed officers were standing guard as a team of a half-dozen crime lab technicians in blue jumpsuits went over his car.

"I guess I won't need your keys after all," Steve said as they stepped out of the elevator.

"You better have a search warrant," Yankton said. He'd watched enough TV cop shows to know that much.

Steve reached into his pocket, pulled out a piece of paper, and handed it to Yankton. "Here it is. Hold on to it for your scrapbook. It will go nicely with the one they issued down in La Quinta, where the police are searching your place as we speak."

"What are you looking for?" Yankton's voice was barely more than a whisper.

"Evidence of murder," Steve said.

"This is crazy. Jimmy could be anywhere. He could be in Vegas right now, have you thought of that? He goes up there for quick trips all the time. Flies up, gambles all night, and straggles in here at ten a.m. looking like hell." Yankton glanced at his watch. "He could be here any minute."

One of the crime lab techs motioned Steve over to the trunk. Her name was Leslie Stivers, and the tech squad jumpsuit didn't do her any favors. But Steve was one of the few in the department who didn't need to use his imagination to know what she looked like without it.

Steve went over to her, gesturing to Yankton to follow.

"What have you got?" Steve asked her.

She aimed a special light into the trunk. Several spots glowed bluish-white.

"What's that?" Yankton asked.

"It's blood, Bert," Steve said. "We sprayed the trunk with Luminol, which detects hemoglobin and makes it glow when hit with the right light."

"I spilled some spaghetti sauce in there once," Yankton said. "Maybe that's what it is."

"It's not," Steve said.

"Someone attempted to clean it off, but whoever did it missed a few spots in the back," Leslie said. "He also missed this."

She reached into a dark corner with a pair of tweezers and picked up something, holding it up for them to see.

"Is that a thumb?" Steve asked.

Leslie shook her head. "Tip of a big toe. Hacked off the left foot, I think."

Steve glanced over at Yankton, whose face was ashen.

"Mondays are hell, aren't they Bert?" Steve said.

DON'T MISS THE REST OF
THE SERIES BASED ON THE HIT TV SHOW

DIAGNOSIS MURDER

BY **LEE GOLDBERG**

DIAGNOSIS MURDER:
THE WAKING NIGHTMARE
0-451-21486-2

DIAGNOSIS MURDER:
THE SHOOTING SCRIPT
0-451-21266-5

DIAGNOSIS MURDER:
THE DEATH MERCHANT
0-451-21130-8

DIAGNOSIS MURDER:
THE SILENT PARTNER
0-451-20959-1

Available wherever books are sold or at penguin.com

S523

SIGNET   (0451)

FROM THE MYSTERY SERIES
MURDER,
SHE WROTE
by Jessica Fletcher & Donald Bain

Based on the Universal television series
Created by Peter S. Fischer, Richard Levinson & William Link

Available wherever books are sold or at
penguin.com

S821/MurderSheWroteList

SIGNET   (0451)

COMIGN SOON
IN HARDCOVER

MURDER, SHE WROTE:
Margaritas & Murder

by Jessica Fletcher & Donald Bain

Based on the Universal television series
Created by Peter S. Fischer, Richard Levinson & William Link

San Miguel de Allende is the perfect place for mystery
writer Jessica Fletcher to soak up the sun, bask in
Mexican culture, and spend some time with her good
friends Vaughan and Olga Buckley. But when Vaughan is
kidnapped for a large ransom, Jessica must put her life on
the line for find her old friend.

0-451-21662-8

Available wherever books are sold or at
penguin.com

GET CLUED IN

signetmysteries.com

Ever wonder how to find out about all the latest Signet mysteries?

signetmysteries.com

- See what's new
- Find author appearences
- Win fantastic prizes
- Get reading recommendations
- Sign up for the mystery newsletter
- Chat with authors and other fans
- Read interviews with authors you love

Mystery Solved.

signetmysteries.com

Penguin Group (USA) Online

What will you be reading tomorrow?

Tom Clancy, Patricia Cornwell, W.E.B. Griffin,
Nora Roberts, William Gibson, Robin Cook,
Brian Jacques, Catherine Coulter, Stephen King,
Dean Koontz, Ken Follett, Clive Cussler,
Eric Jerome Dickey, John Sandford,
Terry McMillan…

You'll find them all at
penguin.com

*Read excerpts and newsletters,
find tour schedules and reading group guides,
and enter contests.*

Subscribe to Penguin Group (USA) newsletters
and get an exclusive inside look
at exciting new titles and the authors you love
long before everyone else does.

PENGUIN GROUP (USA)
penguin.com/news